WHEN LAST I DIED

Gladys Maude Winifred Mitchell – or 'The Great Gladys' as Philip Larkin described her – was born in 1901, in Cowley in Oxfordshire. She graduated in history from University College London and in 1921 began her long career as a teacher. She studied the works of Sigmund Freud and attributed her interest in witchcraft to the influence of her friend, the detective novelist Helen Simpson.

Her first novel, *Speedy Death*, was published in 1929 and introduced readers to Beatrice Adela Lestrange Bradley, the heroine of a further sixty-six crime novels. She wrote at least one novel a year throughout her career and was an early member of the Detection Club along with G. K. Chesterton, Agatha Christie and Dorothy Sayers. In 1961 she retired from teaching and, from her home in Dorset, continued to write, receiving the Crime Writers' Association Silver Dagger Award in 1976. Gladys Mitchell died in 1983.

ALSO BY GLADYS MITCHELL

GLADYS MITCHELL

When Last I Died

VINTAGE BOOKS
London

Published by Vintage 2009

2 4 6 8 10 9 7 5 3 1

Copyright © the Executors of the Estate of Gladys Mitchell 1941

Gladys Mitchell has asserted her right under the Copyright, Designs
and Patents Act 1988 to be identified as the author of this work

First published in Great Britain in 1941 by Michael Joseph

Vintage
Random House, 20 Vauxhall Bridge Road,
London SW1V 2SA

www.vintage-books.co.uk

Addresses for companies within The Random House Group Limited
can be found at: www.randomhouse.co.uk/offices.htm

The Random House Group Limited Reg. No. 954009

A CIP catalogue record for this book
is available from the British Library

ISBN 9780099526223

The Random House Group Limited supports The Forest
Stewardship Council (FSC), the leading international forest
certification organisation. All our titles that are printed on
Greenpeace approved FSC certified paper carry the FSC logo.
Our paper procurement policy can be found at:
www.rbooks.co.uk/environment

Printed and bound in Great Britain by
CPI Cox & Wyman, Reading, RG1 8EX

Chapter One

THE DIARY

But thou, whose pen hath like a pack-horse served,
Whose stomach unto gall hath turned thy food,
Whose senses, like poor prisoners, hunger-starved,
Whose grief hath parched thy body, dried thy blood. . . .

DRAYTON.

THE lunch had consisted of sausage-meat roll, diced swede and mashed potatoes ; these covered with thick floury gravy and followed by tinned plums and custard. The boys had consumed the first course in three minutes, the second in one and a half, and still, to Mrs. Bradley's possibly prejudiced eye—for she had nephews, great-nephews and, now that Ferdinand was married, a grandson—they retained a wolfish aspect which depressed her. Her notions on diet, she informed the Warden, when he canvassed her opinion of the menu, were, she thought, about a century out of date.

The Warden wisely decided to treat this reply as a witticism, and as he was essentially a serious-minded man the subject of conversation languished. Grace, which had, to Mrs. Bradley's embarrassment, preceded the meal, now, with suitable grammatical adjustments, indicated its conclusion, and, with remarkable orderliness and very little noise, the boys filed out except for one child who re-seated himself and continued to eat.

" What on earth is he doing ? " said the Warden. He raised his voice. " Dinnie ! " The boy, with a regretful glance at his plate, stood up. " Why haven't you finished ? "

" Sir ? "

" Why haven't you finished ? Come up here." The boy approached with considerable reluctance. " And step up smartly when you're called. Don't you know we have a visitor ? "

7

" Yes, sir." He shot a half-glance at Mrs. Bradley, contemptuously, she thought.

" Well, where are your manners? Now, then, answer my question."

" It would only have gone into the swill-tub for the pigs," said the boy, in an almost inaudible voice. He had dark red hair and brown eyes flecked with lighter specks so that it seemed as though the sun danced on a trout stream. His brows slanted in an alarmingly Mephistophelean manner, and he had a wide mouth set in a grim jaw. The Americans, with their flair for good-humoured expressiveness, would have dubbed him a tough citizen, thought Mrs. Bradley, for whom bad boys had academic and occasionally—for she was a woman—sentimental interest.

They were all bad boys at the Institution. The Government, with one of those grandmotherly inspirations which are the dread and bane of progressive educationists, had decreed, some ten years previously, that its theories with regard to the preventive detention of delinquent children were a long way out of date, and were to be re-stated in accordance with the facts so far gleaned by child-guidance clinics.

Mrs. Bradley, among other psychologists, had been called into consultation, but her simple suggestion was that delinquent children, who, like delinquent adults, can be divided into those brands which can be snatched from the burning and those which, unfortunately, cannot, should (literally) be killed or cured. The former treatment was to be painless, the latter drastic. This view was received without enthusiasm by the authorities and was treated, even by the Press, with reserve.

Now, ten years later, she had been called in again ; not (be it stated hastily to those who retain the uncivilized view that human life is necessarily sacred) to assist in translating her theory into fact, but because, strangely enough, the Government had discovered that the new methods in preventive detention had again sprung a leak and badly needed plugging.

Why they should have called into consultation one with whose thought upon the subject they would be bound to disagree, not even Mrs. Bradley herself could say, well-versed though she was in morbid psychology, but she had answered the summons as a good democrat should, promptly and with an open mind.

The trouble was, the Warden had explained, that in spite of humane treatment, fewer punishments, better food, and the provision of playing fields, bad boys, on the whole, continued to be bad, and even attempted, more frequently than could be justified, to escape from Elysium—in other words, the Institution —into the wicked and troubled world.

The worst of it was, he continued, voicing his own point of view with a certain naïveté which she found entertaining, that the two boys who had run away a week before Mrs. Bradley's arrival, had not, so far, been traced, and were, as he expressed it, still at large.

It could not be helped, Mrs. Bradley suggested ; for she found that she was sorry for the Warden in his obvious anxiety, although she knew that he did not like her.

No, it could not be helped, the Warden agreed, but it was particularly unfortunate as, some years previously, just before he had been appointed, two boys had contrived a similar disappearance and had never been found.

" What ? Never ? " said Mrs. Bradley, startled ; for the police, she reflected, are noted, among other things, for their bloodhound abilities. " Do you mean to say . . . ? "

" I mean to say," said the Warden, looking, all in a moment, haggard with worry, " that, from then until now, there has been not another sign of either of them. I received my appointment partly on an undertaking that such a thing should never happen again, and I've been careful, very careful indeed, but, if we don't get these two soon, I shall feel that I ought to ask the authorities to accept my resignation. You see, the kind of boy who is sent here—just excuse me one moment. . . ."

He checked further revelations and confessions in order to attend to the matter of immediate moment.

"What do you mean, Dinnie ? "

" You know what I mean," replied the boy.

" Don't be impudent ! Answer me directly ! "

" But you do know what he means," murmured Mrs. Bradley. In spite of her pity for the Warden in his distress, she found that, on the whole, humane though she believed him to be, and a great improvement on his predecessor, whom she remembered very well from her previous visit, she could not approve of all his methods, and this one, of attempting to make a boy look a fool when he was not a fool, she deplored almost more than any other.   She had been an interested but disapproving witness of it several times during her stay.

The Warden, feeling, no doubt, that it was due to his estimate of himself and his position to ignore it, took no notice of the interruption, but addressed himself again to the truculent and obstinate-looking Dinnie.

" Now, boy !   Answer me directly.   Tell me at once what you mean ! "

" There was an extra dinner, and I ate it," said the boy.

" Right.   Go and finish it.   To-morrow do without your pudding.   If you had answered me at first when I asked you, I should not have punished you at all."

He rose briskly.   The rest of the staff had left the high table and had gone out with the boys, so that, except for Dinnie, now busily and hastily gulping down the pig-food, the hall was empty but for himself and Mrs. Bradley.

" Have to be sharp on them," he said, feeling, for some reason, that some justification was needed for the combination of bullying and weakness he had shown.   " No good letting him get away with that."

" How did there come to be an extra dinner ? " Mrs. Bradley tactfully inquired.

" That still remains to be investigated."   He investigated it by sending for the housekeeper the moment he reached his sitting-room.

" It was Canvey.   He felt sick ·and did not go in to dinner. But as we had had no notification, his dinner was sent in as usual," said the housekeeper, looking, Mrs. Bradley thought, in the presence of the Warden like a drab female thrush confronting an imposing frog.

" I had better see Canvey."   The Frog touched the buzzer which had already brought a boy to act as messenger.   " Get Canvey, Williams, please.   All right, Margaret, thank you. . . . We use Christian names with one another here.   It helps the atmosphere," he remarked to Mrs. Bradley when the boy and the housekeeper had gone.

Canvey was a rat-faced boy with handsome, wide-open eyes,

affording a strange impression of cunning and frankness mingled. Call the cunning lack of self-confidence, and the frankness an attempt, probably an unconscious one, to compensate for this, and you had a different portrait of the boy and not necessarily a less faithful one, Mrs. Bradley surmised.

" What's the matter with you that you couldn't eat your dinner ? " the Warden inquired. He prided himself, Mrs. Bradley had discovered, upon taking a personal interest in each boy. That this might prove embarrassing and even disagreeable to the boy, obviously never entered his head.

" Sir, I don't like sausage-meat, sir. It makes me sick, sir," responded Canvey, bestowing on the interlocutor his wide gaze.

" Nonsense, boy. Did you eat your pudding yesterday ? "

" Sir, yes, sir."

" Your vegetables ? "

" Yes, sir."

" No, you did not ! " thundered the Warden. " You did *not* eat your vegetables."

The boy remained silent, but he did not drop his eyes, and he and the Warden stared at one another, until the Warden, apparently the weaker character, added :

" Well ? "

" Sir ? "

" Your vegetables."

" I felt ill, sir."

" No, no. You didn't feel ill. You've been smoking. Have you been stealing tobacco from the staff ? "

" Sir, no, sir."

The Warden produced a cane. The boy eyed it with a certain degree of sullen speculation.

" Well ? " said the Warden.

" I didn't steal anything. It was rhubarb leaves," said the boy.

" Then you deserve to feel sick. See that you eat your tea." He put the cane away, and the boy departed.

" Rhubarb leaves," said Mrs. Bradley thoughtfully.

" Yes. A good many of these boys are inveterate smokers when they come here, and we have to cure them. I have given up smoking, myself. I don't want boys coming into this room and smelling tobacco. I don't feel that that would be playing the game. But I can scarcely help it if the staff have an occasional pipe or cigarette. One can scarcely expect them to adopt all one's own standards."

"One could engage non-smokers, I suppose," said Mrs. Bradley, interested in a system which regarded the powers of self-denial of the staff as being inferior to those of the boys. The Warden, again scenting a witticism, made no direct reply. He said :

"It is very difficult to get these boys to see that certain things aren't good for them, and, of course, if they come here with the craving, they'll satisfy it somehow if they can. It is one of our many difficulties, to eradicate these tendencies."

Mrs. Bradley thought it might be not only difficult but impossible to eradicate the tobacco habit, judging by men, young and old, of her acquaintance, and some women, too, who were addicted to it.

"I suppose voluntary abstinence, for some reason which they can appreciate, would be the only means of overcoming it," she observed. "Athletes, for instance, voluntarily give up tobacco, among other things, I believe."

"It wouldn't work here. These boys have no *esprit de corps*," responded the Warden, looking disfavourably upon her.

"In that case it might be as well to let them smoke, if they can find anything to smoke, or even to offer a packet of cigarettes as a good-conduct prize," she suggested.

The Warden disregarded these flippancies, and asked, rather abruptly, whether she would like to see another group at work.

"No. I should prefer to take over a group myself, for a week," she said. The Warden, looking rather like a snake-charmer who has been asked by one of the spectators for leave to take over the management of his pets, replied vaguely and dubiously, whereat she cackled and did not renew the request. "Why is that boy Dinnie here ? " she asked.

"He was employed by a receiver of stolen bicycles," replied the Warden. "He used to ride away on those left at the roadside. Ladies' bicycles were his speciality. He wasn't caught until he went outside his class and tried to ride off on a motor cycle."

"And Canvey ? "

"Nasty little nark," said the Warden pardonably. "He used

to push away babies left in perambulators, and then ' find them abandoned ' and claim the reward, if there was one."

" And if there was not ? "

" Then he and the woman he worked with used to wait a week and then abandon the babies themselves. One mother committed suicide, and another was injured for life by her husband because of that boy."

" And the woman he worked with," Mrs. Bradley gently remarked.

.Her own methods with the boys were characteristic. She thought they needed stimulating, and applied psychological treatment, to their astonishment and her own amusement. She discovered very soon that they were afraid of her. One even went so far as to ask whether she was there to pick out the " mentals."

" We are all ' mentals,' my poor child," she remarked.

Nevertheless, at the end of two days she could tell the Warden where to lay hands upon his missing boys, for it was common knowledge where and how they had gone, and this common knowledge she soon shared.

" Word-associations," she replied, when, the lambs having been caused to return to their apparently unpopular fold, the Warden asked her to tell him how she had done it.

" My predecessor could have done with the same sort of help," he volunteered abruptly. " You knew, perhaps, that the loss of those two runaways cost him his job ? He was not exactly asked to resign, but—well, it was clearly indicated that there was no future for him here."

" Why ? Surely he was not dismissed because two boys contrived to get away ? "

The Warden shrugged. " He had a private income, I believe. But there was a public inquiry, and one or two things came out. It seemed fairly certain, for one thing, that the escape had been assisted, if not actually engineered, by a member of the staff. That was what went so seriously against him. Of course, he wasn't popular, but still——"

" Extraordinary," said Mrs. Bradley, hoping to hear more.

" Couldn't trace it to anyone, though," the Warden gloomily continued. " But somebody seemed to have supplied them with files, for example."

" Don't they use files in the manual centre ? "

" Yes, of course they do. But those are always checked at the end of one period and at the beginning of the next. They are always in order. No, these files came in from outside. Different make, and so on. It all came out."

" Their associates outside ? "

" Curiously enough, no. They were two rather freakish specimens, as it happened, and had no associates at all in the sense that you mean. One of them had committed a murder. He was quite simply a pathological case, and had no business here at all. On the other hand, there was no trace whatever of a criminal background. He came of the most respectable middle-class people. The other was a bit more up our street, but had no criminal associates. He worked entirely on his own, I understand, and had been employed at racing stables until he got the sack for stealing. He then became the terror of his neighbourhood. Went in for handbag snatching, and once cut a woman's head open. A little beauty, he must have been."

" Most of the staff are new to me," Mrs. Bradley remarked. " But of course, it is ten years since I was here. The house-keeper you have now, for instance——"

" Yes, they are all new except the man who takes the wood-work, and the physical training instructor."

" The kitchen staff, I see, has been augmented."

" Yes. I believe that, before my time, besides the house-keeper, they had no one but a kitchen-maid, which left the unfortunate housekeeper responsible for all the cooking. But now we have two cooks and a scullery maid as well. They all live ' out,' however, except the housekeeper and one of the cooks. Those two have to be on duty for breakfasts."

" Interesting," said Mrs. Bradley. " I wonder whether the authorities would encourage me in making a minor psychological experiment ? I should like to take a house from the beginning of May until the end of September and have some of the boys to visit me there. If I had three boys each week for twenty or twenty-one weeks, that would give a short holiday to about two-thirds of your numbers, would it not ? "

" The authorities would never allow it ; and I should not like it myself," replied the Warden frankly. " We dare not spoil these boys. Sentiment, unfortunately, does not do. I am afraid they would take every possible advantage of such a scheme."

" Including making their escape. I know. That is what makes it interesting," said Mrs. Bradley. The Warden shook his head.

" It would never do. It wouldn't be good for them. After all, they're here as a punishment, you know."

" I am afraid so, yes. A terribly immoral state of affairs."

" And for guidance as well ; and for the protection of society."

" I know. If I were a caged tiger, do you know the people who would have to be protected against me if ever I made my escape ? "

" Yes, yes, all very well. I admit these boys have a grievance against society. But what can we do ? "

" I told the Government of ten years ago what we could do," said Mrs. Bradley. " Well, I shall look about for my house at the seaside, and when I find it I shall come to you again."

The Warden felt that he could afford to smile, and therefore smiled. He even attempted light humour.

" I could tell you of the very place," he said. " I have the address in my desk here. It once belonged to the aunt of the former housekeeper. Perhaps you remember her from your previous visit ? She would still have been here then. About six years ago she retired, having inherited her aunt's money, but was dead within the year. Tried for murder, acquitted, and then committed suicide, poor creature, because people were so unkind. Sounds like something on the films, but it's perfectly true. The house belongs to an old servant now, I believe, who is glad to let it in the summer."

" Boys or no boys, I should like to have that address," said Mrs. Bradley.

" ' No boys,' is more likely to be correct," said the Warden, almost good-naturedly. He could afford to be pleasant to the somewhat terrifying old woman, he concluded. She had brought back his truants for him, and, in any case, she was leaving the Institution in the morning.

" Cynical old thing ! " said Caroline Lestrange, looking up from Mrs. Bradley's letter.

" No," said Ferdinand, glancing at their son, Derek, aged seven, who was advancing purposefully to the table with a set of the game called Tiddleywinks. " No, indeed she isn't. If mother says they ought to be put out, she is probably perfectly sincere and perfectly right. They must be the most unhappy little devils on earth, those delinquent kids. You can't really do anything for most of 'em. They're a mess, like Humpty Dumpty when he fell off the wall. She goes on to ask whether we'd care to lend her Derek for a bit. I'm all for it. She needs him, I expect, to get the taste of the others out of her mouth."

His son came up and planted the game on the table. Then he surveyed his parents sternly.

" You can both choose your colour," he said, " and I'll have what's left. There's blue and green and red and yellow and purple and white. I don't use the white. I only use the green and purple and yellow and blue and red. I don't like white. Do you like white, mother ? "

" No, thank you, darling," Caroline replied.

" I'm not going to play," said his father, basely. " I've got this letter from Gran and I'd better answer it."

He fled, pursued by the joint maledictions of his wife and son, who, thereafter, forgot him, and settled down to Tiddleywinks until it was Derek's bedtime.

" Would you like to go and stay with Gran at the seaside for a bit ? " asked Caroline, when she went in to say good-night. Her son's reply was brief but warm, and so by the middle of the following week all arrangements had been made.

The house which Mrs. Bradley had rented was about a hundred yards from the sea, and was, from the child's point of view, admirably situated. Mrs. Bradley had fitted up her dressing-room for him, and there he had a camp bed and a chest of drawers. On the top of this antiquated but useful piece of furniture he placed the model of a Viking ship made for him by a cousin. This was so much his most cherished possession that it could not be left at home.

The house was that of which Mrs. Bradley had heard from the Warden. Unattractive from the outside, and furnished in accordance with the taste of an earlier period, it was comfortable and convenient enough, and grandmother and grandson enjoyed one another's company and the pleasures of the sea and the shore. Permission had not, so far, been granted for any of the Warden's boys to join them.

George, Mrs. Bradley's chauffeur, one of the servants she had brought with her, had become mentor to the little boy, and introduced him to the wonders of the internal combustion engine and to the vocabulary of the mechanically-minded. The weather, on the whole, was fine, and although Mrs. Bradley deplored the ostrich-outlook of the authorities in refraining from granting their blessing to her holiday scheme for the Home Boys (as they were euphemistically entitled), she enjoyed the sea air, the old-fashioned house, and, until the last week of the child's visit, the innocuous gossip of the village.

During this last week, however, she was surprised and annoyed when the little boy said suddenly, one evening when he was having his supper, and only an hour before his bedtime,

" Gran, what lady was murdered in this house ? "

" Murdered ? " said Mrs. Bradley. She had no time to prepare an answer. " Oh, I expect they mean poor old Aunt What's-it. I've forgotten her name."

" Does her ghost walk ? "

" Why should it ? "

" Somebody told me it did."

" Had this person seen it ? "

" No. What would it look like, Gran ? "

" Exactly like the person, I suppose."

" I don't want to see it, Gran."

" No such luck. I've tried hard to see them, many and many a time. It isn't a scrap of good. I've come to the conclusion there are no such things. People are such liars, unfortunately."

" Do you think Miss Peeple was telling me lies, Gran ? She said Miss Bella killed Aunt Flora, and Aunt Flora's spirit can't rest."

" Well, she's a funny old thing, and not very sensible, you know——"

" George says she's batty and sees double. Is it the same thing, Gran ? "

" Exactly the same thing," said Mrs. Bradley, paying her usual mental tribute to her chauffeur.

"Yes . . . but I think I'm glad I'm sleeping in the next room, Gran. Do you think I could move my bed in beside yours ? "

" I think it would be great fun," said Mrs. Bradley. In the morning she said to the postmistress, in the course of a conversation engineered to lead up to the question :

" What is this tale that the house I have rented is haunted ? "

" It's only Peggy Peeple's nonsense," said the postmistress. " Although you can't wonder at her, poor thing. There's plenty about here to swear the old lady was murdered. They do say it was her niece, Miss Bella Foxley, the one that inherited the money."

" Wasn't someone tried for it ?—the niece, or some other relative ? " said Mrs. Bradley, innocent of all real knowledge of the subject, but determined to get to the bottom of it.

" Oh, no, not for that. It was never brought in as murder, that wasn't. Oh, no ! It's only people's wickedness to talk the way they do, but, of course, she *did* come in for the money, Miss Bella did, and then she *was* tried for murdering her cousin, and that set people off again. But the poor thing committed suicide in the end—drowned herself, so I heard—and some thought it was remorse that made her do it. But all that talk about her aunt, there was nothing so far as we knew, though they *do* say no smoke without fire."

Other customers came in then, and the conversation was abandoned. Neither did Mrs. Bradley find any occasion to resume it during her grandson's visit, for every time after that that she visited the shop, Derek happened to be with her.

At last the time came for him to return home, but he suggested that he should stay another week, so, despite his parents' protests that they missed him, and wanted him back, stay he did until the following Thursday.

During his visit Mrs. Bradley had heard, at intervals, of a holiday task he had been set. He went to school, but Caroline preferred that it should be a day school until he was nine.

The last day of his visit was wet. He woke up to a rainy morning, and although he pressed his nose to the glass of the window for nearly half an hour before he aroused his grandmother, the rain showed no sign of ceasing.

He was a philosophical child, and, when he did wake her up, he merely remarked that it was raining. Mrs. Bradley, however, viewed the inclement weather with some concern, and at breakfast voiced her thoughts.

" Too bad it should be wet for your last day. What would you like to do ? "

Her grandson looked up from his plate.

" It would be a good idea to do my holiday task," he replied in his serious way. " I've got all my scraps ; some I brought with me and the others I've collected down here. But, you see, Gran, I haven't a book to paste them in, and I haven't any paste."

" I dare say we could find a book," said Mrs. Bradley.

" Well, I have *sort* of found a book," said the little boy. " I found it on the shelf in your bedroom cupboard ; only it's partly wrote in."

" Written in ? "

" Yes ; so I thought if I showed it to you and you said I could have it, perhaps we could make some paste and perhaps you've got a brush. A piece of paper *would* do, only I'd rather have a brush. It does it neater. Do you think I'll get the prize Gran ? "

" Do *you* think you'll get the prize ? "

" I expect so. If I could have a brush."

" In that case we must certainly provide a brush. Go and ask George about it. Perhaps he'll run you down to the village in the car, and then you could choose one for yourself."

" Oh, may I really, Gran ? Oh, *thanks* ! "

" Perhaps I'd better see the book before you go. If it isn't quite the thing, you could see what they've got at the village shop."

" They haven't got *anything*, because I asked. They've only got the miserable-est little drawing-books and exercise books and things. This one I found has got stiff-covers and it's *thick*. I suppose," he added, as a gloomy afterthought, " it really belongs to Miss Hodge."

Miss Hodge was the old servant who had inherited the house from Miss Bella's Aunt Flora, who had died (or, if one accepted Miss Peeple's warped view, thought Mrs. Bradley, had been murdered) in it. Miss Hodge was a woman of nearly seventy, and Mrs. Bradley and Derek both liked her.

" Well, we'd better look at this book of·yours," said Mrs.

Bradley, " and then we can judge whether Miss Hodge would be likely to let us have it."

Her grandson led the way upstairs. The book, produced most carefully for her inspection, proved to be one of those large, thick, stiff-covered diaries which are produced, judging from the letter-press, for the use of business men in South Africa. About a quarter of it, or rather less, had been used. The rest was blank. The diary was six years out of date.

" It doesn't look very important," said Mrs. Bradley. " I'll tell you what we'll do. We'll call on Miss Hodge on the way to the village shop, and take the book with us, and see what she has to say."

George had hoped for an undisturbed morning during which he proposed to re-read and to psycho-analyse Nietzsche (for he was an unobtrusive but indefatigable student of Mrs. Bradley's methods, and had attended all her public lectures in England), but he put the book down and rose to his feet when his employer and her grandson entered the kitchen.

" George, I want a brush for pasting my scraps, and Gran wants to ask Miss Hodge about the book in her bedroom," said the little boy. " So we shall have to go to the village, if you don't mind."

" Very good, sir," said George.

" And, George, I shall have to ask your advice about the brush."

" Yes, sir ? "

" And, George——"

" Sir ? "

" Do *you* think I shall win the prize ? "

" I sincerely hope so, sir. But kissing goes by favour, as they say."

" Is that what you say to yourself when you don't get what you want, George ? "

" No, sir. I merely say *Aliud alia dicunt*. That comforts me a good deal, sir."

Mrs. Bradley cackled.

The cottage in which Miss Hodge lived whilst her house was let was about three-quarters of a mile from the sea and on the outskirts of the village. There was no pavement to walk on, but on either side of the front door flowers flourished in their season, as they did in front of all the cottages on that side of the village inn. The front door led directly into the parlour, and was opened to the visitors almost before they had finished knocking.

Miss Hodge, a thin, upright, fresh-faced, pleasant, elderly woman, had come directly from the kitchen, wafted towards the visitors upon an odour of cooking. She wiped her hands on her apron.

" Good morning, madam," she said. " Good morning, Master Derek. A nasty morning ! Will you come in ? Nothing wrong, I hope ? "

" Nothing at all. It is just a question of a book which Derek has found," said Mrs. Bradley.

" You see, Miss Hodge, it would make an awfully nice scrap-book, and I have to give in a scrap-book, as my holiday task, to Miss Winter at school. Now, I've got the scraps—I think you would like to see them . . ."

" I'm sure, Master Derek."

" . . . and all I want, you see, is the book." He produced it. Miss Hodge gave her hands an extra rub on the apron, and then took up the diary, but did no more than glance at the beginning of it.

" Dear me, Master Derek ! Now what can you have got hold of here, I wonder ? " she said mildly. " This isn't the mistress's writing. I don't seem to know this hand." She looked at Mrs. Bradley. " He can have the empty pages and welcome, Madam, if that would do, but I'd better p'raps just see what it is, as it seems to be wrote out so neat. Now, where did I put my glasses ? "

Derek, assisting in the search, discovered them. Miss Hodge, in the laboured manner of an unaccustomed reader, perused a page or two slowly, and then looked over the top of her spectacles.

" It seems as if Miss Bella wrote it. I never knew she could write so nice. It's very like Mr. Tom's hand, now I call his letters to mind. But it's certainly all about Miss Bella, and partly about her aunt, my poor mistress, by the look of it. Ah, I remember now. Mrs. Muriel sent it after Miss Bella died."

" Oh, we can get hold of another book," said Mrs. Bradley quickly. " I am sure you wouldn't want us to have this one."

" Oh, *Gran* ! " said the little boy.

" If Master Derek fancies this one, he shall have it, bless him ! Only, I can't quite fancy throwing away Miss Bella's own words, her having such a sad end and so much trouble," said Miss Hodge, " although they found her ' Not Guilty.' Not that it did her any good, poor soul. I wonder if I could take out these pages that's wrote on without hurting the rest of the book ? "

" Dear me," said Mrs. Bradley. " Well, if you're quite sure he can have the book, Miss Hodge, I'll undertake to remove the written pages without spoiling them, and I'll get them bound for you, unless you'd like to take them out yourself. You see, the diary is very well put together in these sections. We should merely need to cut through the strings here and here . . ."

" I'd much rather you did it, madam, than I. I'm sure you know more about it. And perhaps you'd care to have a read of it, madam. It was quite a celebrated case in its way, poor Miss Bella's case was. . . ."

Mrs. Bradley, perceiving that Miss Hodge proposed to unfold a tale, sent Derek out to find George.

" Yes, Miss Bella had a sad life of it, poor thing," continued Miss Hodge, when Derek and George had gone off to the village shop. " She worked hard at that Home for dreadful boys until her aunt died, and then, when she might have been happy and independent, her gentleman cousin, Mr. Tom, fell out of a window, in what was said to be a haunted house, and then, of all things, if she wasn't arrested for murdering him, if ever you heard anything so wicked ! "

" Why did they think she had murdered him ? " asked Mrs. Bradley, interested not only in the story itself but in the persistent idea of a haunted house which seemed to run through it.

" Oh, I don't know. There was a whole lot of wicked, lying stories getting spread about after the poor mistress's death, and I believe someone wrote some ugly letters. And then, when Mr. Tom died so very shortly afterwards, it seemed that somebody thought themselves clever enough to put two and two together, and so she was arrested, and tried, poor thing. They had to let her off, of course, because nothing was proved against her, but it preyed so on her mind that she killed herself, and the money all went to Miss Tessa, the other niece."

" How long ago was this ? " asked Mrs. Bradley.

" Six years ago this month she was tried and let off," said Miss Hodge. " I remember it by when the mistress died and left me the house and the money."

" I expect I was in America then," said Mrs. Bradley. " I suppose I missed the whole thing. It must have been very dreadful for the people who knew her. I'd like to read the diary, if I may, and I'll bring it back to you the moment I've finished with it and bound the pages, shall I ? "

" No hurry, madam. Keep it as long as you like if it interests you. I just don't care to destroy it. That's all it is. I don't suppose I should ever read it myself, not all that writing. Just the little bits about the mistress."

" I ought to pay you for the pages I'm going to use, Miss Hodge," said Derek, when he returned from the village shop. " I have my own money, you know."

" Good gracious me, Master Derek ! I'm sure you're more than welcome," said the old servant. " Especially," she added, with the sentimentality of her class and generation, " if you'd give me a nice kiss for it, now."

" With pleasure," said Derek gravely, putting his arms round her neck. Mrs. Bradley cackled at this display of social tact by her grandson, and her eyes were bright as a bird's as she looked at the manuscript in her hand.

The diary, as Miss Hodge had indicated, was neatly and legibly written with a fine pen, and some attempt had been made at literary style, as though the diarist, consciously or unconsciously, had hoped that eyes other than her own would read the manuscript. Later on, Mrs. Bradley obtained permission to make an exact copy of it. This ran as follows :

January 17

I dreamt Aunt Flora was dead. They say the wish is father to the thought, so perhaps to the dream as well. It is not that I wish the poor old woman any ill, but there is no doubt that at ninety she is too long-lived. It is no joke for me to be earning my living at the age of forty-seven when I have had expectations (as they say) of two thousand pounds a year since I was twenty.

The chaplain's wife said yesterday that some people (meaning me) had much to be thankful for. A good salary, she remarked, no encumbrances (they have six children and the chaplain's mother to provide for) and a good appetite (I shall never go there to tea again!) are gifts of good fortune which fall to the lot of only one or two. She knows of nobody else, she added, quite so fortunately placed as I am. Detestable woman. I should regard myself as fortunately placed if I had my two thousand a year, and should be thankful—very thankful—for it, but I see nothing else in life to merit or justify my thanks. I responded to the chaplain's wife that a good husband and six olive branches were surely excellent reasons for thanks. Her reply, although phrased in the conventional terms, was extremely wintry.

January 18

I asked Vera, the kitchenmaid, to-day, what she thought any of us had to be thankful for. She said good health, which I believe she enjoys. But I have rheumatism always here, because of these stone floors, and I catch cold easily. The worst of it is that I get no sympathy from anybody. The others are never seedy or off-colour. Besides, I think they dislike me. Aunt Flora does not care much about me, either. Although she is ninety she retains all her faculties, as they say, and I believe she enjoys teasing me about the money. She asked me this Christmas-time what I intended to do with the two thousand when I got it, so I said I should start a restaurant. I should not dream of doing anything of the sort. I am not going to do any work at all when I get that money, and I am going to make quite sure that I spend the whole of the two thousand every year. I cannot touch the capital, of course. That remains for Tessa, and I imagine that her brat will get the income when I am gone unless cousin Tom comes next. As I have not seen the will, I do not know anything about this, but imagine that he is left out.

January 19

The chaplain preached to the boys to-day on Hosea, who

seems to have had a sad life caused chiefly by a bad wife. I do not know what lesson there was for the boys in this. What hideous little faces they all have. It is nonsense to say, as William does in staff meetings sometimes when he thinks we all need a pep talk, that criminals are made and not born. These boys are predestined to crime, and no psychologist or educationist is going to persuade me otherwise. As for wives—a lot they are going to know about them ! Most of these will be in prison a year after we let them out of here.

Denny has a poison bottle in which he places butterflies, moths, and other creatures for his collection. His ' smelling salts ' the boys call it. How they love to watch the creatures die ! And what a good thing it would be if this institution were one gigantic bottle into which we could drop the boys, one by one, as they came into our charge. A little struggling and choking, a fluttering of helpless limbs, and then—a perfect specimen of young criminal ready to be preserved, dissected, lectured upon and buried, according to his uses as an anatomical, biological or psychological specimen.

January 20

I wish now that I had followed my original intention, and kept this diary from New Year's Day instead of waiting until the beginning of the term. One is lazy in the holidays, I suppose.

It was good of Tom and Muriel to invite me to stay with them for the last few days before I returned to the Institution, especially as they have moved recently. I think Tom is overdoing this psychical research business, and Muriel looks a wreck. I am sure that ghost-hunting does not improve her nerves. A nice little modern house at the seaside would be far better for her—and for me, too. I should very much enjoy spending a rent-free weekend or two at Bournemouth, say, or Ilfracombe, during the summer.

Muriel makes a good wife, though, and Tom is so keen on his work that I suppose she feels she must help him all she can. But this dodging from one reputedly haunted house to another must be past a joke, especially as they find out nothing exciting enough for Tom to make into a best-seller. What he wants is a house like Borley Rectory. I often wonder why he never rented it. Can it be that he doesn't really *want* to find an authentic ghost ?

Well, anyhow, apart from the nervous strain, I must say Muriel seems to keep pretty well. A pity they don't have children, but I suppose it must be rather hard on children to have a ghost-hunter for a father, so possibly all is for the best.

January 21

Talking of wives, it appears that unbeknown to everybody except Ronald who acted as best man, Denny was married during the Christmas holidays and has brought his wife to live in a house about half a mile from the front gates of the Institution. I think William is a little worried. He has to give married instructors permission to live out, as that is in the regulations. On the other hand, we can't have too many people living out, otherwise there are not enough left here to look after the boys at night. Therefore the next instructor who wants to get married will have to resign, as already we are what William calls (without mincing matters) dangerously understaffed at nights with Denny off the premises.

This is, of course, an overstatement. Nobody, least of all a man in William's position, is justified in accepting the responsibility of our being *dangerously* understaffed here at any time or under any circumstances, but we all know what he means and are sufficiently uncomfortable about it. Once, before my time, when two-thirds of the indoor staff were down with influenza, the boys made a mass attack on the food stores and the instructors' private rooms, and ten boys got away and were at liberty for three days, during which time they robbed hen-roosts, half-murdered an old woman and held up a village post-office.

January 22

Denny's wife seems a nice enough little thing. I was invited to tea there. I wonder sometimes what kind of wife I should have made, and whether it would have been better if I had married in 1916 when he wanted it. I wonder whether he really was killed, or whether, after he was reported missing, he ever turned up again, a case of lost memory or shell-shock. For all I know (or am ever likely to know) he is in a mental hospital. There was insanity in his family, and these things persist. There was no one but myself to wonder what had happened, and sometimes I wonder also whether I really cared, for I certainly don't care now. It is a very strange thing, when one thinks about it, to be forty-seven years old, and to be quite certain that not a soul on earth cares whether one is alive or dead. I suppose if I left the Institution, or died, the staff here would feel compelled to subscribe either to a gift or a wreath. As it would come to about half-a-crown each in either case, it would not matter to them, I suppose, whether I were going to a new post or to the grave.

January 23

A new post ! Sometimes I used to think that, if only I could hit upon the right place, I might enjoy my job. Nowadays, of course, I know that I should be a failure anywhere ; not a spectacular failure, like poor Justin, who was almost kicked to death by the boys before he was dismissed by the managers, but the sort of failure that rubs along somehow without ever being quite bad enough to get the sack.

" Hangs on by her eyebrows, poor devil," I heard Colin say in the staff-room the other day ; and I am certain he was talking about me. It was kind of him to call me a poor devil. Most of them hate me like poison because, when I take my sick-leave, they are put to a good deal of inconvenience. But I know I could not manage a whole year right through, even with the holidays. I should die without my little bits of ill-health.

January 24

Two boys, Piggy and Alec, escaped last night and appear to have got clean away from the Institution. Both were serious cases. Piggy is in for killing his little sister by pushing her off a bedroom window-sill, and Alec was a thieves' boy, and used to get through larder windows which were too small for the cracksmen. They are nice boys and I hope they will not be caught. Piggy's little sister was a horrid child, he says. We are not supposed to discuss with the boys the reasons for their having been sent here, but when I am superintending the washing-up and the other household tasks they do as fatigues when the better-behaved (that means the cleverer) ones are at football, I hear a good many things which I am not supposed to know.

Alec is a merry little boy. Although he is fifteen now, and has been with us for two years, he does not seem to grow at all. He has told me that when he is released he will go back to his old employment unless he can get into some racing stables and train for a jockey. There is no harm in this boy. Thieves can be as honest as anybody else along their own lines, and it is all nonsense for William to think that boys like these can be reformed, or that the world would be a better place if they were.

January 25

William is spending all his time at the end of the telephone while the search for the boys continues. He looks worried, as well he may, for it proves, upon investigation of the sleeping quarters (we do not call them dormitories here, lest these lads should get ideas beyond their station !), that the bars of F room have been filed through and that Arthur, who is in charge of this room, ought to have known what was happening.

William has interrogated a boy named Larry, and search is still being made for the files, but Larry has said that Piggy and Alec must have taken the files away with them, and he has declared that he knows nothing about the bars.

It is part of William's policy to accept the word of a boy until he can disprove it. When he has disproved it (which he usually manages to do) he has the boy punished. This system is open to two objections. It has undermined William's moral sense, which can never have been very robust, and it disproves any theories that William is a gentleman. William is not a gentleman. He does not even punish the boys himself. This is Arthur's part of the work. He is called the Second Master and most of the boys are in awe of him. It was very daring of Piggy and Alec to make their escape from Arthur's room.

January 26

I received a telegram this morning and have had to ask for special leave of absence. Aunt Flora is seriously ill.

January 27

I have spent most of yesterday and all of to-day at Aunt Flora's bedside. She is unconscious. It appears that she tumbled over her flannel petticoat when she was walking along the landing and hit her head against the bathroom door. She had refused to allow Eliza to dress her and, of course, had not managed the strings. Eliza says that it is a judgment upon Aunt Flora for being so contrary, but she (Eliza) seems, all the same, in good spirits, in spite of the extra work. She is thinking, no doubt, upon the little legacy which Aunt Flora, for decency's sake, is certain to have left her in the will. I do not in the least object to having my money depleted upon Eliza's account.

I find myself wondering (for there is little to do except sit and wait for the end) whether it will be in order to have Aunt Flora's hair washed after she is dead. I have been noticing that her parting is very grimy, and that her white hair is so tinged with dirt as to be rather shocking. I do not like to speak to Eliza about this, in case she should think that I was finding fault, for she is a touchy old thing and I should not care to offend her. Perhaps the dirt is partly the result of the fall, although it hardly looks like it.

January 28

Aunt Flora has recovered consciousness, and this, says the doctor, is the end. He had rather thought that she would never speak again, or recognise any of us, but she has wonderful rallying powers. I only hope that they will not prove too wonderful, for that would be too bitterly disappointing. Tom and Muriel arrived at ten this morning. They had travelled all night, they said, in order to be in at the death. At least, Tom said this, and was immediately hushed by Muriel, who thought it an unfortunate metaphor. It was certainly very clumsy, but what does that matter? It is true—or so I profoundly hope.

January 29

William rang me up on long distance—a pretty penny it cost, but I suppose he will not pay it himself—to ask me when I could conclude my family business and return. There is still no news of Piggy and Alec, he says, although the police are doing their best, but a boy named Dick has bitten Francis in the hand, and the bite has turned septic and Francis is very feverish, and not able to continue his duties. Will I be prepared to ' fill-in ? ' I should like to retort that I cannot hurry Aunt Flora into

eternity, much as I should like to do so, and that even Dick's
bite would not turn septic when applied to an instructor's hand
if the instructor drank whisky instead of taking drugs. (I know
for a fact that Francis does this). But I refrained from both
remarks, and replied that I should return as soon as possible,
and that Aunt had rallied a little.

I went out for a short time this afternoon and brought back a
tin of lobster for Eliza. It is her favourite delicacy, and she was
greatly pleased. Aunt Flora keeps no other servant, and the
house is a small one. It seems strange that she, who has so
much money, should choose to live so simply. It is not a fad of
her old age, either. It has been so since Uncle died.

Eliza was delighted with the lobster and continued to thank
me long after any further thanks were necessary. It became, in
fact, a little embarrassing for us both, but she is a dear old soul,
and I sincerely hope that Aunt has provided for her in the will.

January 30

I am astonished, although, of course, I neither say so nor
let it appear so, that Tom and Muriel took the trouble to make
this long journey, busy as they have been over their moving.
They have no possible expectations under the will, and therefore
must be much more good-hearted than I had supposed.

Tom says that the new house promises well. There are
recorded *poltergeist* disturbances, and, according to the villagers
(who cannot, however, usually be depended upon for accurate
information when hauntings are in question !) something more
interesting still. I have not pressed Tom for details, as I find I
cannot sleep after I have been listening to his stories, incon-
clusive and vague although most of them are. I will let him
unburden himself before lunch to-morrow, and then I can
forget all about what he tells me by the hour that bedtime comes.
In any case, I have enough to think about. Aunt Flora has so
far rallied that the doctor says she is out of danger !

January 31

I can hardly realize it ! In fact, I try not to realize it, because
when I allow myself to think about it at all, I can think only of my
money. Yes, it has come about at last, and nothing but that

strange by-product of civilised intercourse which we think of by the name of " decent behaviour " prevents me from shouting it aloud. At last, at last, after all these lean and dreadful years, and when, after the doctor's report, I had given up hope again, Aunt Flora is dead. It all happened strangely and suddenly. At seven o'clock yesterday evening she sat up and, in her normal voice, asked for some grated carrot. She has taken up this raw food dieting during her later life, and usually attributes her longevity to it. Tom said that he realised it could be nothing but the return of all her normal faculties ; and he thought she must be humoured. We went to the kitchen, therefore, and, Eliza being at chapel for her weeknight meeting, I scraped some carrot on a nutmeg grater. The result was messy, but we hoped that it would do. I put it into a large, deep saucer, thinking that Aunt would manage it best that way, and placed a spoon beside the saucer on the tray, and also a glass of water.

The effort of eating must have been too much for the poor old thing. She had scarcely taken a third mouthful of the carrot—judging by what was left on the saucer—when she must have choked and, after struggling, I should think, to clutch the glass of water—for it was overturned—she must have fallen back dead.

When we came back again a little later on in the evening and saw her, I sent Tom running for more water. He came back with the tumbler, dashed the water into her face and made other efforts to revive her. It was hopeless. The doctor came a quarter of an hour later, but, of course, there was nothing to be done Poor Tom was in tears. He is a good-hearted man. I feel that in the past I have misjudged him sadly. He, with nothing to gain—but I need not dwell on that.

February 1

The doctor's manner has been somewhat off-hand. I asked him rather sharply whether he had any objection to signing the death certificate As he had already signed it, I suppose he thought this an improper and impertinent question, but I did not like his attitude, and took care to let him know it. Aunt is to be buried on Tuesday. There is no one to bid to the funeral except Tessa, and I don't suppose she will trouble herself to come, since Aunt cut her out of her will when she heard that the brat had been born out of wedlock. As though it was Tessa's fault! The man would have married her if he had not been killed in the war. Of course, Tessa was Aunt Flora's favourite until the child was born, but then I took my sister's place in her regard, and the money, which was to have been shared between us, was all diverted to me. Much good it has done me all these years! And Tessa did have her fun—while it lasted! But now . . .! The future seems so bright I dare not look at it for fear that something should, after all, go wrong.

February 2

I have written to Tessa, care of the last address I have (although I know she moved from it just over three years ago) to tell her the news. Poor old Eliza is quite stricken with grief, and says that she shall never get another situation at her age, and that she had "looked to go before the mistress." I believe she is turned seventy, so I do hope that Aunt has done something handsome for her, as she has been in service here, she tells me, since she was sixteen and a half.

It is very useful and nice to have Tom here. He has undertaken all the funeral arrangements, and these are so much more easily done by a man than by a woman. Muriel and I walk about the house and look at the very simple, old-fashioned furniture and effects, and speculate upon Aunt, who has always been, to me, of a most forbidding and incomprehensible age, because, after all, she was forty-three years old when I was born! Muriel knows nothing much about her, except from Tom's descriptions.

February 3

My wreath is to be of white hyacinths and dark crimson carnations. As William has not seen fit to send me on my cheque, I am now very short of ready money, and may have to borrow off Tom for the funeral bakemeats, for which, presumably, I am liable to pay, as there is nothing much in the house or ordered.

February 4

The funeral went off quite well, and a surprising number of people attended; surprising to me, that is, for Tom said he believed that Aunt was greatly respected in the place. The flowers were really good, and the hearse looked quite a picture. It was a fine day, too, which is a great blessing on these occasions. I think a fine day is almost as important at a funeral as at a wedding. In fact, from the point of view of the general health, it is more so. I have heard of more than one person developing a fatal illness from standing at a graveside in the wet.

Eliza had everything ready for us on our return, and Tom and Muriel said that as they had no interest under the will they would not stay to hear it read, and as it was Eliza's afternoon out I sent her off to see her sister who lives in the next town, a fourpenny bus ride, and said that I would tell her any news on her return. The selfless old creature did not give the slightest indication that she thought Aunt might have remembered her in the will, and I said nothing about it, in case my surmises should be wrong. I could not bear to disappoint Eliza. She did say, just before she went (and when I was in a fever lest the lawyer should arrive and she feel bound to stay at home to see to things), that she supposed I would not be keeping the house on. I replied, very gently, that I did not think so, and positively pushed her out. She turned at the last, even then, and asked me whether it looked heartless, her taking her afternoon just as though the mistress had not died. I replied firmly to this, and at last got rid of her.

February 7

I have had no time to write up this diary for the past two days. Now I am back at the Institution, which I cannot leave suddenly without breaking the terms of my engagement. Besides, William asked me as a personal favour to stay at least until the end of the month. Fortunately the news of Aunt was so grave on the thirtieth that I gave provisional notice then, and I am determined not to stay beyond the twenty-eighth of February to please or oblige anybody.

I told Vera to-day all about my good fortune. Aunt's house is in the hands of the agent, and they trust to be able to make a good and quick sale, as the house is small, convenient and easily worked, and is within nice distance of the sea.

Vera was particularly interested to hear of poor old Eliza's fifty pounds a year, and said that she thought she should take a situation in private service. She was very raw and untrained when she was first appointed here, but I have done my best, and I think now that she might get a very good place.

The staff congratulated me on my inheritance, and we had quite a jolly evening with some port (provided by me) and a bottle of whisky. William, however, is very worried, as there is still no news of the missing boys.

Cyril, who cannot take very much to drink, asked me, after his third glass, whether I had sued the *Daily Pennon* yet. I did not know what he meant, and the others seemed so anxious to shut him up that I must make the opportunity to find out what he was talking about.

February 8

I tackled Cyril before supper this evening and he apologised and said he had meant nothing—it was simply a stupid joke. He seemed so anxious to reassure me that I became anxious, in my turn, to find out what the stupid joke is. Perhaps I would be better advised to let the subject drop, however, as, no doubt, plenty of people have been making spiteful remarks since they heard of my good fortune.

February 10

The beginning of a new week. A boy, Jones, has complained of the dumplings. He says they contain screwed-up pellets of paper. William has had a lengthy interview with Jones, but can ascertain nothing, as Jones had swallowed the pellets after chewing them. I was also called upon as cook, to interview the boy, but could get no further details of the complaint, and nothing will shake him in his assertions. It is very curious. I have spoken to Vera, but she declares that after I mixed the paste for the dumplings nobody entered the kitchen, for she was there the whole time until I came back from interviewing the butcher to whom I had complained about the chops the staff had one day whilst I was absent. The staff do not have the same food as the boys, and this is a bitter grievance which is always aired when the boys complain (as they do about once every five or six weeks) about the diet.

William, most unwisely in my opinion, has addressed the Institution publicly, to request that any foreign bodies discovered in the food shall be preserved and handed to the instructor in charge. After tea, therefore, Denny, who was on duty, received five buttons, a decayed tooth, half a dozen teeth from a comb, a small piece of lead pencil, a chip of glass, a fragment of bone, some matted hairs, a couple of match-sticks, some wood splinters and a score of other, more or less horrid, objects. Every boy had made it a point of honour to " find" something.

February 11

William has called another assembly and has announced that the next boy who finds a foreign body in the food will be flogged.

February 12

I have received an unpleasant letter which I have sent on to Tom, requesting his advice. It has a London postmark, but must have been sent by someone who lives near poor Aunt's house.

February 13

My letter has crossed with one from Tom enclosing a communication very similar to the one I have just sent to him. He wants to know what I want done about it, and suggests putting the letter into the hands of the police. I don't quite care for the idea, but probably it is the only way to stop the writer from becoming a serious nuisance. Another plan, he says, is to burn the next one unread—if there is a next one—and so let the writer work off her ill-nature and spite.

February 14

There is some news of Piggy and Alec. Two boys answering the description have been found by the Yorkshire police. William is to go to York to identify them. From the evidence, there is little doubt that these are the right boys. They have remained at large for three weeks. Much seems to have happened since they went. It seems a year to me, because it all happened before Aunt's death.

February 15

My legacy is to be paid quarterly. I had hoped to have it every month, and shall write off straight away to find out whether this cannot be arranged. I do wish I did not feel obliged to work out my month here. I should like to get away at once. For one thing, I have to find somewhere to live, as I do not think I should care for hotel life.

February 16

The boys are not Piggy and Alec.

February 17

I shall go sick for the rest of my month. Why not? It is an easy and pleasant way out, and as William cannot return until this afternoon at the earliest, I shall simply go to Tom and Muriel as soon as I have sent in a doctor's certificate, and write to William from there.

February 18

The doctor was very nice about the certificate and said that a rest would do me good. The certificate will last a fortnight, and that will do beautifully. It is wonderful to think that I shall never darken these doors again, and to work out my notice in sick leave is perfectly permissible. I have told Vera that I am going to be away for a few days, and that she will have to manage. If William has any sense, he will arrange for one or two of the instructors' wives to come in and give a hand with the dining arrangements. The menu is settled. They have only to prepare the food and cook it. Anyway, I cannot help their troubles. Oh, to be free! To be away from it all for ever! I can hardly believe my good luck. I wish I did not keep thinking about those anonymous letters.

February 19

I wish I had never read about Borley Rectory* because I am sure that this house in which Tom and Muriel are living is

* " *The Most Haunted House in England. Ten Years' Investigation of Borley Rectory.*" By Harry Price. Longmans, Green and Co., 1940.

exactly like it. I believe I am psychic. I have often thought so. At any rate, the house affects me most unpleasantly, and the atmosphere is not helped by the attitude of Tom and Muriel, who do not appear in the least pleased to see me, and are treating me so much like an intruder that I think I shall move to the village inn to-morrow, and not trouble them any further with my company.

February 20

I have had a long conversation with Muriel. She is a nice woman, and I made the opportunity to ask her—as tactfully as I could, but, of course, these things have to be expressed in words, and it is not always that the best phrases come exactly when they are wanted most—whether my presence in the house was an inconvenience. To my distress, but not altogether to my astonishment, she burst into tears, and, with both hands clasping my arm, implored me to stay, saying that she knew they had been " horrid " but that the atmosphere of this weird house had quite daunted them and was getting on their nerves to such an extent that they had already begun quarrelling with one another—a thing, she added, with a fresh outbreak of crying, that had never happened before in their married life.

This I can believe. They have always been a devoted couple.

Reassured by her outburst, I reiterated my willingness to leave the house if my presence was the slightest embarrassment to either of them, but she again begged me to stay, and then asked, almost in a whisper, whether I had " seen " or " heard " anything since my arrival. I said that I had been aware of " presences " but had not seen or heard anything which could not be explained away. What did I mean by that, she wanted to know. Bats, rats or mice, I replied, and, of course, Tom coming past my door in his slippers. She looked at me oddly when I said that, and advised me to say nothing about that to Tom, as she had already accused him of walking in his sleep, and he had so vigorously denied it that the argument had been the prelude to their first quarrel.

" And I don't believe now that it *was* Tom," she concluded, " but I daren't say so, *because if it wasn't Tom, who was it* ? "

February 21

A bitter letter from William affecting to sympathize with my illness but written to point out how extremely inconvenient it is of me to have to take sick leave at such a time. I shall not reply to it. A letter from Aunt's lawyer to say that the income can be paid monthly by arrangement with my bank. This is splendid. I have told Muriel privately that as long as I live with them I am going to make Tom an allowance of two hundred and fifty a year. This brought more tears, as she tried to thank me. They must be very badly off for the offer to have affected her as it did. I feel quite a philanthropist.

February 22

The manifestations have begun in earnest. Last night, as I was going upstairs, I heard a slight sound behind me. The house has electric lighting, and so everything was perfectly visible, and I could see that some small object had fallen on to the floor in the middle of the hall. I went down again and picked it up. Tom and Muriel keep no servants, so there was no one but our three selves in the house, and I had just left the other two in the dining-room which we use as a living-room. The object was a small perpetual calendar which I had seen on my dressing-table before I went downstairs that evening. I picked it up and took it upstairs with me.

Scarcely had I replaced it in its usual position when I heard the most appalling crash downstairs. I ran out of the bedroom and Tom and Muriel ran out from the dining-room, all of us anxiously calling out, " Are you all right ? "

Then we saw that the entire contents of the kitchen shelves had been precipitated into the hall—several saucepans, a couple of enamel jugs, kettle-holders, three or four odd cups, a bottle-opener, two frying pans, an earthenware casserole, a fish slice and a porridge strainer were scattered all over the place. Nothing was broken, not even the handles off the cups, but two of the saucepans were dented.

When we had picked them up and put them back on the kitchen shelves—a hateful task, since none of us in the least wanted to enter the kitchen—all the bells in the house began to ring.

February 23

Tom has cut all the bell-wires, but the bells continue to ring. I do not like it at all.

February 24

The slippered footsteps are worse. They follow Muriel everywhere. She is a nervous wreck. Tom is having four people down for a séance. He is like a man with a pet snake—fascinated but frightened. We have now heard ghostly music.

February 25

I have moved to the village inn, and Muriel has come with me. She says she cannot stand the house any longer. The séance has completed her breakdown. The four people, three men and an elderly woman, arrived at four o'clock yesterday, and, after tea, Tom showed them his journal and notebook. He has kept an exact record of all the phenomena of the house. They seemed interested, and discussed everything in a detached, scientific way which was very comforting. Even Muriel cheered up, and was ready to agree that nothing *harmful* had happened. But the effect of all this was suddenly spoilt when, in the middle of the séance, there was a crash and a series of bumps overhead, and when we—or, rather, they—investigated (for Muriel and I remained downstairs holding on to one another for fright), it turned out that all the furniture in the spare bedroom had been overturned, and the electric-light flex had parted, depositing the lamp and shade on top of the dressing-chest which was on its side in the middle of the room. The bedhead fittings were undisturbed except that, as Tom switched on a torch, the bedhead flex began to swing like the pendulum of a clock. As soon as one of the gentlemen put out his hand to switch on the light, however, the swinging stopped, but the music broke out again.

They put the room to rights, but I was far too nervous to sleep in it, so went off to the inn and Muriel accompanied me. Tom and two of the visitors remained in the house. The other two visitors had to get back to town. It was then about half-past eight.

February 26

Muriel has rejoined Tom. She must be a heroine and I hope Tom appreciates the fact. Nothing much has happened to-day, so far as I know. I spent the early part of the afternoon with them, and they had nothing to report except a few bangings upstairs, but nothing had been moved. Tom and the visitors occupied themselves after the séance and our departure with chalking rings round every movable thing in the house—furniture, ornaments, pictures, books (there are no bookshelves here—it makes the house seem very cluttered-up and untidy) so that we can see at a glance whether anything has been moved. Tom has a fanatical gleam in his eye. The London experts have impressed him. He is longing now for further manifestations.

February 27

There are horrid stories round the village of *something that walks in the grounds* of Tom's house at night.

February 28

News of Piggy and Alec. Here in this village, too. Two boys answering to the description have been taken up by the village policeman for robbing a chicken-farm kept by a young couple called Tolleson on the outskirts of the village. As every police station has a description of the lads, they have been handed over to the inspector at Ridge, the nearest town. I have not seen the boys, but have no doubt that these are they. Still, it is none of my business now. William has written to invite me to go back for a " small presentation " if I feel well enough. I do *not* feel well enough. Nothing will induce me to visit the Institution again. They can keep their clock or suitcase or whatever it is. I shall not even answer the letter. It is better to cut all connection.

March 3

The stories in the village become more horrifying. There is now a coach and horses with a headless driver.

March 4

Muriel has rejoined me at the village inn. She says that if she stays in the house any longer she will go mad. She certainly seems almost beside herself. She says that the footsteps get worse. They are no longer quiet, but run all over the house. She lay awake for half an hour, by her watch, in an ecstasy of terror, last night, from half-past twelve until one. Tom came in at one— they share a room, but he had remained downstairs writing up his journal—and asked her whether she had heard anything. He had been out twice, he said, to investigate, but could see nothing, and the noise stopped the moment he opened the dining-room door. In the morning, the spare-room furniture was found piled on to the bed.

March 5

These boys are not Piggy and Alec, either.

March 6

I have received three more anonymous letters. Somebody has discovered where I am living. They are the usual thing, plus a direct accusation of murder. I am supposed to have poisoned Aunt Flora. I took the letters to the police. They have promised to make some enquiries, but I have no faith in the police. They may be able to discover criminals of the ordinary kind, but they will never trace these letters to the sender. And why can't they find Piggy and Alec, if they are so clever? It seems impossible that two boys of that type can remain at large for so long.

March 7

Tom has told Muriel that he will give up his researches at the house.

March 8

Muriel has asked my advice. It would be a pity, she thinks, for Tom to give up the house, which is now attracting a good deal of attention in journals devoted to psychical research, and Tom has already made more money out of his articles than he has made in the past two years. Moving house, too, she points out, is a very expensive business. On the other hand, the house terrifies her. I told her some of the stories which are current in the village, but said I did not believe them. She said again that nothing will induce her to live in the house. She intends to tell

Tom that he can live there alone or invite friends who are interested in the phenomena, and she will live with me for the time, until he has finished with the house.

March 9

Tom has heard all Muriel's arguments and it is agreed that he shall lease the house for another three months, and that if she still refuses to live there he will then move to a place of her choosing. I have persuaded Muriel to agree to this, and I am giving Tom a hundred a year of the money Aunt left to me, although I am no longer the " paying guest " at the house.

March 10

Two vulgar epithets and part of a prayer have been scribbled on the walls of Tom's house. He is tremendously excited, seems to have overcome all his nervousness, and invited us both to come in and see the new manifestations. I went, and, after a bit, Muriel (rather to my surprise) followed suit. She would not stay in the house, however, which, she said, made her want to scream. Tom sent off several telegrams from the village post-office to psychical research people, inviting them to come down and see the spirit-writing. He had a lot of fun this afternoon putting glass over it, as they have done in the Tower of London over prisoners' scribblings and carvings.

March 11

Things are getting worse—and more exciting—at the house. Last night we said good night to Tom at the inn, at which we had invited him to dine, and he left us at about ten o'clock. It was a dark night, no moon and a cloudy sky, and he went off singing. I do not mean, of course, that he was drunk. I will say for Tom that he carries his drinks well. We listened to the singing until we could hear it no longer, and then we went back inside the inn and up to bed. We were sharing a room because of Muriel's nerves, and at about eleven she leaned up, switched on the light and said that she could not bear it ; she was certain that Tom was in some danger.

The house was not on the telephone, otherwise I would have rung him up, so I comforted her and she lay down again. As it happened, however, her uneasiness had now communicated itself to me and I could not sleep. At midnight I got up and dressed. I was now so worried that I could think of nothing except going to see whether Tom was all right, as I knew he was in the house alone.

I reached the house at about twenty minutes past twelve, walked up the drive, and saw a light in the bedroom which I knew Tom usually occupied. I threw some gravel up at the window and called out to know whether he was all right. He opened the window and called out to know who was there. I told him, and he replied :

" Good heavens, Bella ! What on earth are you doing at this time of night ? Of course I'm all right. In fact, the house is quieter than usual."

As he spoke I thought I could see a second figure just behind him in the room, and I called out :

" The headless coachman is just behind you ! "

I heard him laugh, and as he did so the figure behind him disappeared. Then he told me to go back before Muriel woke up and missed me and had another of her nervous attacks, so I called good night up to him, and, suddenly getting very nervous, ran back all the way down the drive to the gate. When I reached a point along the road from which the house can again be seen I saw that the light in his room had gone out.

To-day the boots told me the news that Tom was hurt. He had been found by the boy who brings the milk. It seems that after I left he must have tumbled out of the window. Muriel is prostrate. I am afraid for her reason. She says the ghosts want the house to themselves.

March 12

On my own account I have been to the house to see whether there is any explanation of the mystery. Tom is in bed.

March 13

Tom is giving up the house as too dangerous.

March 14

Another anonymous letter about the death of Aunt Flora.

This time I am accused of having strangled her. Three gentlemen and two ladies interested in psychical research came down by train this morning expecting to be shown over the house by Tom. As I felt sure he would have wished it, I myself let them in and showed them over, but although they stayed four hours and we all lunched off corned beef, bread, and some chocolate, there were no manifestations of any kind. I showed them Tom's journal, which was on the writing-table, and they were very much interested in this, and asked leave to carry it away and study it at their leisure. I obtained a receipt for it, and let them have it. Later I broke to them the news of Tom's accident. It is sure to be in all the papers to-morrow if not to-night. The reporters have been nosing round here already.

March 15

The police have *also* been nosing round. I can't think why, unless Tom sent for them, but there seems no reason for that. They asked to see us, and Muriel blurted out all her fears about the haunted house, but the police, I can see, don't credit the hauntings. They ought to stay a few days and nights in the house !

March 16

The police now think that Piggy and Alec must have got away on a cargo boat or something. I had a letter from Vera to-day sent on from Aunt's house, the last address of mine she had. William, she says, is at his wits' end to find a new housekeeper, and she herself does not think she wants to work under anybody else now, but will give in her notice as soon as the new person is appointed. It seems that Denny's wife has been carrying on with my job temporarily, but, according to Vera, is not much good at it. I wish joy to whoever gets it ! When the muddle about poor old Tom is cleared up I think I shall go and live in Cornwall. I have always loved the Cornish villages.

March 17

Muriel was much calmer this afternoon. She asked me whether I would be prepared to lend her a little money until she can find some work, as Tom is determined to return to the haunted house, and she has refused to live there. Tom cannot afford to pay her bills at the inn if I leave them and go to Cornwall. I said I would gladly help her, and that, if she cared to do it, I would be pleased to take her on as my paid companion. She asked whether she might have time to think it over, not that she wasn't grateful, but she had thought of something more in the secretarial line, or teaching music.

March 18

There is no doubt the police think Tom was pushed out of the window. That means that he must have said so, and is returning to the house to solve the mystery. The police have interviewed a good many people—tradespeople and others—and have again questioned Muriel and myself. How I wish I had never gone near the house that night ! That's what's done it. They think I pushed him out, I do believe ! I wonder what he has against me !

March 19

Muriel told me that they have been asking her whether he had anything on his mind. That would make it attempted suicide. She replied that he was in good spirits with every prospect of making some extra money out of his writings on the haunted house, that he was not financially embarrassed, and that, in any case, he was receiving an allowance. That brought them back to me, and they demanded to know what had made me think of giving Tom an allowance. I explained about Aunt, as briefly as I could, and the inspector rather nastily said : " Oh, yes, the old lady who was choked with the grated carrot. I remember."

In spite of my income and my freedom, I am beginning to wish that that particular carrot was still growing in the garden.

The diary ended somewhat abruptly, and Mrs. Bradley could not help wondering what had caused so assiduous a diarist—supposing the diary to be genuine, a supposition which, on the internal evidence, she was disposed to reject—to fall short of reporting the course of events at least up to the death of Cousin Tom.

She enquired, later, on what date Cousin Tom had died, and learned that it was on the morning of the twenty-second of March that his body had been found on a gravel path outside the haunted house. The ghosts believed in repeating their effects, it seemed.

Chapter Two

REACTIONS OF AN ELDERLY SERVANT

> " And whereas none rejoice more in revenge
> Than women use to do : yet you well know,
> That wrong is better checked by being contemned
> Than being pursued. . . ."
>
> DANIEL.

AT half-past two in the afternoon, Mrs. Bradley drove into the village. The weather had improved. It was no longer raining, although there was no sunshine either. In the distance the sea boomed, a sullen sound in keeping with the lowering sky.

Derek accompanied his grandmother. They were to meet his father and mother at the station and drive them back to the house for an early tea.

The little boy had spent three hours upon his scrap-book, and the result, a little uneven, and marred here and there by the application of too much paste, was creditable enough, considering his age. Mrs. Bradley, in fact, was surprised at the dimensions and variety of his holiday collection when she assisted him in checking, classifying and naming it.

" We're allowed to have any help we can get," he announced. " Miss Winter says that no man is sufficient unto himself when he goes out into the world, and so she sees no reason why we should be sufficient unto ourselves at school. She lets us cheat our mathematics and everything else, if we want to. She says it's too fatiguing to fight against Nature in the raw. I don't know what it means, but she's awfully nice."

Mrs. Bradley inwardly commended Miss Winter for being, if not ' awfully nice,' at any rate the most sensible person she had heard of for some time. She then urged George to drive a little faster, as she thought the train was almost due. George replied with an inspired burst of speed which brought a flush of joy to the clear cheeks of the child, and caused Mrs. Bradley to quote Aristophanes in a dignified but heartfelt manner.

" Be valiant, daring and subtle, and never mind taking a risk,"* said she in Greek, as the car drew up at the station.

It was Ferdinand's habit to travel by train whenever it was possible to do so. Caroline, who detested trains, said that he liked working out the connections from Bradshaw and deciding how much time could have been saved if they had made three more changes. Ferdinand denied this, and said that driving made him sleepy.

At any rate, the train had not arrived when George pulled up, but they could hear a distant whistle.

Ferdinand and Caroline both looked well and were pleased to see their child again. Caroline questioned Mrs. Bradley, Derek supplied vociferous footnotes, and the scrap-book, solemnly brought from the house to the station in brown paper, had to be displayed.

It was agreed that the parents should remain at the house for the night, and should leave with Derek soon after breakfast next morning. Caroline, who was tired, was grateful ; Derek was delighted, and, with his father's assistance, put in a valuable couple of hours after tea on the scrap-book. At eight he went to bed, sleepy, but, as an artist, satisfied.

" Staying on here all alone, Mother ? " asked Ferdinand. " What on earth for ? "

" Well, I'm still hoping that the authorities may let me have my boys. Besides, I've stumbled upon something interesting," replied Mrs. Bradley. She showed him the diary. " I was doing some work at Shafton, the reconstructed institution for delinquent boys, when I came on the story first. It appears that there was a housekeeper there named Bella Foxley. She resigned about six years ago, when she came into some money at the death of her aunt, an old lady who lived in this house, and died in it under, apparently, peculiar circumstances."

---

* *The Frogs*, Act 3. Trans. by D. W. Lucas and F. J. A. Cruso. 1936.

"Do you mean that she murdered the aunt?" asked Caroline.

"Oh, no, she didn't murder the aunt. At least, there was no suggestion of that. But certainly she murdered her cousin," said Ferdinand, before his mother could reply. "I remember the case quite well. She was acquitted, but, all the same, she did it. You were in America, Mother, at the time. I was asked to defend her, but I wouldn't undertake it. However, they got her off. Lack of motive. But the motive was there, all right."

"You mean she did murder the aunt, and the cousin knew it?" said Mrs. Bradley. "I can see all sorts of objections to that theory, and yet there is a great deal to be said in favour of it. The diary gives some very curious sidelights. *Poltergeist* phenomena——"

"Oh, lord, yes! The haunted house," said Ferdinand. "The prosecution didn't care for the *poltergeist* at all, I remember, but the defence produced some pretty good stuff on the subject. Their theory was suicide whilst the balance of the mind was affected. They tried to prove that the haunted house had got on Cousin Tom's nerves, and he'd chucked himself out of the window in a fit of panic. You know, Mother, you ought to meet Pratt, if you're interested in the case. He covered it for one of the evening papers. Of course, he's given up reporting ever since he brought off that record-breaking play, but I daresay he could give you a pretty good idea of how the trial went. Conscientious bloke, too. Wouldn't invent anything or distort anything—knowingly!"

"How was Cousin Tom supposed to have died?" asked Caroline. "Just by falling out of the window?"

"Well, that was the contention of the defence, but the prosecution got hold of medical witnesses who declared that a blow on the head was struck before he ever reached the ground. It became a battle of the experts in the end. I think that's why the jury let her off. The average person is suspicious and upset when expert witnesses can't agree, you know."

"I'm going to stay on for a bit and pump Eliza Hodge, my landlady," said Mrs. Bradley. "She used to be a servant here before the old lady died."

"But I still don't understand what your object is, Mother,

in going back over all this," said Ferdinand.   " What has struck
you about it ? "

" While I was at the Institution I helped to trace two boys
who had broken out," replied Mrs. Bradley. "When Bella
Foxley left the Institution two other boys had disappeared, and
were *never* traced. That seems to me a most extraordinary
thing."

" Why ? Do you think she helped them to run away ? "
enquired Caroline.

" There is little to lead one to such a conclusion, but she
mentions the boys several times in her diary, and the present
Warden thinks that some member of the staff connived at the
escape. If he is right, one wonders what could have been the
motive. These boys were anti-social and degenerate. One of
them had committed murder. It seems odd that any responsible
person should think it desirable to have them at large. Especially—although this is not mentioned in the diary—as Cousin
Tom did die."

She spoke with her usual mildness, and Ferdinand looked at
her sharply.

" What are you getting at, Mother ? " he demanded.   " You
don't think one of those boys did the murder, do you ? "

" Oh, no. I am prepared to believe that Bella Foxley did
the murder. I think, too, that she murdered her aunt. And I
think she contrived the escape of the boys. All of that is implicit
in her diary, as I read it. Do you read it, child, before you go
to bed. You will find it more than interesting."

It was to Miss Hodge that she took herself straightway when
the guests had driven off in the morning. She had made up
her mind that she would approach the subject bluntly, and she
did.

" I was interested in the diary, Miss Hodge," she said.   "I
wonder . . . ."   She looked into the eyes of the old servant.

" Yes, madam ? " said Miss Hodge ; and her eyes flickered
nervously, Mrs. Bradley noticed.

" An impertinence on my part, perhaps, but—were you very
much attached to Miss Bella and Miss Tessa ? I suppose, by
the way, that you *are* the Eliza of the diary ? "

" Yes, madam, of course I am. As to Miss Bella and Miss

Tessa—well, I was very fond indeed of Miss Tessa, and terrible grieved when she was so unfortunate."

" Unfortunate ? You mean . . . ? "

" Yes, that's it, madam. Her husband turned out badly, I'm afraid. In fact, it proved he *wasn't* her husband. Such a nice fellow he was, too. But I suppose these bigamists often are, and that's where they lead themselves astray. I don't really think he meant Miss Tessa any harm, and fortunately— *most* fortunately as it turned out—nothing came of the marriage——"

" No children, you mean ? "

" That's right. So it wasn't as bad as it might have been ; and when it all came out he went away to South America before he got himself arrested, and there, it seems, he died of being attacked by a crocodile or a snake or something of them kind of horrible things."

" Is it certain that he's dead ? "

" Oh, yes, madam. No manner of doubt, and really, for poor Miss Tessa, the best way out. But she always kept up her married name, I believe, although she never came back here no more. I did just write to her once, getting the address— although I suppose it was not my place—out of the bureau drawer where I knew the mistress kept it, for all she had said she would never see Miss Tessa again. . . ."

" But surely it wasn't the girl's fault ? "

" Well, she wasn't so much of a girl, if you take me, madam. She would have been all of thirty-five when she married him, and the mistress never liked the marriage anyhow, and when it came out what he was, she said she had always known something would happen, and Miss Tessa was old enough to have had more sense about men."

" Yes, I see. So she cut Miss Tessa out of her will, and left all the money to Miss Bella."

" Well, she did and she didn't. She left the money to Miss Bella, but Miss Tessa was to have it after her, unless Miss Bella should have got married, which there wasn't much chance she would. But, much to everybody's surprise, madam, Miss Bella gave Miss Tessa to understand that she was to have half the interest on the capital straight away. Of course, after the death of poor Mr. Tom, we heard no more about it, but I dare say she did it, all the same. Mr. Tom's death, and then Miss Bella being put in prison and tried for her life, took all our thoughts, as you can fancy, and . . ."

" The sisters got on well together, then ? "

" Well, I can't hardly say, madam. They didn't quarrel, that I know of, and I suppose Miss Bella must have been fond of Miss Tessa to share the interest with her like that ; although, as she said to me herself, ' Why shouldn't a thousand do me as well as two thousand, Eliza ? After all, I've never had more than two hundred up to now.' As, of course, madam, no more she hadn't, and a job that ate all the heart out of her, too, and all, even to get that much. But I was sorry to think Mr. Tom never came in for his share."

" You were very fond of both of them, then ? "

Eliza hesitated for an instant, and then seemed to make up her mind.

" I'm not ever one to speak ill of the dead, madam."

" I am glad to hear you say that," said Mrs. Bradley. That this was a cryptic utterance was lost upon Eliza. She replied :

" No, that's not my way, madam. What's buried should bury our spite with it. That's what I always say. All the same, I was very, very glad when they let Miss Bella off. It would have been a most terrible thing, that would."

Mrs. Bradley agreed, and then said, changing the subject, it seemed :

" I wonder whether you'd care to come to tea with me at your house this afternoon ? I shall be quite alone now that my grandson has gone back with his parents."

" That would be ever so nice, madam," said Eliza immediately. " Mrs. Bell is going over to Hariford, so I shall be all on my own, too."

" Good," said Mrs. Bradley. " I shall expect you early, then."

Eliza arrived at half-past three and found her hostess in the garden. Together they walked up the path and talked about the plants and flowers. The rockery particularly attracted attention. It had been one of Aunt Flora's hobbies, and Mrs. Bradley encouraged a subject of conversation of which she had

some knowledge in order to keep the memory of Aunt Flora
well in the foreground of her companion's mind.

These artless tactics were successful, and by the end of her
visit she had a clear picture of the household just before the old
lady's death.   Eliza was not garrulous, nor did she make too
many tiresome repetitions.   She seemed to welcome questions,
and was obviously so much interested herself in what she was
talking about that Mrs. Bradley's curiosity did not strike her as
excessive.   It seemed perfectly natural to her that other people
should be fascinated by stories about the tragic household in
which she had had a place.

They had tea in the garden.   It was brought out by the young
maidservant who had come down with Mrs. Bradley because it
was thought that a fortnight by the sea might do her good.   It
was doing her good, Mrs. Bradley had been glad to notice.   She
had taken Derek for some of his walks while Mrs. Bradley, who
enjoyed what she called ' pottering about the house,' had done
the dusting and had cooked most of the meals.

During tea Eliza's anecdotes were chiefly based upon the
small and harmless eccentricities of her late mistress, but, later
(for the evenings were not very warm), when they went into the
house to a small but cheerful fire, the trickle of reminiscence
gradually rose to flood height, and by the time the visitor left
at half-past eight Mrs. Bradley's curiosity was satisfied to the
extreme limit of whatever satisfaction Eliza was able to provide.
In fact, Mrs. Bradley felt that if there was anything she had not
been told, it was because it was something which the old servant
herself did not know.

The fire had been lighted in the drawing-room, a room which
had been furnished too heavily for its size.   Heavy mahogany
chairs, a sideboard (in the same kind of wood) which occupied
almost the whole of a wall so that there was scarcely enough
room to open the door, a dark red carpet with a thick pile, a
mahogany bureau, an overladen mantelpiece and dark red
velvet curtains which hung from the ceiling to the ground,
created an impression of stifling and strangely hellish gloom
which was not discounted, but, on the contrary, enhanced, by
portraits of a gentleman with side whiskers and a lady wearing a
bustle ; by a couple of large fish labelled respectively Uncle

Percy and Uncle George ; and, finally, by a repellent arrangement of Wedgwood dinner plates affixed to the walls by wire brackets.

" The mistress loved this room," said Eliza, looking round it with affectionate pride. " It was here that she died, madam. Had her bed brought down here and the dining-table and chairs moved out to get it in. What a job it was to get her downstairs and into it, too. She was a big, heavy woman, you know, madam, and had had her hair dyed dark red, which nobody really cared for, not even herself when it was done. ' I've made a fool of myself, Eliza,' she said to me when she came home— went up to London, she did, to have it tinted—' and I wish now I'd never had it done. But you can take it that nobody but myself is ever going to know that. I shall keep it touched up now I've taken the plunge.' And so she did, to the last. Ah, she was a wonderful old lady ; eighty-one when she died, and all her faculties, as you might say. Nobody thought of her going like that at the end. It was on the Wednesday that she tumbled over. She wouldn't have me help her dress, and so, of course, it happened ! The very first time I hadn't tied her strings for her—for she wore the old-fashioned petticoats to the end, two flannel ones and one white one in winter, and just the two white ones in summer—and down she went. I'd helped her ever since her rheumatism began to make her what she called fumble-fisted.

" I was down in the kitchen when she fell, but of course, I heard the crash, and her calling out as she tumbled.

" Doctor was very grave at first ; a young doctor he was then, although we've got quite used to him in these parts by now. He said she'd never work off the effects like younger people can, so, when he put it like that, I said, ' Oh, doctor, you don't mean she won't get over it ! Because if you mean that,' I said, ' I really ought to send for her relations.'

" He looked at me very sober at that, and said, ' You'd better send for them, then.' That was on the following Saturday morning.

" With that, he went, and I went straight to the bureau for the address of the Institution where Miss Bella was gone to be housekeeper. The mistress saw me, of course, and she called out from the bed, ' Don't you go writing to that addle-headed niece Tessa of mine ! I'm not that far gone, Eliza, that I don't know how you favour her above Bella.'

" ' I thought you'd like Miss Bella to know you weren't quite yourself, mum,' I said ; and at that she tried to raise herself a bit on the pillow and said, speaking sharp-like, as she always did when she wanted a bit of an argument,

" ' What do you mean—quite myself ? I'm not in my dotage yet, thank goodness ! Don't be a fool, Eliza ! '

" ' No, mum,' I said, quite meek, for I'd found Miss Bella's address by that time, so I wanted to humour her a bit. But she saw I'd got it. Her eyes were very quick. Still, she said no more, except to tell me to put *Care of the Warden* on the envelope. It was that, I think, her wanting Miss Bella to come, that made me sure how very bad she was, and made me turn the letter into a telegram, to fetch her as soon as might be."

" And I suppose you sent, also, to the other relatives who came ? " said Mrs. Bradley.

" No, that I didn't, madam. I wouldn't have taken the liberty. Not that Mr. Tom wasn't very fond of the mistress, although he wouldn't go in and see her, and as for his wife, well, she was more like an angel of mercy, because she hardly knew the mistress at all, and yet, when it came to the come to, she was far more help in the sickroom than ever poor Miss Bella was. But there ! The married women are the handiest (although I'm not married myself), when it comes to looking after things in the house."

" I don't quite understand, then," said Mrs. Bradley, " how Cousin Tom and his wife Muriel happened to be there at that very crucial time."

" You may call it that," said Eliza. " The mistress rallied nicely, and the doctor, you could tell (although, of course, he wouldn't say so, taking to himself all the credit, as young men do), was wonderfully surprised at how she was getting over it. He said she must have had, for her age, a fine constitution, but, myself, I call it more the will-power. She could be very determined, the mistress, when she liked. I say it was her will-power pulled her round. But as for Mr. Tom knowing he ought to be present if it meant the poor mistress's deathbed, I said to Miss

Bella to send a telegram if she thought he ought to be present, and so I suppose she sent it, which I wouldn't venture to do."

" Where exactly in the house did your mistress have her fall ? " Mrs. Bradley enquired.

" Why, in the bathroom passage, to be sure."

" Ah, yes, of course. Now what was that about the tin of lobster which Miss Bella brought back with her after she had been out for the afternoon ? "

" Crayfish, not lobster, madam. She asked me to have some, but it always gives me such terrible indigestion that I asked her to excuse me, and she ate it all herself for her tea. I remember thinking it was too big a tin for one person, but there ! Miss Bella would sooner belly bust than good stuff be lost, as my Yorkshire uncle used to say when we were children and didn't want to finish up our food."

" Splendid ! " said Mrs. Bradley, leaving the old servant with the impression that the exclamation referred less to the Yorkshire uncle's proverb than to some secret satisfaction which she felt over something else which had been disclosed to her. " And then, of course, came the extraordinary business of the grated carrot."

" Extraordinary you may rightly call it, madam," assented Eliza immediately. " *I* can't imagine the mistress calling for such heathenish food. She liked carrot well enough in a stew, but never in my life had I known her eat them raw."

" Raw carrot is good for the system," observed Mrs. Bradley. "Perhaps one of the relatives persuaded her that it would be good for her to eat some."

" Well, Miss Bella actually grated it for her, I think, because she asked me for the nutmeg grater to do it on, but Miss Bella wasn't a vegetarian or anything of that, that I know of. In fact, I don't see how she could have been, living in the Institution like she did. I'm sure she had no time for fads and fancies there."

" Mr. Tom, perhaps, was a vegetarian ? " Mrs. Bradley suggested.

" Mr. Tom ? Oh, no, madam. He might hunt ghosts and the like rubbish of that, but he was always one for his cut from the joint and two veg., with anybody. And with him like that, I don't see how his wife could have been anything but a meat-eater too."

" Well, then, who do you suggest is the author of the grated carrot, Miss Hodge ? "

" I couldn't say, I'm sure, madam. It seems out of all reason, as I remember saying at the time, that she should have ate such stuff. My poor mistress ! I only hope she died easy of it, weak as she was with the fall."

Mrs. Bradley concurred sympathetically in this pious wish, and then added that she supposed Aunt Flora had been a churchwoman."

" Indeed not, madam, no. Not if she was ever such friends with the vicar. Which she was. Friendly enemies they were, so to speak, both being interested in rock gardens, and the vicar having more knowledge and the mistress more money. Oh, many's the time, as I remember well, that he would call, and they would go over the rock garden plant by plant, and some-times he would bring her nice little white painted bits of pointed wood with the Latin name on in black, and stoop down and push them into the ground, so we always knew what we were looking at, even if we couldn't pronounce it. But Church ! Oh, no. No more than me, and I, I am rather ashamed to say, have never gone anywhere since I was about twenty, although brought up to it by a pious father and mother. I was jilted at twenty by a young fellow. We used to sing out of the same hymnbook, and I never fancied Church after that. But the mistress—if she ever went anywhere those last years—she went to the Congrega-tional at Raddleton in Mr. Tripps' car. One of her uncles was a Congregational minister, or so she told me once."

Mrs. Bradley glanced at the portrait of the gentleman with whiskers, and Eliza, following her glance, exclaimed :

" Oh, no, that wouldn't be him, madam ! But he's in the family album if you'd like to have a look. That there was the mistress's husband. That was before I knew her. He died when she was sixty. I've only been with her the last twenty years."

She went to the bureau, unlocked one of the drawers, and, after removing various books and papers, came over to Mrs.

Bradley with a black-bound, Biblical-looking volume with thick, gold-edged leaves.

" Don't be alarmed when you first open it, madam. It's got one of those little musical-boxes inside the front cover. Very pretty it plays."

Mrs. Bradley turned back the cover, and a small prickly metal cylinder was disclosed under a sheet of glass. The cylinder revolved, and the thin sweet tune it played was *Annie Laurie*. When Mrs. Bradley turned the leaves over to look at the photographs, however, the music ceased.

Eliza came over and stood beside her, laying work-roughened fingers on the pages as she talked. Anecdote followed description, and Mrs. Bradley was taken relentlessly from photograph to photograph, and was not allowed to miss one. She did not object at all to this, however (but only begged Eliza to draw up a chair so that they could rest the book on the table and both look at it in comfort), because a great many of the photographs, which were mainly of groups of people, showed either Aunt Flora or one or both of the nieces. Miss Tessa figured more often than Miss Bella, but never, when only one of them was in the group, did the old servant falter, even for so much as a moment, in naming which niece it was. They were, Mrs. Bradley could see, women of widely different appearance, the one large, square and resolute, the other smaller, more timid, more completely feminine.

It took more than an hour to go through the whole of the album, and at the end of it Eliza said how much she had enjoyed herself, and that she supposed she ought to be going. At this, Mrs. Bradley produced two decanters, one containing port and the other sherry, and a tin of biscuits. Possibly under the influence of the port, Eliza suddenly said :

" You know, madam, there was something very funny about that carrot. I don't say Miss Bella exactly forced it on the poor mistress, but I do say it was funny."

" Yes, if she had never eaten such a thing before, it does seem odd, but sick people take these fancies," said Mrs. Bradley.

" But she wasn't all that sick, madam, not at that time. It was when the doctor told us she would recover. And she was perfectly sensible ; not wandering in her mind, or anything. And it wasn't like when one might be expecting. I grant you people do have strange fancies *then* in the eating line. I remember my own sister. Nothing would content her but duck eggs, although she never would touch one at other times. And the job we had to get them for her, us then living in London ! Such nasty, indigestible things ! I can't abear them myself. I said to her, afterwards, a wonder the baby wasn't born with webbed feet, I said. And the queer thing about that is that he became quite a champion swimmer, madam. So it all goes to show, doesn't it ? "

" Yes, indeed," agreed Mrs. Bradley politely.

The next day she called in the doctor because her maid complained of a sore throat. He had heard of Mrs. Bradley and was anxious to make her acquaintance. As there was no servant except the maid who was ill, Mrs. Bradley herself opened the door.

" Ah, Doctor ! " she said.

" Ah, Doctor ! " he replied. Then, when he had examined the patient and prescribed for her, he remained for a bit to gossip, confessing that the village never troubled him much throughout the summer, and that he had plenty of time on his hands.

" A good many months since I was here," he said. " The last time was when Eliza had an accident with a gardening fork and stuck it into her foot. That would have been two years ago last Easter. And before that—no, I don't believe I was in this house between that time and the previous time when the old lady choked herself with the carrot. I'd only just come here then. Hardly knew a soul in the village. I was called in by Eliza, of course, to see her mistress after a fall she had had. Tripped over, or something. I forget the details. They don't matter, anyway, because she was soon on the highroad. Must have had marvellous recuperative powers, considering her age. Can't think how she got over it as she did. Anyhow, point is, she *did* get over it. I tell you I was absolutely staggered when she pulled round. Then came the knock-out—that beastly grated carrot."

" Yes, I've been hearing about that from Miss Hodge. I'm her tenant here, of course. She came to tea yesterday, and told me a lot about it. It appears it was a sudden fancy on the part of the patient. She had never eaten raw grated carrot, and seems to have conceived a desire to try it."

" Or someone else conceived the idea for her," said the doctor. Meeting Mrs. Bradley's sharp glance, he smiled, shrugged, and then said, " Oh, yes, I admit it. If I'd had the guts I'd have said the old lady was murdered. Trouble was, I knew I couldn't prove it. No marks of violence ; no cause of death beyond the simple one that she had choked herself. And doctors who have much to do with bringing accusations of murder aren't popular, as no doubt you know. No ; there was no proof, and I didn't know the people, either. It just seemed like asking for trouble. Funnily enough, the niece knew I wasn't satisfied. Put it to me, point-blank. Proved her own innocence, anyhow ; and nobody would be fool enough to suspect old Eliza of murder. Left the married couple. Nothing there to get hold of, so I signed the certificate. I think the majority of people would have done the same. Still, I was a bit taken aback when I read about the arrest of the niece for murdering the cousin."

" Yes ? " said Mrs. Bradley.

" So the doctor wasn't satisfied ? " she said abruptly to Eliza Hodge when next she saw her.

" Wasn't he ? Poor young girl," responded Eliza. "I do hope she isn't sickening for something, madam."

" I meant about the grated carrot," said Mrs. Bradley, even more abruptly ; but the old servant's face did not change, except that the concern in her eyes deepened.

" I believe you're right, madam," she agreed. " He asked me, I remember, a whole lot of questions, funny enough."

" What sort of questions do you mean ? "

" Well, who gave it to her."

" And you weren't prepared to say."

" Well, Miss Bella said she was going out shopping in the village, and Mr. Tom and his wife said they were going out for a walk along the shore, so I suppose, if anyone gave it to her, it must have been me," replied the old servant, with a peculiarly hard expression on her face.

" And was it you ? "

" You don't need to ask that, madam. You know it wasn't."

" Yes. Even the doctor knew that," said Mrs. Bradley. "But, since the subject has come up, Miss Hodge, I do wish, if it wouldn't cause you too much distress, you'd tell me what you really think."

" Well, I'm not going to speak ill of the dead, but I'll tell you one thing straight away, madam. *One of them didn't go out.* At least, I didn't think so. Mr. Tom, he went, and I see a flick of the blue dress his young wife had been wearing—or it might have been Miss Bella ; she wore blue. But there was the sound of a sewing machine in Miss Bella's room, her having borrowed mine to run herself up an apron—one of mine, altered, it was."

" And she *did* grate up the carrot, using the nutmeg grater to do it."

" Well, yes, I think so, but, of course, I can't be sure. For one thing, although she *asked* for the nutmeg grater, I didn't actually see her use it. Still, there was carrot on it when I came to wash it. And as for the shopping, and being out of the house when her poor aunt died, well, she said she'd been out, and I couldn't contradict her."

" Perhaps," suggested Mrs. Bradley, " she grated the carrot for her aunt, and took it up to her so that she could help herself to it. That's what she suggested in the diary."

" It might have been that way, madam. I really couldn't say. Still, it seems funny that if the mistress wanted grated carrot, she hadn't said so to me and let me do it for her. Besides, I will say this : Miss Bella was perfectly open about the carrot when she spoke to me about the grater."

" Was your mistress at all fond of any kind of food which could *look* like grated carrot at a distance ? " Mrs. Bradley enquired.

" Only pease pudding, and that's not *very* like," Eliza replied. " You mean Miss Bella thought it would do her good, and didn't tell her what she was going to do until it was all made ready ? I couldn't say, I'm sure, madam. Anyway, it was a very great relief when she was found Not Guilty of Mr. Tom, although the suicide so soon after was very dreadful."

" The suicide ? " said Mrs. Bradley, anxious to hear more about this.

" Oh, yes, madam. She took a little house down in the country, Miss Bella did, far enough away, you would think, for her to be able to forget all about the trial and what she'd gone through. But it seems some ill-natured people got hold of the tale and spread it all round the village. She left a farewell letter, poor thing, saying she had been driven to it by gossip. It was read at the coroner's inquest."

"Oh, dear me! What a very dreadful thing!" said Mrs. Bradley. "How did she do it? I suppose she drowned herself?"

"Yes, that was what she did, madam; she was found in a pond on the common, I believe."

"Dear, dear!" said Mrs. Bradley. "Not far from her house, I presume?"

"I couldn't say how far, madam. Probably not very far. She was never much of a walker. But I don't know the district at all. I didn't even go to the funeral, not knowing how I was to get there and back the same night, her living all alone as she did, and me hardly one of the family to go poking myself in if not invited; although, really, who could have invited me I don't quite see, I'm sure."

"Did Miss Tessa go to the funeral?"

"There, again, I couldn't say, madam. I've not had a word from Miss Tessa since poor Mr. Tom's sad death. In her last letter she mentioned she was going to move. I kept the letter. I expect I've got it somewhere, if you'd like to see it. It's nice for me to talk to somebody who takes such an interest in it all."

Mrs. Bradley, who still wondered whether her apparently insatiable curiosity about the whole affair would not, at some point, strike Eliza as unnecessary and impertinent, was relieved to hear this last statement. She said immediately that she would be very glad to see it, and, upon its being produced, she noticed that, as Eliza had indicated already, it was written in a far more careless and dashing hand than the neatly written diary which she had already seen. In fact, it bore most of the indications of a singularly ill-balanced personality. Had it been the writer who had committed suicide, it would have been most comprehensible, thought Mrs. Bradley. "The sisters must have been women of widely different temperament," she remarked.

"Temper, too," responded Eliza. "Miss Tessa would fly off the handle, as they say, over anything. But I never knew

Miss Bella to be angry. She was sort of sharp and abrupt, but never lost control like Miss Tessa. I liked Miss Tessa the better for it. Give me somebody that speaks their mind, and perhaps has to apologize afterwards for being over-hasty. Still, that isn't everybody's taste, and I dare say Miss Bella might have been a lot easier to live with in the long run."

Mrs. Bradley consulted the diary again that evening. The wish-fulfilment dream and the self-pity so frankly expressed seemed ingenuous enough, but there were other passages over which, comparing them with Eliza's version of the facts, she frowned in concentration for minutes at a time.

How, for instance, could Bella so have misinterpreted the old servant's feeling for her mistress as to suggest that Eliza considered the fall a "judgment" on Aunt Flora for being contrary? Nothing in Mrs. Bradley's conversations with Eliza had led her to believe that such a remark could possibly have been made, least of all to Bella, whom, it had become very clear, she did not like very much.

Then the beginning of the entry for January the twenty-eighth was puzzling. It did not seem at all likely that the doctor had diagnosed Aunt Flora's recovery from the fall as " the end," and Mrs. Bradley had made up her mind that the rest of the entry, referring to the arrival of Tom and Muriel after " they had travelled all night " was pure fiction.

Again, there was the ridiculous entry about the lobster and Eliza's delight when she was given it. This, however, could be dismissed as more cloud-cuckoo-land on the part of the diarist, and was not more important than it appeared on the surface to be. But the entry about the grated carrot was very interesting. There was, first, the discrepancy in the time. According to the diarist, it was not until seven o'clock in the evening that there had been any mention of grated carrot. Then, again upon the authority of the diary, it had been Aunt Flora herself who asked for it. Eliza's story, on the other hand, contradicted both these assertions. Aunt Flora had had the carrot during the afternoon, and yet, it seemed, knew nothing of grated carrot and certainly would not have suggested partaking of it. It was interesting, too, to note the awkward sentence in which Cousin Tom's name appeared. ' Tom said that he realized it could be nothing but the return of all her normal faculties and he thought she must be humoured.' Further, ' *we* (Mrs. Bradley added the italics) went to the kitchen, therefore, Eliza being at the Chapel for her week-night meeting . . .'

This was more than interesting, as Eliza, upon her own showing, was not a chapel-goer, and certainly was not likely to have attended, of all things, a weeknight meeting at a town some distance inland.

Then, (extremely suspicious this), there was the careful suggestion of what had happened when the old lady had been left with the saucerful of grated carrot and the spoon. ' The effort of eating,' the diarist had pronounced on what seemed almost a judicial and was certainly a remarkably detached and objective note, ' must have been too much. . . .' The careful dissociation of the narrator herself from the dreadful event she was describing was obviously intended to indicate that poor Aunt Flora had been alone when she died. But, unless there were guilty knowledge of the means which had encompassed her death, and unless the diary had not been written for the usual personal reasons, but was intended for a wider circle of readers than is usually the case, why this elaborate and stiffly-phrased disclaimer of all knowledge about the choking fit which had caused Aunt Flora's demise ?

There followed, then, the information about the sister. According to Eliza, Tessa had had no children, but had married a bigamist. According to Bella, her sister had not been married at all and had had an illegitimate baby. There were discrepancies, too, between what Mrs. Bradley had heard from the Warden of the Institution and what Bella Foxley had written.

Strangest of all, perhaps, was the extremely odd entry referring to Aunt Flora's dirty hair and head. She re-read that several times, trying to connect it with Eliza's statement that her mistress had had her hair dyed dark red and had kept it this unbecoming tint until the end.

There were other mistakes, notably the one which referred to Eliza's term of service. Between the twenty years mentioned by the old servant herself and the years between the age of sixteen and almost seventy referred to by the diarist, there was a substantial difference.

Then there was the reference to the Aunt's house having been put in the hands of the agents. The house had been willed to Eliza, and it did not seem as though the diarist knew this ; yet Bella, as the chief inheriter, must have known it.

On a par with this small yet significant error, was the one about the files. According to the diarist it seemed as though the files used in the escape of Piggy and Alec had not been traced. According to the Warden, they must have been ; otherwise the make could not have been compared with that of the files in use at the Institutional manual centre. Yet surely Bella would have known that the ' escape ' files had never left the building ?

Then came the incredible entry which referred to the inspector of police who investigated Cousin Tom's first fall from the window of the haunted house. It was inconceivable to Mrs. Bradley that he should have made any mention of the old lady and the grated carrot. There was no reason for his doing such a thing, for the old lady's death certificate was in order, and, except for the reference to a remark in the *Daily Pennon*, there had been no official suggestion that the old lady had died from anything but natural causes.

(Mrs. Bradley, incidentally, was so much interested in this point that she took the trouble to go up to London specially to consult the files of the newspaper in question. To her great interest, there was not a single reference to Aunt Flora's death in any of its columns for the whole year in which that death had occurred, for she went carefully through the lot.)

Then there was the slip in describing the pre-Institution activities of Alec. Either the diarist or the Warden was wrong, and, in view of the exhaustive records of each boy which were kept in the archives of the Institution, Mrs. Bradley did not, somehow, think it could be the Warden who was at fault. Of course, Bella Foxley *might* have been misinformed . . . but, added to the rest of the evidence that the writer of the diary had made mistakes which the ex-housekeeper of the Institution ought not to have made, and, in most cases, Mrs. Bradley decided, *would not* have made, it was curious and very interesting.

She locked and bolted all the doors and fastened the down-stair windows—actions which, in that innocent countryside, she rarely troubled to perform—that night before she went to bed.

Chapter Three

COUNSEL'S OPINION

How in my thoughts shall I contrive
The image I am framing,
Which is so far superlative
As 'tis beyond all naming?

.   .   .   .   .   .

It must be builded in the air,
And 'tis my thoughts must do it,
And only they must be the stair
From earth to mount me to it."

DRAYTON.

FERDINAND'S friend stretched his legs and smiled at his hostess.

" I've been longing to meet you," he said.

" Flattering," said Mrs. Bradley. " I hope Ferdinand told you why you've come ? "

" Oh, yes." He nodded his handsome head. " Bella Foxley. Interesting case. Curious that she committed suicide. Still, quite the type, of course."

" I should be interested to know exactly what you mean by that."

" I can't explain—exactly. But we see a lot of suicides, unfortunately, in our job. When I was a cub I had a regular Embankment beat for a fairly lurid sort of rag—the old *Gimlet*. You wouldn't remember it. Anyway, you can divide humanity into suicides and non-suicides. You ought to know more about it than I do ! There is the person who would commit suicide no matter how life seemed to turn out, and there is the person who wouldn't, whatever sort of hell on earth he suffered. Bella Foxley, to my mind, belonged to the first group."

" Thank you," said Mrs. Bradley. " But why did she choose to commit suicide at that particular time ? "

" Well, some unkind people suggested that it was remorse, because, although she was acquitted, she was guilty. Most people thought she was guilty, you know."

" Why did they think that ? "

" She made an unfortunate impression in court, I think."

" Yes. Reason enough. People *will* jump to conclusions, and the awkward part is that, as often as not, they are justified. It makes the scientific mind appear cumbersome and rather unnecessarily slow. Did *you* think it was remorse, as well as that she was guilty ? "

" I thought she was guilty, but I don't think it was remorse that caused her to drown herself. I think she received anonymous letters."

" Yes, she would do, of course. There are always lunatics at large, and they have brought about the suicide of an innocent person before now. But we seem to have begun at the end. It was the trial I wanted to hear about."

" I remember it very well indeed," said the ex-journalist. " The case was most interesting to me. She was quite a tall woman, you know—five feet eight, I should think—and a bit bloated, with a bad skin—greasy and blackheads—rather repulsive, really. Besides which, she looked every inch a spinster, if you know what I mean. She was not at all nervous, either, and that was what impressed people most unfavourably, I think. Everybody still seems to think that the bold ones are guilty and the furtive ones innocent, although I don't pretend to know why. People don't change their nature or their general mental attitude because they've been accused of a crime."

" Of what did the accusation consist ? How did they state it ? "

" Well, the story told by the prosecution was that this woman had been blackmailed by her cousin, a man named Turney, and that she went to the house that night, and, pretending that she had come to pay up, took the opportunity of pushing him out of the window."

" How did they get hold of the blackmailing theory ? " Mrs. Bradley inquired.

" That came from the wife, who was the chief witness for the prosecution. Her story was that she did not know why the prisoner had been paying certain sums of money to her husband, but that he had told her that the rent of the house and some money for psychical research had been provided by Bella, and that 'Bella would have to cough up a lot more before he was through with her.' "

Mrs. Bradley thought of the admission in the diary that Bella had become a lodger with Cousin Tom and his wife Muriel, but she said nothing.

"The defence pressed Mrs. Muriel Turney hard, of course, to declare how much money had changed hands between the prisoner and her husband, and scored quite well when they forced her to admit that her husband had once shown her five pounds, on another occasion three pounds ten, and lastly a further five. If the prisoner were interested in the experiments he was making in connection with the so-called haunted house, these sums, the defence suggested, were not excessive subscriptions from a woman with an income of a thousand a year.

"They also dug up the prisoner's sister and got evidence from her of the prisoner's generosity. Weak-looking, faded sort of woman. You'd never have connected her with Bella. It appeared that the prisoner thought her sister had been treated badly by being cut out of the aunt's will, and had made over half her income to her. In the light of this really rather magnificent gesture, the small sums paid over to the cousin seemed almost negligible, especially as the defence found witnesses to prove that the prisoner was paying for board and lodging whilst she was staying with the cousin and his wife, and that the sums mentioned might have been nothing more than these payments."

"They seem to have been made on rather a generous scale," Mrs. Bradley suggested. "She was only with Cousin Tom and his wife a week or two, I believe."

"Still, it seemed absurd to talk of blackmail when the sums were so trifling. If they weren't actual payments they were probably small loans. The defence tried to establish the financial position of the cousin at the time of his death, but didn't get much change there, because the prosecution were able to show that the fellow had no outstanding debts, and was, in fact, rather better off than he had been for some time, so they dropped that pretty quickly, for, without the blackmail theory, they couldn't find a motive."

"How did the prisoner herself account for her actions that night?" Mrs. Bradley enquired.

" Oh, well, of course, she was asked that by the prosecution. She went into the box all right. No trouble about that. She said that she and the wife had become very nervous in the haunted house and were unwilling to remain there, and so had gone to the inn. There the cousin came to see them several times, and had dinner, and then, after he had returned to the haunted house to continue his researches, which Mrs. Muriel was no longer willing to go on with, Mrs. M. became agitated, said that she knew something dreadful was going to happen, and that she felt she ought to go to the house and see whether all was well. Apparently she said this several nights."

" But she didn't go ? "

" No. What is more, her story and the story told by the prisoner did not agree. The wife said that on one occasion the prisoner refused to let her go, flung her back on her bed, darted out and locked the door behind her. The next morning the husband was found hurt, but not seriously. The prisoner, on the other hand, stated that the wife said she was too nervous to go to the house alone and yet was in ' such a state '—the prisoner's words—that she offered to go with her. The wife then said, ' What good would any of us be against those awful things ? ' Therefore the prisoner, much against her inclinations, but to pacify the wife who was ' in a terrible state of nerves ' went alone to the house, and, throwing gravel up at the bedroom window, attracted the attention of the cousin and conversed with him. She declared upon oath that she did not enter the house, but that, ' finding he was all right and had got over his drinks,' she returned to the inn and reported to the wife that all was well.

" Well, that was where, I imagine, all the fun and most of the lying began. Next morning the boy who delivered the milk found Tom Turney lying on the gravel path outside the front windows of the house, and the man said that he had fallen from the bedroom. Apparently he soon recovered, but the curious thing is that he was lying on almost the same spot and was found by the same boy not so many days later. The only difference was that the second time he was dead.

" The wife's story here was about the blackmail. She declared that the prisoner had insisted upon going to the house after dark ; she asserted that this was to pay over some money for which she was being blackmailed by the husband, and she gave it as her view that Bella Foxley, to rid herself of a nuisance and a drain upon her income, had pushed the chap out of the window and that in this second fall he had struck his head and had died.

"Bella's rather feeble reply to this was that *it was the wife who had gone to the house that night*, but I don't think anybody could swallow that."

"How many visits is Bella Foxley supposed to have paid to the house at nights between the two falls?" inquired Mrs. Bradley.

"I can't say. According to her own story, she did not go again after that first time. According to the wife she went two or three times.

"Well, the greatest fun was provided by the medical witnesses. Both sides had a regular platoon of them, and such a battle of the experts followed that one began to wonder whether the whole profession knew anything for certain about anybody's anatomy, or whether it wouldn't be better to go to a faith-healer or something if one had anything wrong.

"I really think it was the arguments between the doctors which got Bella off, you know. The jury, strongly directed, gave her the benefit of the doubt, although my personal feeling still is that she was guilty."

"What did the doctors say?" asked Mrs. Bradley.

"Well, one lot declared that if the chap had pitched out on to his head, even from a first-floor window, he could have received the injuries which the police doctor had already described to the court, and which nobody on either side disputed. The prosecution, however, put in a couple of surgeons who declared that the injuries could not have been caused by the fall, but that the fellow must have been hit on the head and his skull smashed before he was pushed out at all."

"But . . ."

"Yes, I know. But, you see, their contention was that a struggle must have taken place for her coat button to have got into his hand the way it did. I didn't tell you about that, did I? But the defence contended that a man who is falling from a height instinctively clutches out at things, or even makes clutching movements at the air. That being so, his hands would have been open, not clenched, and so the button must have been planted in his hand after death."

" The wife ? " said Mrs. Bradley, who had not heard of the button before.

" Exactly. Although they left that to be inferred. My private opinion is that the prisoner had made a pass or two at the husband, and that the wife didn't like it and was ready to blacken her in any way she could. Nevertheless, that wouldn't necessarily affect her guilt. On the contrary."

" But . . ."

" Yes, I know. The point was that he had already tumbled out of the window shortly before. Both sides put their own interpretation upon that, of course. The prosecution contended it was either a rehearsal or a boss shot at the murder which Bella eventually brought off by the same means, having corrected the errors. On the other hand the defence argued that it proved the bloke was off his chump. Besides, they further contended that the button had not been in the dead man's hand when first he was found by the milk boy. It appears that the village policeman, having telephoned his inspector, hopped on his bike and came bursting up to the inn to tell the wife what had happened. His tale was that he found the wife alone, and that she went with him immediately—on the step of his bicycle, in point of fact—to the haunted house, and was left alone with the body, having promised not to touch it. Very irregular, and the bobby was well cursed for it, but he was a nice, simple, country chap, and as it couldn't be proved that she *had* touched the body, his sentimental action was overlooked by his superiors. Nevertheless, she had the opportunity if she wanted it."

" And what was the prisoner's explanation of the button ? " asked Mrs. Bradley.

" The prisoner ? She was very vague about it. In fact, she hadn't an explanation, really. But that, in itself, didn't prejudice the jury. They probably thought it looked more innocent that she couldn't explain it. Anyhow, her counsel managed to make a point with them there. One of the prosecution's own witnesses was wearing a cardigan which had a couple of buttons missing. Counsel had noticed this, and suggested that the juryman did not know when he had lost the buttons or where they were. Sheer bluff, of course, because he might have known exactly, but, as the buttons had not been sewn on again, even for him to appear in court—and most witnesses like to be a bit dressy to make their public appearance—counsel deduced—not that it took much doing ; it was written all over him—that he was probably a careless sort of bloke who'd simply let the buttons drop off and hadn't bothered any further about them, and, sure enough, he got away with it. His point, of course, was that the button had been lost from the prisoner's coat some time previously, and had been planted in the dead man's hand either by some spiteful person or by the real murderer. Still, as I said before, I think it was the battle of the doctors that got her off. Juries don't care to give a verdict on expert testimony, anyway, and when the experts can't even agree among themselves it's rather optimistic to try for a conviction."

Mrs. Bradley assented. Then she said :

" And, apart from the button, why were *you* convinced that she was guilty ? "

" Her demeanour, chiefly, and the fact that I knew the story of the grated carrot—the aunt's death, you know. She had nothing to gain by the murder, of course, unless one believes the blackmail story. We had evidence of character and disposition from people who had known the dead man intimately, and he could have been a blackmailer, I thought. His psychic stuff was obviously completely phoney, I should say. Then, too, she could not tell a straightforward story which held water. It was rather too unusual a thing to leave an inn round about midnight to go and find out whether a ghost-hunter was all right. But, of course, it's not *impossible* that, having decided to do such a batty thing—not that I believe it !—she did exactly what she said she did—spoke to him and came away again."

" But that only refers to the first time, the time he was hurt but not killed," said Mrs. Bradley. " I suppose," she added, " he really was killed on the spot where the body was found ? "

" You mean . . .? "

" Supposing, for the sake of the argument, that she did murder him, did he die just where he was found ? "

" There was no evidence offered to the contrary by the prosecution, but I see what you mean. There were some very rum stories round the village—probably rot, but you never quite know—about cries and moans and what-not, a day or two after the death, by the way. But I only got that on the side. It didn't come out at the trial."

Mrs. Bradley was silent for about a minute. Then she said :

" It seems to me that Bella Foxley was arrested on insufficient evidence."

"Not if you read what the wife said at the inquest. She practically accused Bella Foxley of the murder, and the coroner's jury brought in a verdict accordingly. She let out—only, of course, it had to be suppressed—that she believed the real motive was that Tom knew Bella had murdered the ancient aunt. He was murdered to shut his mouth, and to put an end to the blackmail. She wanted to shout the same thing at the trial, and it was with the greatest difficulty that she could be persuaded to be quiet about it, because, of course, the aunt's death was all signed up and generally accounted for by the local doctor, and as there was no question of poison or violence, and the death certificate was in order, it was hardly possible to drag it up again. Would have meant an exhumation order and all that, so, although the prosecution knew all about her ideas on the subject, they didn't feel they could possibly admit her theories—because, dash it, that's all they were !—as part of the evidence."

" I see," said Mrs. Bradley. " The wife appears to have adopted a very biased, not to say spiteful, attitude towards Bella. It seems odd, considering that Bella had benefited them since she had come into the money."

" I know. I think she really had got a bee in her bonnet about Bella's having been the murderess, but I believe she thought, too, that there was something between Bella and her husband. Anyway, she was so much incensed against her that one of the solicitors told me the prosecution had grave doubts about calling her at all. They were afraid she would prejudice their case. Juries detest a spiteful witness, and rightly. Spite and truth are never too closely related, even though the one may be based upon the other."

" How true," said Mrs. Bradley, sighing. " And I suppose, whether she murdered her cousin or not, there isn't much doubt that Bella really did murder the aunt ? "

Mr. Pratt shrugged and smiled.

" One thing I can tell you," he said. " We were all after her for her story when she was acquitted, but she wouldn't give us anything at all. Said she wanted to get away and be at peace."

" She went to her sister, I suppose."

" Well, no. Some of the reporters lay in wait for her there, but, although the house was fairly persistently haunted, she did not turn up."

" How long after the trial did she commit suicide ? "

" Oh, about a year. She took a cottage—two cottages turned into one, it was—not far from the New Forest. The reporters trailed her, but she still held out on them, and after a week or two she ceased to be news, of course, and so they went away. She didn't become news again until she committed suicide, and then she only got a line or two, because most people had forgotten all about her by then. Funnily enough, she had then joined forces with the sister. They were living together when it happened."

" Really ? " There was a lengthy pause.

" She may have murdered the cousin, but she hadn't dismembered the body," said Mrs. Bradley, referring to the fact that a fickle populace had so soon forgotten Bella. " That always keeps a murderer's memory green. The public has a passion for horrors ; although how they think most murderers can dispose of a body neatly and successfully without dismembering it I can't imagine."

" The haunted house was the only interesting and unusual feature in Bella Foxley's case," said Mr. Pratt. " But, you know, some quite ordinary murders remain in people's memories. Take the case of Jessie M'Lachlan, for instance. . . ."

" The details were inclined to be unsavoury," Mrs. Bradley remarked. " And, of course, from the criminologist's point of view, what a beautiful case ! You have not chosen a good example. Two hundred years hence the case of Jessie M'Lachlan will still fascinate, tease, beckon, and defeat the student of crime. It was a case in a million. No, not even that. I believe it is, and always will be, unique."

The conversation turned easily, from this statement, to a discussion of the verdict in the case of Ronald True, and the problem in English law of the criminal lunatic ; the eternal query in the case of Madeleine Smith ; the vexed question of Thomson and Bywaters ; and the talk continued into the small hours.

The next day was Sunday, and at half-past five in the evening the guest departed regretfully for London.

On Monday morning Mrs. Bradley telephoned her son.

" I am eaten up with curiosity," she said. " Can't you find me somebody else who was mixed up with it all ? "

" Would one of the jurors do ? " Ferdinand inquired. " I think I could get you a perfectly good juror. As a matter of fact, he's my barber."

" Ah, an artist. Most satisfactory. When and where ? "

" I'll tell him you're coming, and let you know the arrangements. I suppose your time is your own ? "

" Better than that : my time is his," said Mrs. Bradley. She hung up and rang for Henri. Her cook appeared, preceded, in the manner of the Cheshire cat's grin, by an expression of marked anxiety.

" Ze 'addock, madame ? " he enquired, spreading his hands disconsolately. " What I 'ave said to ze fishmonger ! "

" No, no, Henri, dear child ! This has nothing to do with the haddock, which was eaten in its entirety by Mr. Pratt. It is simply this : do you know any hairdressers ? "

Henri gazed at her stupefied. Then he began to talk in French and continued to do so for nearly ten minutes.

" Ah," said Mrs. Bradley, who was old-fashioned enough to believe that French is the most civilised language on earth (except, possibly, for Chinese, which she did not know), " then you will agree with me, Henri, when I suggest that a hairdresser must be, of necessity, an artist."

Henri agreed in another burst of idiomatic rhetoric. His employer nodded and dismissed him. Next day Ferdinand rang up to say that his barber, whose name was Sepulle, would be delighted to recall, for her benefit, his experiences at the trial of Bella Foxley.

Mrs. Bradley met the barber in a room at the back of his shop. It was during business hours, but that, said Mr. Sepulle, mattered nothing. He himself had no appointments that afternoon, gentlemen being, on the whole, more prone to the 'drop-in' than to making appointments, and as to serving on a jury, well, appointments or no appointments, that had had to receive attention before anything.

Not that it was altogether a waste of time, he continued ; no, he should be sorry for anybody to think he thought that. We all had a duty, and ought to be prepared to face it. No shirking ; that was his motto, peace or war. And it had been a very interesting case, although, in his opinion, it had been 'messed up.' "

" Messed up ? " Mrs. Bradley inquired.

Well, there was this woman, Bella Foxley, brought in and charged with the wilful murder of her cousin, and pleading 'Not Guilty,' and then a whole lot of disagreement among a lot of doctors, and then all this stuff about Reasonable Doubt from the judge when the evidence had been completed, and then the jury sent out to consider their verdict.

" We were out about an hour and three-quarters," concluded Mr. Sepulle, " arguing the point, with seven of us for an acquittal and five against. I was against."

" Why ? " asked Mrs. Bradley. The barber had believed Bella Foxley to be guilty because he did not like her face. That, surely, was not part of the evidence, Mrs. Bradley suggested, but he denied this. Her appearance was a fact, he protested, and, as such, it had importance. Then he added that the police knew what they were doing when they arrested her. To this Mrs. Bradley agreed, but very cautiously. What, in the end, she enquired, caused the five jurors who were against an acquittal to join those seven who were in favour ?

Well, Mr. Sepulle had always believed that there were two ways of looking at everything, and the judge *had* stressed giving the prisoner the benefit of the doubt. The doubt in his own mind, he confessed, was rooted in the story that the house was haunted. He did not believe in haunted houses, he explained. Why should not the 'ghost' have committed the murder, and, that being so, there was nothing to suggest that the ghost had been Bella Foxley. Then there was the question of the time. That was extremely important. The medical evidence—not contested by the defence—suggested that death had taken place between eleven o'clock at night and two in the morning. Well, this Bella Foxley was supposed to have been visiting her cousin at this haunted house between those times. The wife swore to it.

Now, he, (Mr. Sepulle), was a married man, and what he wanted to know was, was it likely that a wife was going to let some other woman go gallivanting off at that time of night to visit her husband in an empty house? She had done it once—granted. And, funny enough, the chap fell out of the window. But did it seem reasonable to suppose that the wife would let her do it more than once? Was it sensible to suppose the wife would have it? Not on your life it wasn't. Scared of the haunted house she might have been—thin, whining little thing—but she'd be a darn sight more scared of having some other woman larking about in an empty house with her husband, or he (Mr. Sepulle) was no judge of women.

Then, again, would the prisoner really have been such a mutt as to repeat herself like that? And then, that blackmail stuff. That got nowhere with him. When you talked of blackmail you meant really fleecing people—draining them and draining them like a foul leech sucking blood. You didn't mean a little bit of a five pound note here and there from a woman who'd got a sackful of the ready, and was sweet on the chap anyway.

"So there it was," Mr. Sepulle concluded. "I swallowed my doubts and gave her the benefit of them."

"And how did she take the verdict?" asked Mrs. Bradley, somewhat overcome by Mr. Sepulle's piling of Pelion upon Ossa by following his ripe simile with an unimaginable metaphor.

"She said her prayers," replied the barber, "and, somehow, that seemed to me unnatural."

"Interesting," said Mrs. Bradley. "And was she—in spite of the fact that you did not like her appearance—a striking-looking woman? Should you know her anywhere, as the saying is?"

"She was nothing much to look at," the barber replied, "except she was big and heavy enough to have done it. One of those local permanent waves, and not set fit to speak of, but perhaps she'd had no chance to do much with it while she was awaiting her trial. I am not informed as to that, although you'd have thought that anybody would just have gone in and touched it up for such an important occasion."

" Ah ! " said Mrs. Bradley, interested in this professional point of view.

" Yes. About a twenty-five to a thirty-shilling touch," the barber continued. " Not that I do ladies now, but I used to be a ladies' hairdresser when my old father was alive. Ours is a family business, you see, and he always did the gentlemen himself, right up to the last. He only retired four years back, and died last year, so I got a good knowledge of the ladies' side of the business, being in it twenty-two years, and also of all the other little extras that go with it, manicure, face-packs—Ah, and that reminds me, speaking of this Bella Foxley. She could have done with a mud-pack or two herself, and some mercolised wax, but that's neither here nor there."

Mrs. Bradley rang up Mr. Pratt and invited him to spend another week-end at the Stone House. Mr. Pratt accepted gracefully, and on the following Friday evening came down from London in time for dinner.

" More Foxleyana ? " he inquired, lighting one of the special cigars selected by Ferdinand for his mother's guests (including himself) and then lying back in the very comfortable chair. " What have you been doing since I left you here last time ? "

" Talking to my son on the telephone, and to his barber in person," Mrs. Bradley replied. " The barber was on the jury which acquitted Bella Foxley."

" The deuce he was ! " said Mr. Pratt, deeply interested. " Did he give any special reason for the acquittal ? "

" It appears that the judge was in the prisoner's favour and almost instructed the jury to bring in the verdict which was pronounced as the result of the trial. The barber himself was not at first in favour of acquitting her. He thought her face was against her."

" So it was, but that's not evidence."

" He said it was. After all, he is a student of personal appearance, don't forget."

Mr. Pratt chuckled.

" I've brought a book with me," he said. " It's the reminiscences of Cotter, the prosecuting counsel in the Foxley case. He's got a chapter—half a chapter, actually—about

Bella. I thought you might like to read it. I don't agree with all he says, but there's no doubt that if they could only have proved motive (which, he hints, they could have done if only they could have referred to the death of the aunt) they would have got Bella hanged all right."

" So the prosecution had got hold of the grated carrot, had they ? " said Mrs. Bradley. " From the report of the inquest, I suppose ? "

" Must have been—unless one of their witnesses spilt a few beans in private which they couldn't very well spill in court."

Meanwhile, there was Mr. Cotter's book, and whilst the ex-journalist and Ferdinand played golf on Sunday morning, she spent an interesting time with *Catalogue of Crime* (a handsome twelve and sixpenny volume), and obtained, she told Ferdinand later, Counsel's opinion upon the case.

The eminent gentleman had intended a popular book, and had attempted to govern his literary style in accordance with this aspiration. His matter, however, was sufficiently interesting to be erected on almost any foundation or to carry almost any super-structure, and she not only read his remarks upon the Foxley case (to which he had given the title *Ghaists or Bogles or*——), but his reports and remarks upon a dozen other cases, with close interest.

Of Bella Foxley he said : " We were concerned throughout almost the whole of this baffling case with the contradictory testimony of the medical witnesses, and our hands were tied because we could not allow what, in some circumstances, might have been a telling point against the prisoner, namely, the extraordinary death (by natural causes) of her aunt, to be used in evidence. This deprived us of the possibility of showing a more powerful motive for the death of the cousin than that of a determination to be rid of a blackmailer. This motive, had it been put before the jury, must inevitably have influenced them when they came to consider their verdict.

The aunt, a woman approaching eighty years of age, had died as a result of choking herself with some grated carrot prepared for her by the prisoner, who inherited almost the whole of the aunt's fortune—a considerable amount for one who had always earned her own living. The cousin may have had some information about the aunt's death which he did not disclose but for which he died.

Still, these are but speculations. It is likely that the old lady's death was as accidental as the coroner said, but, lacking ability to show what, in the opinion of the jury, could be regarded as a powerful motive, our case was made very difficult from the outset.

The arrest of Bella Foxley was fully justified, however, and the evidence was clear. It was stated that she had visited the ' haunted house ' as the newspapers called it, between those times when, according to all the medical witnesses (whether they had been called for the prosecution or for the defence) death could have taken place, and she could give no convincing denial, as it was known she had been there before.

In spite of the fact that there was some slight suggestion of a love affair between her and her cousin, the evidence of the wife went to show that she herself was fully cognisant of this visit, and, apart from the fact that she ' thought Bella was foolish to go,' had made no objection to it, except that she ' thought Bella was rather rough with her, the way she threw her down on the bed.'

The fact of this first visit, which was paid on March 11, was not denied by the prisoner, but she contested the further statement by Mrs. Turney that, later, similar visits had been paid, ending with the one which resulted in the death.

The defence attempted to show that no wife would have countenanced assignments with her husband in an empty house at such an hour, but we replied—I think with justice—that the prospect of monetary gain would overcome all such scruples.

However, to revert to the question of what we felt sure in our minds was the true motive for Thomas Turney's murder, it is reasonable to suppose that, at the inquest upon Mr. Turney, the coroner, an experienced man and a solicitor, had conducted his enquiry properly. There was no doubt, however, that the very evidence which the prosecution could not use at the trial, that is, the wife's evidence referring to the aunt's death, was, if not admitted, at least expressed at the inquest, and, although the coroner had begged the jury there to disregard it, it is perfectly certain that, being sensible men, they did not.

The wife, who had ' turned against ' Bella Foxley (to use the prisoner's own words), had let her tongue run away with her at the inquest in a way which was deplorable but undoubtedly interesting, and this tattle, coupled with the evidence of the police doctor (who was also called at the trial), caused the examining magistrates to commit Bella Foxley for trial.

Her counsel (wisely, in my opinion) decided to put her in the box. She made a fairly convincing witness, and stressed that she had gone to the ' haunted house ' that first night merely to make certain that the deceased was ' all right.' Her story was that she left as soon as he (speaking out of the window) had convinced her that all was well. Beyond that she refused (either on advice, or from sheer commonsense combined with a strong instinct for self-preservation) to be budged. The case for the defence was, quite simply, that the prisoner's declaration that that was the only night she had gone to the house ought to be believed, and that there never had been any case to go before the jury. From this position they did not permit themselves to be shaken, for my good friend Godfrey Wenham, now Sir Godfrey, who led for the defence, absolutely refused to allow us to jockey him into the position of trying to prove his client's innocence. It was for us to prove guilt, and, in spite of the testimony of our medical witnesses, who demonstrated clearly that the dead man had been attacked and had received a severe blow on the head before he fell from the window, we were unable to do this.

Nevertheless, I believed fully that the prisoner was guilty, and, although we lost, I shall always regard it as one of my most interesting cases. I was further cheered by the announcement to me (in private) by Sir Godfrey that he had not anticipated an acquittal, and thought that they had been very lucky to obtain one.

Such evidence as was offered against the prisoner by the wife of the dead man, Mrs. Muriel Turney, prejudiced the jury by showing too great an animosity. Had it not been entirely necessary to call her in order to establish the time at which Bella Foxley left the inn, and the fact that more than one such visit had been paid, together with the secondary motive for the crime, I should have been in favour of keeping her out of the box, for she was that most difficult and unsatisfactory type of witness,

an hysterical subject. This, added to her unconcealed hatred of
the prisoner, went sadly against us. Remarks made afterwards
proved that, even without the conflicting testimony of the medical
witnesses, she probably damaged our case irretrievably.

Another controversial point of which much was made on both
sides by the use of those two-edged tools, the expert witnesses,
was that of the button found in the dead man's hand. Even now
I am not convinced in my own mind which side was right over
this. The defence claimed, possibly quite justly, that a man
falling from a height instinctively opens his hands to make
clutching movements as he falls. This theory, of course, depended
upon their premise that the man was alive when he began to fall.

Our own point was that, even if they were right in their
' clutching ' theory, the man was already dead when he fell and
that, therefore, his hand, clenched round the button from the
murderer's coat, would remain closed. This suggestion was weak-
ened by the evidence of one of our own witnesses, the police
doctor, who was compelled to disclose that the button was not so
much clenched in the dead man's hand as resting lightly on the
palm which was ' slightly folded over it.'

The testimony of the youth who found the body was of no help
to either side on this point, as he deposed that he ' was frightened
to see the poor chap lying there all knocked out,' and went at once
for help. Incidentally, we were unfortunate with this witness,
too, for he was so flustered that throughout his evidence he often
confused the two occasions on which he had found Mr. Turney
lying on the path. Help, on both occasions, was not immediately
forthcoming, for the superstitious villagers, who have always
believed the house to be haunted, refused to go anywhere near it
when they heard that someone had been found hurt there, and the
only person at first to respond was the village policeman.

An interesting detail contributed by the prisoner herself
was that the cardigan from which the button came had been
given by her to Mrs. Muriel Turney, and that when she
presented it all the buttons were in place, although she agreed
that it was not then a new garment but was ' one she did not like
the colour of, and Cousin Muriel fancied it.'

Mrs. Turney, on the other hand, while not denying the gift,
stated that when Bella Foxley left the inn in such a hurry that

night she said, ' Oh, my coat's downstairs ; never mind ; this will do.' As she said this she snatched up the cardigan from the foot of Mrs. Turney's bed (the women were sharing a room at the inn), and put it on. In reply to a question from the judge, she said that Bella was fully dressed, except that she had not troubled to put on her stockings, and, in reply to a question from the defending counsel, she agreed that both of them had gone to bed previous to Bella Foxley's having left the inn, and that Bella had awakened her by her preparations for going. ' She did not tell me what she intended to do, until I asked her,' the witness continued, ' and it is my belief that she proposed to sneak out without letting me know where she was going. Unfortunately for her, I am a light sleeper, and I woke up and asked her what was the matter. She said she was worried about Tom, and was going to see if he was all right. As Tom had already once fallen out of the window, I could see what she had in mind.'

In reply to another question she said, ' Yes, of course I offered to go with her. It is all nonsense for her to say I was too nervous to go. She said it would take me too long to get ready, and that by then the mischief would have been done. She then pushed me back on the bed.'

She was asked what she thought this remark about mischief meant, and replied that she supposed at the time that it referred either to the hauntings, or to Tom's previous fall. She added that they had had a good deal of trouble with *poltergeist* phenomena, for which reason she and the prisoner had gone to the inn, being unable to stand the continual nervous strain.

Being asked, further, whether she had ever considered that what she called the *poltergeist* was more probably some mischievous person who was taking advantage of the fact that the house had a ghostly reputation among the villagers, she replied that she ' had thought of it, of course,' and added, ' We always investigated each house we took of this kind to make sure nobody was playing about. My husband was quite experienced with haunted houses. He made his living by them, and had to be careful.'

Explanation of these statements took up what I regarded as an unnecessary amount of the court's time, but the judge ruled that all was admissible. Sir Godfrey Wenham was justified, of course, in exploiting this witness to the full, for she prejudiced our case with almost every word she spoke, although she was our witness. Incidentally, she blamed me bitterly afterwards for not having secured a conviction.

A curious point which did not come out in court but was told to Bella Foxley's solicitors by the youth Hodge who discovered the body, was that the ' hauntings ' were always believed to take the form of a headless huntsman dressed ' like Robin Hood,' but having deer's antlers sprouting from his shoulders—a local variant of the legend of Herne the Hunter, apparently. The *poltergeist* phenomena were ' a new one on we,' the youth averred. He proved to be an earnest patron of the nearest cinema. He added that cries, groans and a kind of miserable wailing had been heard to come from the haunted house a few days previous to Thomas Turney's death, and that when people heard of the death they ' said there had been warning of it.'

The sequel to the case is well known, but it deserves to be detailed here, if only to show that in prosecuting Bella Foxley for the murder of her cousin the Crown was not entirely in the wrong, despite her acquittal by the jury. Almost a year after her release she was found dead in the village pond which was near the house she had taken in a remote part of Hampshire, far from all her old haunts, and where, presumably, she thought the past could be safely forgotten.

It was explained at the inquest that anonymous letters were the cause of her suicide, but it seems more likely that remorse had at last overtaken her, and that she had expiated her crime in the only manner which was in keeping with what she knew were her just deserts."

Mrs. Bradley shook her head in denial of this conclusion and returned the book to its owner when he and Ferdinand returned from golf. She announced that she was going to solve the mystery of Bella Foxley.

" Oh, Mother ! That wretched woman ! After all, she's dead and buried. Why don't you leave well alone ? " enquired her son.

" So said the ghost of Joan of Arc to George Bernard Shaw," Mrs. Bradley replied, with a chuckle.

Chapter Four

THE WIDOW'S MITE

Who can tell what thief or foe,
In the covert of the night,
For his prey will work my woe,
Or through wicked foul despite?
So may I die unredrest,
Ere my long love be possest.

CAMPION.

THERE were several avenues of approach (as the politicians might say) and it remained to arrange them in order. Mrs. Bradley gave this arrangement some thought whilst enjoying to the full the delightful early summer and the no less delightful results of it which were to be found in the garden of the Stone House and in the country around Wandles Parva.

At the end of a week she had made her decision, having put before herself in judicial manner all the alternatives.

There was the widow of Cousin Tom, the prejudiced and apparently spiteful Muriel. It was more than probable that she knew more than she had been permitted to disclose either at the inquest or the trial. It would be interesting to find out where she was living—Eliza Hodge might know—and to find out, too, whether, with the passing of time, her views had become modified in any way.

Then there was the sister Tessa, who had inherited all the aunt's money following Bella's barely comprehensible suicide. Mrs. Bradley would have said that the suicide was entirely incomprehensible but for the evidence of the diary which revealed its author as anti-social, introverted and somewhat defeatist by nature. Possibly the sister could throw more light upon these idiosyncrasies.

There remained the Institution. There Bella had worked as housekeeper and she had hated it with great intensity. Fortunately Mrs. Bradley was in a position to re-introduce herself there without being under the necessity to state her real errand.

She decided to take Muriel first. Her behaviour at the inquest and the trial scarcely accorded with the somewhat mouse-like character which Bella had given her in the diary, but that was not necessarily surprising. Bella, possibly, had never seen her roused. And yet—hadn't she ?

Before she tackled Muriel, however, Mrs. Bradley decided to take a look at another factor in the case, one with a personality, possibly, of its own ; to wit, the haunted house.

She drove first to the inn at which Bella and Muriel had lodged. It was an old place pleasingly reconditioned, and George drove in through an ancient gatehouse arch and drew up in a gravelled courtyard.

Mrs. Bradley, bidding George put the car up and go and get himself a drink, went into the lounge and ordered a cocktail which she did not really want. While it was being brought, she looked about her.

The lounge was an oak-beamed, low-ceilinged room with the huge open fireplace of the original house and the comfortable armchairs and handy little tables of modernity. The order for the cocktail had been taken by a young girl who had come out from behind the reception desk, and who proved to be the daughter of the house. As she did not look more than eighteen it was unlikely, Mrs. Bradley thought, that she retained any memory of guests who had been at the inn six years before. The drink was brought by a waitress, who said pleasantly :

" Taking lunch here, madam ? "

" Yes," said Mrs. Bradley.

" Straight through the door at the back, madam. Only I thought I'd ask, because we shall fill up in a few minutes, and I could see you get a good table."

Lunch offered no opportunity for the kind of conversation Mrs. Bradley had in mind, so when she received her cocktail she scribbled a note which she gave to the waitress to deliver to George in the bar. It was to tell him to get his lunch, and take the car back to Wandles for a suitcase. She proposed to spend at least one night, possibly two, at the inn, to make certain of the local geography before she interviewed Muriel, whose address, so far, she did not know.

After she had had lunch, a short walk, described by the girl who was now back at the reception desk, brought her to the haunted house. The owner of the house, with commendable commonsense, had decided to commercialise its reputation following the acquittal of Bella Foxley for the murder, and it was with little surprise and a certain amount of amusement that Mrs. Bradley found that she could enter the house upon payment of a shilling, and that in return for her entrance fee she was to be escorted round the building by an old man who pointed out the spot where the body had been found, the window from which it had fallen, the Haunted Walk (a picturesque addition, Mrs. Bradley surmised, to what had previously been known about the hauntings) and the Cold Room (further embellishment of an old tale?), where, sure enough, it was possible to feel a draught of air which came through some crack impossible to perceive in the dim light of the landing.

" Is that all ? " she asked, when this conducted tour was over, and she found herself back at the front door.

" There's nothing else, without you can get a special permit, like they ghost-hunting gentlemen have that comes here sometimes in the summer," the old man answered.

" And from whom do I get such a permit ? You see, I used to know something of the people who lived here. I was abroad at the time the thing happened, but it was a great shock to me to hear of the gentleman's sudden death."

" Ah, sudden it was, to be sure," the old man answered. " A kind, good gentleman, too. I remember him well. But murdered ? Not unless the spirits did him in. Ah, that's what it must have been ! " He chuckled, and then added, to Mrs. Bradley's gratification :

" Not as we heard much of the hauntings before he came here, mind you, though there was plenty·to swear to the moanin' and 'owling that set up just after he died, and before it, too."

" Oh, but I understood that the house was haunted by a horned huntsman," said Mrs. Bradley. "Somebody with no head."

" Rubbage," said the old man sturdily. " Village chatter. Though, mind, it be a very old 'ouse ; older, a sight, than what you can see of it now."

" But it had been empty for a long time, surely ? "

" Ah, but that was on account of the damp. Do what you would, that damp would come up, and where it rises from is more than I can tell you, for there ain't no water near, except for a well, but I never 'eard that was the trouble."

" Does the water still come up ? "

" Ah, that it do, but not this time of the year. Come October, though, if we gets any rain, the water will be marking all those walls."

" What a pity. Can nothing be done ? "

" I don't know, I'm sure. One house I was caretaker of, well, you could account for that being damp. Built over a river, that one was, on account the first owner was a little bit touched, it seems"—he tapped his forehead—" and said a witch was after him but that she wouldn't cross water—well, not running water. But there is nothing of that sort here. Nobbut this yere silly tale about a man with no head."

" I wish I could find out when the stories of the hauntings first began," said Mrs. Bradley.

" Oh, that would have been donkeys' years ago, before I come here to live, and that were fifty year, nigh on. But when it comes to crockery and furniture thrown about, and writing on the walls, like what that Mr. Turney, him that fell out of window, used to say, well, I dunno, I'm sure. And that reminds me. Would you like to see the writing on the walls ? Cost you another threepence. I'd almost forgot. Funny, too, because most of 'em wants to see it."

Mrs. Bradley produced the threepence and received a second printed ticket. The whole thing was run on very businesslike lines, she perceived. She wondered who the owner might be, and thought she might as well enquire. The reply she received surprised her.

" Why, the lady that got all the money. The sister of the one that was tried for the murder and afterwards drownded herself. She bought the house, and left it to her sister in the will—or, anyway, left it."

" Oh ? Miss Tessa Foxley owns it ? "

" Foxley. That's the name."

" And she pays you your wages ? "

" Ah."

" Why doesn't she allow the whole of the house to be inspected ?   Why do you keep some of the rooms shut up ? "

" Nothing of interest in 'em, that's the reason.   But you can see 'em, if you have a mind.   I got no orders about 'em either way.   I keep 'em locked because it makes less cleaning, and that's the truth.   Folks don't often complain.   They reckon they've had their money's worth with what we calls the Death Room and the Death Spot and the Cold Room and the Haunted Walk.   All them bits I've showed you already, see ?   Then generally the visitors haven't got no time to look at any more. It's all this rushing about with motors does it.   They've just got time to see the Abbey Church and the ruins and this house, you see, in the afternoon, because they have to start rushing theirselves back to London, and there it is.   Americans is worse than the English.   Never knew such people to hustle you off your feet.   And always ask for a *Brochure*, and taking either no interest at all in what you tell them or else too much, and asking you all kinds of things you don't know."

" Is there such a thing ? " asked Mrs. Bradley, referring to the pamphlet.   "I myself should like a copy if there is."

" Another sixpence.   'Tain't worth it.   Keep your money is my advice."

" If it happens to have a plan of the house, it is what I want."

" Oh, ah, yes, it *has* got that."

" With the various places marked ? "

" Oh, ah.   Here it is.   You can have a look at it, and then, if you don't want to buy it, you can give it me back, so be you haven't made it dirty.   I generally charges a penny a look, but you needn't pay it, seeing you takes an interest."

" I'll buy it," said Mrs. Bradley firmly.   " And I want Miss Foxley's address."

At dinner that night she had the booklet open upon the table, and affected to study it while she was drinking her soup.   The waitress, whose custom it was to converse with the patrons if they were staying in the house, bent over it too, and observed, as she took up Mrs. Bradley's plate :

" Been to take a look at the haunted house ?   Waste of money, isn't it, madam ?   I went once, with my young man, when it was first opened to the public, and I can't say it was much of a thrill.

I went to see Boris Karloff that same evening, and, believe me, there wasn't no comparison."

"No, I suppose not," said Mrs. Bradley. When the plates next were changed and she was being helped to fruit pie and custard, she said :

"Are you a native of these parts?"

"Well, yes, I am, really," the girl answered, "though I was in London for three or four years and lost the talk. They think you're kind of funny in London if you talk like you came from a village, so I picked up their way instead. Have to keep your end up, don't you, madam, if you want to get on in the world?"

Mrs. Bradley said that she supposed so, and then asked whether the house had had its present reputation very long.

"Well, I never heard much about it when I was little," said the girl. "It was always a coach and horses then, and it didn't do anything except go along the road that turns off just above the house to the right. I don't know whether you noticed? But I did hear that what is now part of the garden did used to be the road, till they brought it round a bit to make a less dangerous corner by them crossroads."

"How long has the house been there?"

"Oh, years and years, madam."

Mrs. Bradley waited for the introduction of the cheese course before continuing the talk. Then she said :

"The house was there, then, during your early childhood?"

"Oh, yes, madam. My grandmother remembers the alterations being made. She says there's been a house there hundreds and hundreds of years, only now it's been so altered and rebuilt and that, you'd hardly see the old bits unless you were something in the building line yourself."

Mrs. Bradley spread out her plan again and looked at it while she ate cheese and biscuit. She was still looking at it while she had her coffee. She took it upstairs with her when she went to bed, and placed it on the bedside table so that she could look at it again in the morning.

She was up early next day, but she did not go in immediately to breakfast. She walked up the village street and out on the common, and returned to call in at the Post Office, which opened at nine o'clock. She bought some stamps and then a postal order for her grandson (who liked to have the pleasure of exchanging postal orders for money), and, finding the village postmistress inclined for conversation, remarked upon the tragedy of the haunted house, observed that she had visited the house, and then added that she had once known the people slightly and had often wanted to write to the widow, but had been in America at the time of the husband's death. After her return to England, she had lost track of ' poor Muriel,' she remarked.

This slightly mendacious narrative had the desired effect. The widow, it appeared, had left at the Post Office an address to which letters could be forwarded, and although (as the postmistress painstakingly explained) it was some years now since any letters had had to be sent on, the address, no doubt, was still ' in the book.' The book was produced, and the address triumphantly dictated.

"Although, of course, she may have moved again," said the postmistress.

Mrs. Bradley returned to the inn with a hearty appetite for breakfast. When she had finished she walked over to the haunted house. This time it was not the old man but his daughter who showed her round.

"I was wondering," said Mrs. Bradley, as she paid her threepence to see the writing on the wall, " whether any of the people who go in for that kind of thing ever hold séances here. I rather gathered from your father that they did."

" Oh, yes, we've had half a dozen or more," replied the woman. " They have to get special permission, and they generally hold them in the Death Room, but I never heard that anything much ever came of it."

" I thought some very strange things used to happen before the last owner's death ? At any rate, I should like to make some experiments myself," said Mrs. Bradley. " Is it very expensive ? "

" I couldn't say, I'm sure. Folks from London do seem to have plenty of money to throw about, certainly, especially them that's got a hobby-horse, as you might call it. But you'll have to write to Miss Foxley. She does all the fixing herself. She don't leave it to we."

" When did the last séance take place ? Do you happen to know ? "

" Oh, less than three months ago, I think. Yes, it was well after Christmas. There's one gentleman has been twice. He's got some notion the ghosts might be more active, like, at some parts of the year than what they might be at others. Sounds cranky to me, but there ! If you've got time on your hands and money to spend, I suppose it's an innocent kind of an amusement. Anyway, he was very unlucky both times, and said he couldn't understand it."

" Have you yourself ever noticed anything queer about the house ? "

" What, me ! I should think I was going off my onion if I did. Besides, you wouldn't find me caretaking here, not me, if anything turned up to frit me. Although they do say there was funny things seen and heard after the poor gentleman's death."

" You don't believe in ghosts ? "

" I should think not, indeed ! I wonder what parson would say ! I'm his cook when I'm not here with Dad."

" Were you living in the village at the time when the tenant was killed ? "

" No. I was in service in Warwickshire."

" Was the house said to be haunted when you were a child ? "

" Oh, yes. Nobody much liked to come by at night on account of a coach or something. I never heard the rights of the tale, and I never met anybody who could say they had ever seen the coach. I don't hold with such truck. It's ungodly."

" Did you never hear of the ghost of the huntsman, a headless man with horns ? "

" Oh, yes. But that's only what they frighten the little 'uns with round here."

" And you don't mind taking people's money to show them over a haunted house which isn't haunted ? " Mrs. Bradley enquired.

The woman showed no ill-feeling over the question. She merely replied, with indifference :

" It isn't my job ; it's my Dad's. I only come along on my afternoon off to keep him company, or let him go off for his pint. I suppose people can please themselves whether they come here or not. If they like to be fools and throw away their money for nothing, it isn't my business to stop them, and most of 'em seem to be interested. Have you seen all you want in here? Because I'm bound to lock the door up again before we go."

" I should like to see the Haunted Walk again," said Mrs. Bradley. " I noticed a summerhouse there. How long has that been built?"

" Oh, before the new owner bought the house."

" Yes. I wonder why she bought it?"

" She never bought it. It was left her. Come to think of it, there was some tale she wanted to live in it in memory of her sister that was accused of the murder, but it turned out to be too damp, so she hit on this idea of getting her money back, but she don't see much return, with Dad's wages to be paid all the time."

" Did she live in it at all, do you know?"

" No, not that I know of. No, I'm sure she never did. She never even came to see it when she engaged Dad to look after it, nor have him go there to see her. Just got his character from the vicar."

" Your father didn't know her at all, then, before that?"

" No, he'd never seen this one. He'd seen the one that was had up for the murder, of course. She was about here quite a bit. But from this one he even gets his wages by post. He gets paid by the quarter, though I don't know that it's any odds to anybody."

" I wonder how she knew it was so damp? I still don't see why she ever wanted to live in it, anyway," said Mrs. Bradley. The woman shook her head.

" People take these funny fancies. Morbid, I call it," she said. " But she always refuses to sell, although, on the whole, she must be losing money. She's had one or two offers for it from people who write books and all that. Sort of people who think it's romantic to live in a haunted house. They write and tell her so. She could have got rid of it twice, to my certain knowledge, because the offers went through Dad, and so we know. And she may have had others direct. Anyway, she wrote to Dad after he'd sent on the second one, and said to him to discourage anybody else who spoke to him about it. Said she wasn't going to sell, and that was flat. She said to tell 'em she had a sentimental interest. That always chokes people off."

"I see," said Mrs. Bradley. "Well, no doubt you'll be seeing me again, for I shall fix up a séance before the end of the summer if I can get Miss Foxley's permission."

She spent the rest of the day in discussing the haunted house with anybody who would listen, and among these people was a certain Miss Biddle, a spinster, who lived in a small house at the end of the village near the church. She was the daughter of the late vicar, and, according to the landlady of the inn with whom Mrs. Bradley had discussed the subject, the chief village authority upon the haunted house.

With this amount of introduction only, Mrs. Bradley intruded upon Miss Biddle at three in the afternoon, and was warmly welcomed.

"Not *the* Mrs. Bradley! Oh, I am delighted! This is so nice! Such a treat. I read all your books with the very greatest interest. I get them all from the London Circulating Library. Such a good one! Do you know it? One has only to ask for a book, never mind the price, and it is sent the very next time! A very dear friend of mine, blessed, I am glad to say, with this world's goods, pays the subscription for me every year as a Christmas present, and I can't tell you *what* it means to me, dear Mrs. Bradley, buried alive as we are in this little corner."

Mrs. Bradley rightly observed that it was a very beautiful and interesting little corner.

"Now you must have had some reason for calling, I can't help thinking," pursued her hostess helpfully. "I can't flatter myself that you so much as knew of my existence. Now did you?"

"I am delighted, at any rate, to make your acquaintance, Miss Biddle," replied Mrs. Bradley, sincerely and in the beautiful voice, which, like all beautiful voices, managed to convey something more than the actual words spoken. "It's about this haunted house you have in the village, or, rather, just outside it. Miss Foxley's place, you know."

"Very interesting," said Miss Biddle. "Rather sinister, too, by all accounts. And, of course, that unfortunate death! I am so glad they let that poor woman off, although I believe she did it. Yes, very interesting indeed. I remember my dear father, who was the vicar here at the time, saying that there had been none of this *poltergeist* nonsense in England in *his* young days. It was all on a par with this modern psychology. Quite wrong, of course, because, as everybody knows, there were the Wesleys, and although it might seem a great pity that John Wesley should have been driven out of the church by the violence of his own convictions, I am sure that a more upright and truthful family could not be found, and when there is evidence from such a source of *poltergeist* activities, well, I, for one, do not feel that it can possibly be disputed. As for my poor dear father's views on modern psychology, well, they were really amusing. One could not take them seriously, poor dear. He was dreadfully taken aback by Freud's theories of sex, I remember, and was so distressed by them that he could not bear to have them discussed. Havelock Ellis, too, he did not like. ' So noble a head,' he used to say, ' should have housed the brain of a benefactor of mankind.'

" ' So it does, father,' I used to reply ; but he would not have it so. I suppose he would have been equally opposed to Darwin, and, in his youth, probably was."

It was amazing, Mrs. Bradley agreed, how soon the apparently revolutionary theories of succeeding generations of philosophers and scientists were absorbed and taken for granted when one remembered and realized the opposition offered to them at their inception.

" *Poltergeist* phenomena, now," she proceeded to argue, " are generally accepted by the present generation as scientifically demonstrable, although they are not yet subject to scientific explanation. But," she continued, " I understand, from gossip I have heard in the village, and from what the old caretaker and his daughter up at the house were able to tell me, that previous stories of hauntings betray no conception of *poltergeist* activity, but refer to such old superstitions as a phantom coach, a headless hunter, and so on. I was taken to see the Haunted Walk in the garden, although no one seems to know exactly when, how and why it received its title."

" Oh, I can explain that," said Miss Biddle eagerly. " But

do let us have some tea. I get it myself, you know. I have a daily woman, but she goes as soon as she has washed up after lunch. I find it much nicer to have my little nest to myself for the afternoons and evenings, and, of course, it does come a good deal less expensive this way, especially as I do not give her her dinner. Servants, I always used to find, when I kept house for my dear father, do eat such a lot compared with ourselves, and if they are given inferior cuts of meat they are apt to become discontented."

Mrs. Bradley agreed. Her hostess then went off to get the tea, and after she had brought it in Mrs. Bradley returned to the question of the hauntings.

" Ah, yes, the haunted house," said Miss Biddle. "You were saying that you had heard the village stories."

Mrs. Bradley added that she had also read the story of Borley Rectory, and that some of the features of the haunted house seemed to bear a remarkable similarity to what was described in that book.

" Yes, and the queer thing about our haunted house is that, as I was saying, there is no tradition of *poltergeist* activity until just a month or two before the death of that unfortunate man, Mr. Turney, who was supposed to have been murdered by Miss Foxley's sister. So dreadful, after all that, that she committed suicide ! But I have heard of similar cases. People are so terribly malicious, and they write those shocking anonymous letters. Enough to get on *anybody's* nerves, let alone on those of people who have been through such an ordeal as a trial for murder, especially if she was guilty, which many of us still believe she was."

" So I understand," said Mrs. Bradley. But, wishing to settle first the very vexed question of the *poltergeist*, she added, " I have read that cases have been known of *poltergeist* phenomena commencing in a place where they have been unknown up to that time, on the occasion of an adolescent coming to live in the house. There is that strange but authentic case of the Rumanian girl Eleonore Zugun, in 1926, for instance. You remember that she came to live with the Countess Wassilko-Serecki, who had heard of her extraordinary powers, and that whilst she was with the Countess the most astonishing amount of *poltergeist* activity took place, ornaments and toys flying over partitions and from room to room, pins and needles burying themselves in the girl's flesh, hairbrushes and stilettos dropping, apparently from nowhere, and all that kind of thing."

" Ah," said Miss Biddle, " yes. I grant you anything you like about Eleonore Zugun. A most fascinating case. But there was no question of any adolescent being present in *our* haunted house. There was nobody but the tenant, Mr. Turney, his wife, and that unfortunate Miss Foxley. They were the only people living there while the *poltergeist* was active. It was all most unaccountable. But it all ceased soon after Mr. Turney's death."

" Do you happen to know for certain when the manifestations began ? "

" Yes, I do. At least, let me try to be quite accurate, because I can see that there is something behind all this, dear Mrs. Bradley. You are more interested in Bella Foxley than in psychical research, I am sure."

With this shrewd comment, she went to a small *écritoire*, opened it, and produced a leather-bound notebook.

" I call it my common-place book," she remarked. " I put down in it all the really interesting things that happen, with the dates. I am hoping I shall have something to publish one day. Now, let me see. . . ."

She turned over the pages. Mrs. Bradley watched anxiously.

" Here we are," said Miss Biddle. " I knew I had noted it down. Six years ago, wasn't it ? And the first date I have for the *poltergeist* is January 12th. I put : So the haunted house really is haunted ! Samuel Kindred was passing the house at sunset yesterday, and heard the noise of loud quarrelling. As the voices were speaking ' like Londoners ' he stopped to investigate. There was nothing to be seen, but he could hear loud thumpings and bumpings which seemed to come from the back of the house. He knew the house was supposed to be empty, so he went round to the window and peered in. The glass was dusty, however, and he could see nothing. Nevertheless, he did not think there was anybody there. It being none of his business, as he afterwards said, he went on his way.

"Next day, being Saturday, two or three of the school-children came into the garden of the haunted house to play hide-and-seek among the shrubs and trees. They became frightened, however, by loud, heavy noises inside the house, and one child declared that she had seen a ghost at one of the upstairs windows.

" As Samuel Kindred's story was public-house gossip by this time, four or five men armed with sticks, accompanied by Farmer Stokes with a shot-gun, went to the house on Saturday evening, having had a drink at the public-house first, to see what they could find. There was nothing to be seen, but the heavy noises were heard, and a half-brick, which came sailing through the air, struck one of the men on the shoulder and bruised him badly. What they described as ' mad bellows and screeches ' of laughter followed, and in the end they broke a downstairs window and entered the house. As soon as they were in the hall, some furniture near them began to move about in an unaccountable manner, and they retreated, telling each other lurid tales of traditional hauntings. Farmer Stokes loosed off his gun, and the result was a perfect cascade of small articles down the stairs. He proposed to mount the stairs, but finding that the others had all deserted him, he gave up the idea and followed them back to the road.

" There the whole group waited for about twenty minutes, but he could not persuade the others to return with him to the house. Next day, after Evensong, my dear father, with Farmer Stokes, Mr. Morant from the Hall, Mr. Carter and old Everett, the shoemaker, went to the haunted house, but found it perfectly quiet. They climbed in, but the furniture was all in place, and everything seemed to be in order.

" The moment they turned their backs on the house, however, and were walking down the weed-grown drive towards the road, the most unearthly pandemonium broke out behind them. They hastened back, but all was quiet again, and nothing found out of its place."

" Amazing," said Mrs. Bradley.

" Was it not ? " said Miss Biddle, very much pleased by this reception of her account of the hauntings.

" And how long after that was it that the news of the *poltergeist* became general ? In other words, what made Mr. Turney decide to rent the house in order to study the hauntings ? " Mrs. Bradley enquired.

" Now it is very interesting and curious that you should ask that," replied Miss Biddle. " He must have had hearsay of it, for nothing had appeared in the papers then. All the same, it was not more than three or four days after that Sunday that we heard the house had the *To Let* board taken down, and that the owner, who was living at Torquay, had told old Joe to go in and cut the grass and tidy up the borders. Then, funnily enough, the *To Let* board went up again, but only for about ten days."

" And did Joe experience anything strange whilst he was attending to the garden ? "

" Nothing at all, except that he declared he kept hearing voices which seemed to come up from his feet."

" Is Joe the present caretaker ? "

" Oh, no. He's an almost witless old fellow who lives in that yellow cottage by the crossroads."

" I wonder how much he remembers about it ? " said Mrs. Bradley thoughtfully.

" I'm afraid he's not to be depended upon," said Miss Biddle. " He's given to inventing his information. Nobody would have believed him about the voices if it could have been proved that he'd heard about the *poltergeist*. But it really didn't seem as though he *had* heard, so some people thought there might be something in his queer tale."

" I agree with them," said Mrs. Bradley. " Voices from under his feet . . . a house with foundations very much older than the present superstructure . . . a house so damp that the water marks the walls . . . bellows and screeches of laughter . . . *poltergeist* activity . . . very interesting. Very interesting indeed."

Muriel rented a room. This fact she referred to at once. Mrs. Bradley imagined it was her way of introducing herself. It was a large room on the first floor of the house and at the front, and its only disadvantages, from her point of view, continued Muriel, were, first, that it had a bedroom fireplace (which she intended to have replaced by a ' proper one ' as soon as she had enough money, provided that she could get 'the people down-stairs' to agree), and, second, that it was not two rooms.

"I tried to get them to throw in the box-room," she explained, when the visitor was seated, "but they wouldn't part with it. Of course, they are very untidy, so I dare say they feel they must have somewhere to poke all the rubbish. They didn't want any more rent—not that I could have paid it ; I have all my work cut out as it is—they simply wouldn't part with the room. I have all my meals with them, that's one thing. Now, when would your daughter want to begin ? I'm afraid I couldn't reduce the fees very much, because my terms are by the term, if you understand what I mean, and not by the week. And would you want her to use your piano or mine ? Because I can only take just so many pupils to use my piano, not that I wouldn't take more, but I've had to promise not to have the piano played here for certain hours of the day, and as it's an Agreement, I could hardly be expected to break it."

Mrs. Bradley, who had been wondering why she had been accepted, so to speak, at her face value, escorted into the house before she had stated her business, and installed in the best armchair, now briefly explained that she had no pupil to offer, but had come about something quite different.

"Oh, dear ! How silly of me," said Muriel. Then, with the nervous purposefulness of the indigent, she continued hastily, "But if you're selling anything, I really don't need it, thank you."

She rose, as she said this, with the object of showing Mrs. Bradley out, but the visitor remained seated, and replied :

"I have nothing to sell. My errand is a painful one. If, when you have heard what I have to say, you still wish me to go, I shall go at once."

Muriel, looking extremely frightened, sat down again.

"Oh, dear," she said. "No, I didn't think you'd come to sell anything, although really they employ the most respectable people, I'm sure. In fact, I did a little canvassing myself after—after my husband's death, but I didn't like it at all. Some of the people were very rude and unkind. I suppose they have to be, with people bothering them all day. Still, it wasn't very pleasant."

"It is about your husband's death that I have come," said Mrs. Bradley.

"I don't understand. He died—several years ago. There couldn't be—that dreadful woman hasn't left a confession?"

"No, nothing like that. Mrs. Turney, I am investigating matters connected with the trial of Bella Foxley. I wonder whether you would tell me one or two things I very badly want to know?"

"Well—I don't know. You see, I don't want to get into any trouble. After all, the jury did say she didn't do it, although I know she did."

"There will be no trouble, I assure you. I have already had a long conversation with one of the jurymen who acquitted Bella Foxley. And I am in touch with certain aspects of the case which seem to me significant. Mr. Conyers Eastward——"

"But he defended her!"

"Yes, I know he did. But never mind that now. The point is that he is a person of repute, and I am going to re-open the case, to some extent, with him."

"Yes, I see. I'm sure you're quite respectable. But, after all, that awful woman is dead, and, even if she weren't, she couldn't be tried again for the same crime, could she? Oh, I could have done anything to her! You should have seen her look at me when the jury brought in their verdict! She knew she'd done it, and she knew *how* she'd done it! And yet they let her off! And I used to dream night after night that poor Tom was calling me, trying to get me to understand something about that terrible house where it happened. But I always woke up just as I was on the point of understanding what he meant."

"That is very interesting indeed," said Mrs. Bradley. "You dreamt that your husband was trying to explain something to you about that haunted house, and you always woke up just as you were on the point of understanding what he meant."

"Why do you look at me like that!" cried Muriel. Mrs. Bradley's bright black eyes began to sparkle.

"I beg your pardon," she said. "I don't think you understand the importance of those dreams, but that doesn't matter now. Tell me this, Mrs. Turney. Would you want people to be convinced, even all these years afterwards, that Bella Foxley was a murderess—if she was one ? Or are you willing to leave things as they are ? "

" I don't believe Tom fell out of that window, either the first or the second time, and I don't believe the haunted house had anything to do with his death," replied the widow. " But as for Bella Foxley—if I could blacken her name even now that she's dead, I'd do it. It was something she knew, and something Tom knew, too ! That's why she killed him. It was the grated carrot, you know. That's what it was. Tom knew. Oh, how I wish we'd never gone ! It was the telegram that decided us, although Tom knew better than to expect anything under the will. Poor Aunt Flora ! She hadn't very many relations to go and see her ! But we weren't well off, you know, and Tom said she might think we thought we'd got expectations, and he wouldn't go anywhere near. We had no expectations of any sort, and didn't want to have any, and he knew what people would think—especially Bella—if they got to hear.

" Well, Bella was there already. She had arrived the day before. She was quite nice, and she and I went up to see Aunt Flora, who looked very, very frail and very much older than when I had seen her last, for all she had dyed her poor old hair since we were there before, although I didn't like to tell Tom that, and he wouldn't go in to see her. He couldn't bear illness, poor man."

" When had he seen her last ? " Mrs. Bradley enquired.

" When Tom and I were married. I was Tom's second wife, you see, and we had only been married four years. Aunt Flora did not come to the wedding, but we sent her a piece of the cake —Tom *would* have a cake and orange blossom and everything, for *my* sake, because he said I was only a girl, and that, after all, it was my first marriage, even if it was his second. He was full of little jokes like that about it. I never felt his first wife came between us at all, although I believe he had been quite fond of her. But, after all, she had been dead for nearly twenty years when he married me. He was nearly sixty, you see, and although people made some remarks about December and May, it really wasn't like that at all. Tom was really very young for his age—

more like a man of forty-five, I always thought—and I've always been rather reserved and sort of *old* for mine, so it was a more suitable marriage than you would think, considering I was only twenty at the time. I am only thirty now, although people have taken me for thirty-five or six."

She did look that age, thought Mrs. Bradley, but the fact had no importance. It might be important to know that Tom was so much older than she had imagined, though, she decided. A man of sixty-four or five might tumble out of first-floor windows and hurt or even kill himself where a man much younger might sustain no lasting injury. Curious he had not hurt himself the first time, all the same, at any rate, not seriously."

" Had you met your husband's cousin before ? " she enquired, as Muriel paused. The widow nodded.

" Oh, yes, several times. She and Tom got on quite well together. She put him in the way of renting these haunted houses from time to time. She had even come away with us for part of her summer holiday, I remember. We were very hard up that year, and she said that if we would let her join us she would pay half the expenses and we could pay the other half between us. It was quite a generous offer, because, although we had two bedrooms, the one sitting-room did just as well for three as it would for two, so we actually saved a little more than you would think, especially as the rooms came a little cheaper, taking the two bedrooms with one sitting-room, you know. It was then she gave us the first news about this last haunted house. Tom was pleased. We had a happy time. I liked Bella then, and Tom liked her right to the end."

" Even after he knew . . . ? "

" That she choked poor aunt ? Well, perhaps not quite so much then, but, of course, he couldn't be sure."

" But I thought he *was* sure ? "

" Well, you see, what really happened was this : "

" We are coming to it at last," thought Mrs. Bradley.

" You see, Aunt Flora was so much better that we thought we might all venture to go out for a little while in the afternoon. A sickroom can be very monotonous, and poor Aunt Flora's (I don't mean it was her fault, of course !) was really rather stuffy and smelly. Well, Tom said he wouldn't be a minute, and

Bella seemed to be hanging about, almost as though she wanted me out of the way. . . ."

"You thought of that later," thought Mrs. Bradley. She grinned, and the narrator looked disconcerted. "Wanted you out of the way, yes?" said Mrs. Bradley, nodding.

"So I decided I wouldn't be in a hurry, and, anyhow, I was waiting for Tom. Tom came out—I was waiting by the front door—and said that Bella seemed to have found herself a job in the kitchen. I couldn't understand that, because, Bella spending all her life in kitchens at that time, being housekeeper at that dreadful Home, you know, I didn't think she would want to go into one when she need not, so I went and looked through the window and tapped on the glass. She looked up, and I could see that she had a carrot in her hand. . . ."

"I don't think she denied that she grated the carrot," said Mrs. Bradley, gently interrupting the narrative.

"Oh, I see. No, she didn't deny it. But I always say that Aunt thought she was getting pease-pudding. She would never have taken raw carrot; of that I'm very sure. Anyhow, Bella didn't come, so Tom and I walked on for a bit, and then Tom remembered that he'd left a letter for the house-agent up in our bedroom, and he badly wanted it to catch the post. He decided to go back, but told me not to come, but to wait for him at the bottom of the hill if I liked.

"Well, I did wait for him, but he was so long that I began to get chilly, and I walked back towards the house. There was no sign of him until I got right up to the porch, and then I saw him. He looked terrible. He said, ' Oh, there you are, Muriel! A dreadful thing has happened. Poor Aunt is choked to death. You had better go for the doctor.'

"I didn't know where the doctor lived, but he gave me quite a sharp push—he was always so gentle as a rule—and told me to hurry up.

"' I'm not going to leave that hell-cat alone with her,' he said. I couldn't think what he meant, but now I know."

"What did he mean?" asked Mrs. Bradley.

"Why, Bella, of course. He meant he knew Bella had done it, don't you see? And he wasn't going to give her a chance to remove anything which might give her away."

"But you couldn't have thought that at the time, you know, Mrs. Turney," said Mrs. Bradley, even more gently than she had yet spoken. Muriel looked at her, and then agreed.

"No, perhaps not; but I think it now," she said. "Well, I fetched the doctor. Poor aunt *was* choked with the carrot. The doctor confirmed it at once."

"But you can't prove, and your husband couldn't have proved, that Miss Foxley did the choking," said Mrs. Bradley. "He didn't see her do it, and, even if he had, I doubt whether her word would be considered less valid than his if she declared that he was lying. Why did you hate Miss Foxley at that time, Mrs. Turney? She had never done you any harm."

"I know she hadn't," agreed Muriel, "but, looking back, I can see it all."

Mrs. Bradley thought she herself could, too, but she did not say this. Believing, however, that no logical answer would be forthcoming to her question, she asked another:

"How long had you been in the new house when Bella Foxley came to stay with you?"

"Well, she came almost at once; that is, once the funeral was over. Tom and I did not stay for that. Then we heard about the will, and when we knew that poor Aunt Flora had left the house and furniture to Eliza, it was difficult, I thought, for Bella to remain. She ought to have gone back to the Home, of course, to work out her notice. . . ."

"Ah, yes," said Mrs. Bradley. "She gave in her notice before Aunt Flora's death, I believe."

"Yes, I suppose she must have done, to get in the complete month." She paused. Then she exclaimed, "But that's a proof, surely, of what I've been saying! She *did* kill poor Aunt! She must have had it all planned before she went down there! Wicked, wicked thing! Didn't I tell you!"

Mrs. Bradley did not take up the challenge. She merely remarked that Bella hated the work she had been doing, and to this Muriel agreed.

"I suppose another post of the kind she had held would be comparatively easy to find," Mrs. Bradley added; but Muriel could offer no opinion on this.

"At any rate," she said, "she had no home to go to, and she

said she felt bad, after Aunt's death and the funeral and everything, so we agreed to put her up, although we didn't really
want to ; but she kept hinting and hinting, in the way relations
do, and in the end we felt we had to invite her, especially as she
had found the house for us, and had visited us before.

" She was very good about everything, I must say. She paid
well for her board and lodging, and I shouldn't have minded
keeping her on for a month or two if it hadn't been for the way
the house behaved."

" The way it behaved ? " said Mrs. Bradley, intrigued.

" Oh, yes. It was dreadful. Not only frightening but dangerous.
Things thrown about and furniture upset, and people creeping
about in slippers after dark. It terrified me so much that I had to
leave, and Bella was frightened, too, and she came with me.
But Tom wouldn't leave—he said it was the most interesting
house he had ever known. He researched, you know, in such
things, and wrote books and articles. It didn't pay very well.
We were always rather hard up. Still, the rents for those sort of
houses are always very low, so we hadn't the usual expenses,
and my poor Tom was very, very happy."

She paused again, looking sadly back at the difficult but, seen
in retrospect, desirable, happy past.

Revenge, thought Mrs. Bradley, might appease whatever
strife was hidden behind that weak, anxious and, if one had to
admit it, rather peevish little face.

" I thought," she said aloud, " that Bella did return to the
Institution for a time ? "

" Only to get her things. She stayed one night, that's all—
or was it the week-end ? It's so long ago now, and what happened
later was so awful, that I really don't remember every little
thing."

" I think it must have been the week-end," said Mrs. Bradley,
thinking of the diary—although, as she immediately admitted
to herself, it would have been easy enough for Bella to have
transferred the episode of the boy Jones and the foreign bodies in
the food from the time when it had really happened to the date
on which it was chronicled in the diary. She was greatly intrigued
by the diary. Its frankness, lies, evasions, and inventions made up
such a curiously unintelligible whole.

"·Did you see the two boys whom the police interviewed in your village ? " she inquired.

" Boys ? " said Muriel. " I don't remember any boys." Yet her colour rose as she spoke.

" Two boys had escaped from the Home at which Bella Foxley was employed, and at one point it was thought that the police had found them in that village."

" Oh ? " Muriel looked thoroughly alarmed. " Oh, really ? I never heard anything about it. How funny—how curious, I mean. No, I had no idea——"

" Naturally," said Mrs. Bradley, as one dismissing the subject. " I suppose there is no complete and exact record of the happenings in the haunted house, by the way ? "

" Record ? . . . Oh, yes, of course there is ! But . . . oh, well, you could see it, I suppose. There is a typed copy somewhere, but I don't know where it went. The psychic people—the Society, you know—had one copy, and then there was a carbon. The copy I've got is in Tom's own handwriting, and I don't know whether I ought to lend it. Besides—forgive·me ; I don't mean to be rude, and I can see you take a real interest—I mean, not just curiosity and all that—but what are you trying to do ? Even if it could be proved that Bella did push Tom out of the window, it wouldn't help. She's dead. She committed suicide, and, as I say to people (when I mention the subject at all) if that wasn't a confession, what could be ? "

" 1 see," said Mrs. Bradley, " and I know I'm tiresome. But if I could just see the entries about the hauntings I should feel so very grateful."

" Well—all right, then," said Muriel, " but I can't let you take it away."

" It is very kind of you to let me see it at all," said Mrs. Bradley. " Is it a complete record ? "

" You'll see that it goes right up to about—well, when Tom fell the first time."

She went over to the writing desk in the corner, rummaged, and brought out a stiff-covered exercise book containing perhaps a hundred pages of thick, blue-ruled paper. She looked at it, turned the pages ; then thrust it back into the drawer.

" I've remembered where the typed copy is," she said. She

took the cushions off an armchair and removed a brown-paper package.

" Here you are," she said. About forty sheets had been used, and Mrs. Bradley read them carefully. Then she turned to the last page. Upon this a summary of the hauntings had been worked out, dated and timed.

" I should be glad to be allowed to make a copy of this summary," she said. " It may be extremely important."

" Important for what ? " inquired Muriel. Mrs. Bradley, making rapid hieroglyphics in her notebook, did not reply. When she had finished she read through all the entries once more before she put the typescript together and handed it over. It tallied pretty well with the diary.

Muriel put it into the desk, and came back to the hearth.

" He was murdered," she said. " Blackmail."

" I know," said Mrs. Bradley. " Just one more point. You knew of this haunted house, how long before your husband's aunt died ? "

" About a month."

" As long as that ? By the end of December ? "

" Yes. It must have been as long as that, because we had to give a month's notice where we were. That was in the haunted flat in Plasmon Street."

" Yes, I see. That seems quite clear. It's been very good indeed of you, Mrs. Turney, to talk to me like this, and I am interested—more than I can tell you—in your story."

" Well," said Muriel, rising with the guest, " won't you stay and have a cup of tea or something ? I'm sure it's been really nice to have a chat with somebody about it. But nothing can bring Tom back. Still, it's very kind of you to take an interest. I am ever so glad you called."

Mrs. Bradley was glad, too. Dimly she was beginning to see quite a number of things, all of them interesting ; some astonishingly so.

Chapter Five

THE HAUNTED HOUSE

" Tell zeal it wants devotion ;
    Tell love it is but lust ;
    Tell time it is but motion ;
    Tell flesh it is but dust ;
    And wish them not reply,
    For thou must give the lie."

RALEIGH.

MRS. BRADLEY'S application for permission to hold séances in the house at which Cousin Tom had met his death was granted by Miss Foxley, and the séances were duly held. They were not conducted by Mrs. Bradley, although she was an interested participant.

She went twice to the house before the first séance, and contrived to dispense with the services of the caretaker as guide.

" Just as you like, mum," he said, when she pointed out that his voice and familiar tread did not give the spirits, if there were any, a chance, " although I didn't think, when I first had the pleasure of showing you round, as you was one of them fakers."

" One of those what ? " said Mrs. Bradley.

" Well, you've heard of poodle-fakers, haven't you ? I calls these here ghost-hunters spirit-fakers."

" Oh, no," said Mrs. Bradley. " A spirit-faker, in the full technical sense of the term, is a person who fakes, or manufactures, spirits for the purpose of deceiving the earnest seeker after psychical phenomena."

" Oh, ah," said the old man, deflated. He handed her the keys. " No good me telling you which is for which door. You'd never remember 'em all," he continued. Mrs. Bradley accepted the formidable bunch.

" I shall proceed according to the method of trial and error," she said. Lugubriously the old man watched her approach the drawing-room, and then he shuffled away to his dinner.

Mrs. Bradley had chosen her time carefully. She had discovered the hour at which the custodian dined, and the average amount of time he spent over his meal. She knew that she had approximately two hours at her disposal. It was her intention to make a thorough examination of the house and to repeat this examination, if she thought it necessary, once more before the first séance was held. She had arranged that this séance should be held after dark, and had rented the house for the twenty-four hours beginning at ten in the morning.

She did not go into the drawing-room until the caretaker was out of sight. Then she unlocked it and went straight across to the window. It was in front of this window that the body of Cousin Tom must have fallen. Taking a folding ruler from her skirt-pocket, she measured the height of the room. She had already formed a mental estimate of the height of the bedroom window-sill from the ground, and her measurements showed the drawing-room ceiling to be twelve feet high.

She wanted to go upstairs and measure the height of the bed-room from which Cousin Tom had fallen, and prove to her own satisfaction that, allowing for flooring, there was no secret cavity between the rooms. She was trying to account for the *poltergeist*.

If, as she supposed, the phenomena were not genuine, then it was necessary to discover some hiding place from which the perpetrator of what had turned out to be a very grim joke could have emerged and to which he could have returned whilst ' haunting ' the house.

There was the possibility, of course, that the phenomena might be genuine, and this point she did not overlook. Neverthe-less, in as much of the literature relating to *poltergeist* activity as she had been able to procure, there seemed no evidence of anything beyond mischief and a certain amount of childish spite behind the *poltergeist* manifestations. Murder, for instance, seemed quite outside the scope of *poltergeist* behaviourism, and she had not the slightest hesitation in accepting, as a working hypothesis, Mrs. Muriel Turney's conviction that Cousin Tom had met with foul play.

The house itself, as she had realised upon her first visit and in spite of the somewhat irritating presence of the old man, was a most extraordinary place. Stone-built in the most hideous and uncompromising style of the middle of the nineteenth century, it retained evidence of having been erected on the site of a very much older building, for in some respects it adhered to the Elizabethan ground-plan upon which an earlier house had been built.

Of all the picturesque features of its foundation, however, it retained nothing but some panelling by the side of an obviously reconstructed fireplace in the dining-room.

The windows were large and rectangular, and opened up and down by means of sashcords, some of which were in need of replacement. The staircases were narrow and Victorian, even the front one. On the servants' staircase there was not room for two people to pass.

It was a cheerless house ; sinisterly cheerless, for the bright sunshine streamed in through the windows, particularly of the drawing-room, which faced south, and of the bedroom immediately above it, and yet a kind of spiritual dankness seemed to permeate every part of the building.

Mrs. Bradley was particularly free from morbid fears and nervous fancies, but she would not have been in the least surprised, she felt, as she went from room to room, tapping, pacing and measuring, to turn round and find the ghost of Cousin Tom, of Bella Foxley, or even of Aunt Flora, standing in the doorway watching her. As for the front stairs, she stood quite two minutes in the bare and chilly hall looking at them before she could bring herself to mount.

Once on the first floor, however, she shook off this irrational sensation, and explored as fully and measured as carefully as she had done down below.

In connection with the alleged activities of the *poltergeist* she did establish one thing. That was that the contents of the bedroom from which (or in which) Cousin Tom had met his death could be shot over the banisters into the hall without trouble, and that anybody decanting furniture, ornaments or anything else portable into the well provided by the turn of the stairs, would have ample time to escape before the investigators could catch him. As for the sound of his footsteps, that, to a convinced ghost-hunter, would not necessarily convey any doubts. *Poltergeists* can be heard to move about, she had read, and, in fact, their footsteps were often audible without anything being visible.

The route taken by a person playing practical jokes or hide-and-seek with a victim would most likely be along the passage to the bathroom, she deduced. This passage, unlighted for about half a dozen yards beyond the bedroom door, proceeded, under a square-topped archway and down one step, to a fairly large bathroom and to the back stairs. These stairs led down to the kitchen and up to the attics, and were lighted at the top by a large window which overlooked the almost enclosed courtyard. This window, oddly enough, could be closed by shutters on the inside of the glass.

The bathroom door opened on the right of the passage, at the end of which was another bedroom which overlooked the garden. There was a rather similar passage at the opposite end of the landing, but on this side there was no bathroom, and the bedrooms were considerably smaller.

There was one item of particular interest which she had over-looked on her previous visits. This was that a small room, apparently a dressing-room, opened off the side of what, to herself, she called Cousin Tom's room, but the communicating-door had been papered over, so that, at a casual glance, it was unlikely that the fact that it was not quite flush with the rest of the wall would be apparent.

She went over and examined it again when she had explored the bathroom passage to its end. The job of disguising the doorway had been so well done that it almost seemed as though deliberate thought had been given to the possibility of hiding it. She ran her finger round the opening, being very careful not to press hard enough to break the wall-paper, and then went into the adjoining room to study the doorway from that side. The same neat, careful job had been made, and she now noted more particularly a fact which had struck her before—that the opening from the passage leading into this smaller room was not, and never had been, a doorway in which to hang a door— it was merely an arch which had been formed by removing bricks from the passage wall.

Whether these alterations had any sinister implication still had to be discovered. She noted them, and passed on. The attics, which she thought might repay inspection, proved disappointing in that they were entirely empty. Whatever lumber the house might once have harboured was not now on this top floor. She inspected the boards closely. They were dusty, but not unduly so, and she supposed that these rooms, in common with the other parts of the house to which the public were not usually admitted, received attention at intervals from the caretaker and his daughter. There was an absence of cobwebs which suggested that the last cleaning of the attics had been of fairly recent date.

She walked over to the window in each room and looked out, but beyond an extended view of the country around the house, the windows had nothing to offer. She tested the catches. They were rusty, and it did not seem as though the windows could have been opened for some considerable time, certainly not when the rooms had last been cleaned.

The attics did not cover the whole of the floor beneath, but belonged, it seemed, to the older part of the present structure, for the rooms on the opposite side of the house had no attics built over them. The lower roofs could be seen from two of the attic windows. The courtyard could not be seen from any of the upstair windows except the shuttered window on the stairs.

She was about to descend the narrow stairs when she noticed what seemed to be ventilation holes in the partition wall at the top of the staircase. When the attic doors were shut this partition wall was in darkness. She looked back, and saw that one of the doors which she believed she had shut and locked was swinging slowly open.

With a feeling more of interest than of anything approaching alarm, she went back to find out what had happened. She had not anticipated anything in the way of a supernatural occurrence, but she was relieved, all the same, to discover that the trouble was due to a defective lock and did not emanate from the realm of the spirits.

She pushed the door wide open, and went back to examine the air-holes. It was now obvious that they ventilated a large cupboard, or small, unlighted room, on the opposite side of the passage. The door of it had been papered over to match the rest of the decorations of the attic corridor, and again, like the door into the dressing-room on the floor below, would, in the ordinary way, pass unnoticed. She traced the outline of the door beneath the paper, closed the attic door again, and this time, fastened it securely, and then, with some part of her theory if not proved, at any rate capable of proof, she returned to the first floor and made an exhaustive search.

Nothing further was to be discovered there, however, and she spent the next three-quarters of an hour in checking the plan of the house which formed the only illustration to the little guide-book she had purchased on her previous visit, and in preparing a sketch-plan of her own on which she marked the door with the faulty lock, the position of the two attic cupboards, the blocked-up and papered-over communicating door between the largest bedroom, and the window with the inside shutters and the dressing-room at the top of the stairs.

Her next objective was the courtyard. This was a rectangular strip of garden which had been made almost into a quadrangle by the addition of the newest wing. It was overgrown with tall weeds, the willow-herb flourishing particularly. There was a well at one corner, close to the scullery door. A couple of boards formed the cover. She removed them, peered into the well and then replaced the boards.

Although it was broad daylight, the courtyard looked eerie and desolate. It was silent, too, and the surrounding buildings seemed to shut out the sun. It was curious, she thought, that none of the windows, even of the new buildings, overlooked it. It seemed chilly out there. Mrs. Bradley made a careful exploration, even parting continually the long weeds to make certain that the surface of the courtyard was everywhere the same. This examination yielded nothing.

She left the house before the caretaker returned to it. Then, later in the afternoon, she sought him out, and asked him one or two trivial questions before she put to him the important query suggested by her visit.

" What has become of the well-cover, I wonder ? " she said, in the most casual tone she could command.

" Well-cover ? It was covered with two planks last time *I* were here," he responded stupidly. " What do you mean about a well-cover ? "

"I shouldn't have thought two planks would have been sufficient to cover so deep a well, and one which has the opening level with the ground," replied Mrs. Bradley. "But, of course, it's no business of mine. One thing, I see that you are able to keep the flap of the cellar staircase screwed down. That's something."

"If any of the visitors brings childern, I keeps my eye on things," said the old man. "Anyway, this yere courtyard beant on the reg'lar routine. Nothing to see out here. I've give up most of the garden, too, I 'ave. Just keep the front a bit tidy. I thought maybe some of them it belonged to might pay a jobbing gardener to come in now and again. It's a mort of work for an old fellow like me, and I can't keep upsides with it nohow. Barring the little wife of that poor gentleman as was killed, and she only come the once, I don't believe anybody's took that much interest in doing a bit of spade-work. Seems a shame, like, don't it?"

Mrs. Bradley emphatically dissented from this view, but she did not say so. As soon as she left the haunted house this time she went back to Miss Biddle.

"I'm becoming a nuisance," she remarked, "but there is one thing I want to know, and I don't know of anybody else who can help me. These screamings and knockings that seem to have been heard before the death of Mr. Tom Turney . . . ?"

"I'never heard them myself," Miss Biddle confessed, "but I know who did, and that's my daily woman. But weren't they heard *after* the death?"

"What kind of witness would she make? I mean, is she the kind to exaggerate what she heard?"

"Oh, yes, certainly. On the other hand, she certainly did hear something. I put down in my commonplace book what she said at the time, and I attach importance to it because it was the first that anybody heard, it seems, of that part of the hauntings, so that it could not have been the result of hearsay, or owing anything to village gossip."

Mrs. Bradley mentally blessed the commonplace book, of which she had heard on her previous visit, and begged that it might be produced. The entry was not dated—a point not of very great importance, since Cousin Tom's death was referred to, and this fixed the time sufficiently for those circumstances which she suspected that she was investigating.

The entry read : *Mrs. Gubb very excited and upset. She says she heard screams and yells from the haunted house as she came past this morning on her way here. The other day the new tenant, a Mr. Turney, fell out of a bedroom window and was killed. Mrs. Gubb says that what with one thing and another, nobody will want to go near that house, even in daylight, soon.*

Mrs. Bradley asked permission to make a copy of the entry, and, having made it, autographed a copy of one of her own books at Miss Biddle's deprecating but eager request, departed, went back to the inn, carefully collated such information as she now possessed, heard half a dozen more legends of ancient hauntings from the villagers, and went off again to interview Mrs. Muriel.

"I want you to come back to that house with me, Mrs. Turney," she said. A request couched in such terms was almost bound to be refused, and Mrs. Bradley was not at all surprised to hear Cousin Muriel reply :

" Oh, no, really, really, I couldn't. You don't know what you're asking ! I'll tell you anything you like about the house, but I couldn't possibly set foot in it again, and nobody ought to expect it."

As Mrs. Bradley did not expect it she inclined her head sympathetically and added :

" You came to hear of the house through Bella Foxley, and you say that she had recommended houses to you before ? "

" Well, yes. She had rather a flair, Tom used to say. She found Hazy for us. You know—that house where two men of the Plague Year walk about and say, " Bring out your dead." Of course, they never *did* say it while we were there, and so Tom couldn't put much about it in the article he wrote. We only stayed a month, but it was a *very* interesting old house, and we had a good deal of success with *planchette* there. Although, I might tell you, I don't really like *planchette*. It makes me think— it almost makes me believe——"

" Did your husband ask a fee for admission to his séances ? "

" Why, how else could we have lived ? " asked Cousin Muriel. " He certainly did not get very much for his writing."

" Then—if you don't object to the question—did he never

encounter people who were disappointed when the séance, we will say, produced no results ? "

" The séances *always* produced results," responded Muriel. "If it wasn't one thing it would be another. That was what was so wonderful, and rather frightening, really. Tom never had what you might call a *barren* séance."

" Really ? " said Mrs. Bradley, noting down this extraordinary fact.

" Oh, no," said Muriel eagerly. " I don't know whether you've attended many séances, but Tom could *induce* the spirits. He had the most wonderful powers."

" Oh ? So your husband was a medium ? "

" No. I was. But I could only work through him. He always said he got wonderful results with me. They used to scare me sometimes, all the same. I mean, you can go too far . . . that's what people say."

" Tell me," said Mrs. Bradley after a pause, " did Miss Foxley have mediumistic powers ? "

" Bella ? Oh, dear no ! She was terribly materialistic. She used to sit with us——"

" Always ? " asked Mrs. Bradley sharply.

" Well, if she was staying in the house. Not otherwise, of course. Although Tom did say once that when I was in a trance Bella came and *spoke*. Oh, only her astral body or something, of course. I'm afraid I don't remember all the terms. But, at any rate, she projected herself, it seems——"

" By means of the road or the railway," was Mrs. Bradley's mental note upon this——

" And *appeared*. Tom said it was very interesting, and that he telegraphed to the Institution next day to know whether Bella was very ill or even dead. Of course she wasn't either the one or the other, but they did say, funnily enough, that she'd fallen off her bicycle in the grounds as she was making a quick dash into the village that morning for some shopping that hadn't turned up. She was in a fearful state, and complained about her ankle, although she wouldn't have the doctor to it."

" Strange that a figment of that kind could travel all that way," said Mrs. Bradley.

" Oh, it wasn't *all* that way," Muriel put in brightly. " It was only about twelve miles as the crow flies, which is the way such things would travel I suppose."

"I don't know" said Mrs. Bradley soberly. "Wouldn't they perhaps be earth-bound to the roads?"

"Even if they were," said Muriel, who seemed oblivious of the purport of these suggestions, "they would only have had to come about seventeen miles, I believe."

"Ah?" said Mrs. Bradley. "And now, about this particular haunted house in which we are interested."

"Oh, nobody *appeared* there. It was simply a *poltergeist*," replied her victim.

"In what way?"

"Raps, footsteps, raucous laughter, writing on the walls, bell-ringing, throwing things about, moving objects from one place to another, cold air, lights in windows—that sort of thing."

"How many of the things you have just mentioned took place in the haunted house?" asked Mrs. Bradley, who, in flying hieroglyphics, had taken down the entire list. "Raps?"

"Oh, yes, ever so many times."

"Footsteps?"

"Both light and heavy. Sometimes it sounded like somebody in great boots, sometimes more like stockinged feet. Sometimes they ran, and sometimes they walked, and once they just scuffled about over our heads as though two people were fighting."

"You said raucous laughter. Can you substantiate that?"

"I don't know what you mean, but it sounded more like costermongers."

"Writing on the walls?"

"Oh, yes. But I cleaned it all off. It wasn't—it wasn't very nice."

"Are the spirits in the habit of being obscene?"

"No, that's the funny part. They're not.* I mean, they usually write things you can't make any sense out of. I've never known them to be really *rude*."

"Did your husband object to having this writing cleaned off the walls?"

---

* Apparently a mistake on Muriel's part . . . ." The rappings answered back with obscenity or blasphemy." *Poltergeists*. Sacheverell Sitwell. Faber and Faber, June, 1940.

"No, he didn't mind once it was photographed. But the photographs looked even more horrid than the actual scribble, so Bella persuaded him to throw the negatives away and destroy the proofs. She said no one would believe they were spirit writings, and anyway they were embarrassing. Which it is quite true, they were."

"Do you remember them ? " asked Mrs. Bradley.

"Oh, yes, of course I do, but I wouldn't repeat them to you."

"Write them down, then," said Mrs. Bradley, offering her a notebook and pencil. As Muriel hesitated she added with a cackle, " Don't worry. I expect I've heard worse things from some of my mental patients. . . . Now let us continue : bell-ringing ? "

"Well, no, not at this house. At least—not after Tom cut all the wires. At least, I don't believe so."

"Was there a bell in every room in the house ? "

"No, only in some of the rooms. I think there had been bells, but they were all out of order when we got there, but some we had repaired, but I don't remember which."

"I see. Now I know there were things thrown about and things moved, and I know there is a cold draught at one spot in the passage, so I need not ask you about those. What about lights in windows ? "

"Yes, those have been seen from the road at times when both Tom and I—and Bella, when she was with us—were all downstairs, and we knew no one else was in the house or could have got in."

"The lights were always from the bedroom windows, then ? Did the lights show at the same window each time, or was a different window ever used ? "

"Oh, it was always the same window, so far as I know. Of course, people may not always have told us, but we asked them to, as soon as it was known the lights had been seen, because we did not use any of the bedrooms, after that, if they fronted the road. So we knew that if lights were seen it was not any light that we ourselves were using."

"Very interesting," thought Mrs. Bradley, " considering that the hauntings were a source of income."

"When Bella came to live with us," Muriel continued,

" it was arranged that we should take it in turns in the evening to go out into the garden and see whether the lights were visible. If they were, then the one outside was to throw gravel at the drawing-room window, and the other two would rush upstairs to investigate."

" Oh? You took it in turns, did you? " said Mrs. Bradley.

" Well, when it came to the point, Bella said she was far too nervous to go tearing upstairs and bursting in on a ghost. She said if she saw one she'd die. So actually she used to be the one to go out into the garden, and Tom and I were the ones who always rushed upstairs."

" I wonder she wasn't afraid of the garden in the dark if she were so very nervous," said Mrs. Bradley.

" Oh, but she was," said Muriel. " She always took a loaded stick out with her—a cosh, she called it. One of those terrible boys had made it for her in the Institution workshop. Tom used to tease her about it, and ask her what good she thought it would be against a ghost, but she said it gave her confidence and she would always take it with her."

" And did you and your husband ever see the lights independently of Miss Foxley? " Mrs. Bradley enquired.

" Yes. Twice. But we weren't there so very long without Bella, you know. Of course, she only spent the one week-end there before aunt's death."

" Ah, yes," said Mrs. Bradley. She glanced at her watch. " I must go, I'm afraid, Mrs. Turney. My son has booked seats for a revue. Do you like that kind of thing? Some people are so ponderous nowadays. Now in my opinion, the modern revue approximates more closely to the ancient Greek idea of comedy than serious thinkers would suppose."

Muriel nervously agreed.

The séances, one conducted by amateurs, the other by a famous member of the Society for Psychical Research, continued to have negative results. This, of course, proved nothing, although one, at least, of the sitters, would have been very much surprised at any manifestations.

Mrs. Muriel Turney, invited to the second of the séances, again declined the invitation, stating that she really did not think her nerves would stand it. The medium at the second séance said that her ' control ' had been out of temper for some time, and probably would give nothing to the sitters that evening. She then fell into a trance, and the sitters waited for an hour and a half, by which time it was discovered that the medium had passed from her trance into natural sleep. She was gently awakened, and everybody went home or to the inn.

There was, however, one interesting and illuminating occurrence which followed the second séance. Mrs. Bradley made a detailed note of it. The entire house had been locked up and the doors sealed, and the windows, except the one in the séance room, had been sealed also, before the sitters took their places. This was an obvious precaution, and caused no surprise to anybody. The séance was held in the drawing-room, and during the period of silence which followed the beginning of the medium's trance, everybody in the circle was not only watching the medium, but (having been informed of the probable nature of any activity which might occur in this particular house) was alert to any noises which might come from other rooms.

No sounds were heard, but before the other visitors and the medium left the drawing-room, Mrs. Bradley made a thorough exploration of the house. On the wall of the bathroom passage was written in pencil the word *Bread*. The writing was either that of an illiterate, or else it had been done by a normally right-handed person using the left hand (or vice-versa). It had not been there before the séance began, for Mrs. Bradley, who had sealed up the doors and windows, except for the front door, before the other sitters arrived, had also made a careful search and inspection of all walls and passages.

She mentioned her interesting discovery to no one but her son Ferdinand, who, with Caroline, his wife, had come, at her request, for the séance.

" And what do you make of it, Mother ? " he enquired, when the circle was broken up and the other guests had gone.

" What do you ? " asked Mrs. Bradley.

" That the house must have a secret entrance, I suppose. But, even if it has, why should anyone bother ? Or is it in the contract that people who pay to be allowed to hold séances here must get some return for their money ? "

Mrs. Bradley put the question to Mrs. Muriel Turney in a letter, but did not reveal the nature of the ' return.' The teacher of music replied on a postcard :

" Lots of people get nothing. My husband and I were both sensitives."

Mrs. Bradley went to see her again, but did not tell her precisely what had happened.

" Will you allow me to borrow your husband's records of the phenomena ? " she asked. Muriel agreed to lend the typescript from which Cousin Tom had worked up his reports of the *poltergeist*.

" I suppose," said Mrs. Bradley casually, before leaving, " Miss Foxley took no particular interest in spiritualism ? "

" It frightened her," replied Cousin Muriel, in emphatic re-affirmation of what she had already said upon this subject. " She says that if she ever sees a ghost it will be someone come to fetch her, and it will mean her death. I've tried to tell her that that's a very old-fashioned idea about ghosts, but she clings to it and can't bear the subject mentioned."

" Ah, but you are speaking now of Miss Tessa, not Miss Bella. But it has to be mentioned, surely, when the house is let for these sittings ? "

" No. The caretaker always writes to say that it has been ' requisitioned.' That's the word he has to use."

" Interesting," said Mrs. Bradley. She looked thoughtfully at Muriel. " I thought you said you had not visited Miss Tessa since her sister's suicide ? "

" Oh, I haven't, no. I did write to say I would attend the funeral if she wished it, but also said it would probably be painful to me to pay my respects, even my last ones, to Bella. Since then I have not been invited, and, of course, as I am only a relative by marriage, I should not dream of visiting her *without* an invitation, not even to drop in. I think in-laws make mistakes about that kind of thing. After all, they can't expect to be treated *quite* like the family, can they ? Especially when their husband, like poor Tom, isn't there to go with them or anything."

Mrs. Bradley said that she quite understood, and that she would take very great care of the typescript. She returned to her own house at Wandles Parva, and made diligent comparison of Cousin Tom's notes with Bella's diary, bearing in mind the various types of *poltergeist* activity which, according to Muriel, had existed in the house. If these had been faked, had Cousin Tom faked them? Had Bella? Tom, apparently, was a fraud, yet the haunted house had a queer sort of reputation.

Again, there was the story that Tom had rented Hazy. Had Bella Foxley nerve enough to perform in that way in a house which had (Mrs. Bradley had read) a very impressive record of supposedly psychic occurrences? For Hazy had been ' written up ' in most of the journals devoted to ghosts and ghost-hunting. True, Bella was probably a murderer, but murderers sometimes suffer from nerves, and many of them are supremely super-stitious. Perhaps there had been no manufactured evidence at Hazy. Perhaps it had frightened Cousin Tom.

This part of the business seemed insoluble without more evidence. Mrs. Bradley got out the diary again, and settled down to minute comparisons of facts and dates. With the knowledge she had gained since the case had first intrigued her curiosity, she could not avoid the conclusion that the diary, although it could not be said to incriminate Bella Foxley, did make very plain certain tendencies of thought, and did hint with horrid clarity at certain courses of action which made its genuineness even more suspect than she had supposed when first she read it.

Comparison with the copy of Cousin Tom's journal which was typewritten throughout—even the infrequent and neat correc-tions having been made on the typewriter—revealed another curious fact. Wherever the diary and the journal covered the same points, they tallied with one another, and the odd thing about this was that the noticeable errors of fact in the diary—errors of fact over which Bella Foxley ought to have made no errors—were repeated in Tom's journal.

Mrs. Bradley returned to her own notes upon the subject, written after she had read the diary and had questioned Eliza Hodge. Of course, the old servant might have forgotten, or deliberately lied about, some of the occurrences which took place about the time of the old lady's death, but, even allowing for this, the extraordinary similarity between the diary and the journal led to an obvious conclusion.

Of course, certain facts in each might be expected to tally ; the cause of death, for instance, and the doctor's doubts and fears.

As for the *poltergeist* phenomena, they also might be expected to reveal themselves similarly to two careful and experienced observers. The fact that they had occurred, according to Cousin Tom's journal, exactly as the diary stated, was not a reason for surprise. Tom's entry for the nineteenth of February, for instance, was :

" Bella has turned up here, and may check the run of pheno-mena. This would be a great pity, as we have been getting on so wonderfully well until to-day, when there has been nothing much. I talked to Muriel about it, and I am afraid we did not see eye to eye. I believe she is thoroughly alarmed, and would be glad of an end to the manifestations, but John and Elvey were delighted, especially with the music."

" Dear Muriel is sometimes a little nervous about the more noisy manifestations, and I have had to take a strong line with her. All the same, we cannot turn Bella away. The night has been better than the day. Slippered or naked feet have walked past all the doors. This is encouraging, but I have advised the women to keep the doors locked. They think it is a safety measure, but I am interested to know whether this kind can be barred out."

The entry for February 22 also bore out the diary.

" This has been a splendid day," observed the typescript for this date. " We have had various kinds of phenomena of the true *poltergeist* type. Objects such as a small calendar have been displaced and even projected. Before we retired to bed the entire contents of the kitchen shelves were flung out into the passage. It is most gratifying, but the two women are extremely upset by it. There has been a new outbreak of bell-ringing, too, and the women declare that they cannot stand the noise of this. I shall make the experiment of cutting the wires to-morrow, as I am anxious to know whether the entities we are housing here are dependent upon mechanical aid for producing their effects, or whether their supernormal powers can ring bells which are not connected up."

This covered the diary entry for February 23, and the journal for February 24, like the diary, commented upon the sound of slippered footsteps. For February 25, when the four members of a society for psychical research had visited the house, Tom had typed ecstatically :

" A truly marvellous experience ! Mr. W., Lord X., Mr. T. and Mrs. D. were here, and professed themselves delighted with their evening. I was afraid at first that we were going to get nothing at all, but then the noises commenced overhead and, upon going up the front staircase, we saw that all the spare bedroom furniture had been overturned and the electric light flex over the dressing-table was damaged. The lamp and shade were on top of the chest of drawers, and this was on its side in the middle of the room."

Mrs. Bradley cackled, and made a note in her own notebook. It read—if anybody could have deciphered it : " Fingerprints ? " She then added, " Two electric lights in the spare room. · Flex could have swung in breeze from window if open. Test."

The reference to the mysterious ' something ' which walked in the grounds at night was missing from the journal. It had been regarded, for serious purposes, as an old wives' tale by Cousin Tom, Mrs. Bradley surmised. The coach and horses with the headless driver were also not the subject of comment or even mention in the journal.

The flight of Muriel and Bella to the inn was mentioned, and the ' footsteps ' were described, under March 4, as ' almost a nuisance now, as they have become so disturbing, and more often run than walk.' There were other references to them on later dates up to and including March 10, and then the wall-writings were mentioned but were not given in detail. Bella's night visit was mentioned, but only perfunctorily. Strangely enough, Cousin Tom made no reference whatsoever to his own fall from the bedroom window. The journal continued :

" After she had gone I found a woman's suspender, a piece of paper which appeared to have been wrapped round some fish, and a good deal of horse manure in the spare room. These manifestations seem to show that the entity is not altogether friendly towards us, but I am in hope that no mischief will ensue, as this type is usually mischievous and does not always mean to be annoying."

Mrs. Bradley returned the journal by registered post. She was deeply and sincerely obliged to Cousin Muriel, she said, for the loan of it. It had cleared up several very doubtful points.

It had, at any rate, cleared up one. The *poltergeist* was human.

There remained the minor problem of whether to tackle the sister, Miss Tessa, first, or whether to have what Mrs. Bradley described to Ferdinand as ' another go ' at the haunted house. She found herself to be slightly in favour of the visit to Miss Foxley. It would be interesting to visit one who had had, it seemed, so great an interest in Bella's death. Mrs. Bradley also hoped (merely to satisfy her own curiosity, for she could not believe that it would affect the investigation very seriously) to deduce which of the two accounts of Tessa's unhappy affairs was the true one, the bigamous marriage or the illegitimate child.

George first drove her through part of the New Forest to the house which Bella Foxley had purchased, and even past the dirty little pond (they afterwards discovered) in which Bella's body had been found. They also passed the village hall in which the inquest had been held. But they had little time to spare, and had too few details of the suicide at their command to do more than take a slight and morbid interest in the locality. Miss Foxley had sold the cottage, however. This was no news to Mrs. Bradley, for the address she had obtained from the caretaker was in Devon.

" Not Cornwall," she thought, remembering one of the entries in the diary. She ordered George to pull up at the cottage. It was still untenanted. Mrs. Bradley amused herself by peering in at the dirty windows, both front and back, by dabbling her hand in a large rain-water butt which was just outside the back door, and by carefully pacing, checking and timing the distance between the cottage and the scum-covered pond.

Whilst she was thus engaged, she discovered that she was the focus of attention (although that was an exaggerated description of the owl-like staring which she encountered as she turned to saunter back to the cottage) of a loose-mouthed, pallid, puffy-faced idiot boy, who proceeded, in an ungainly manner, to follow her to the gate.

He grinned in a sickly, shame-faced, leering manner when she looked at him.   Mrs. Bradley leered back.

" Pullen ur aid onder wartur," he said, pointing to the rain-water butt.

" Good heavens ! " said Mrs. Bradley, greatly impressed. She walked round to the water-butt, to the great delight of the idiot, and peered into it again.

He repeated his assertion, grinning.   Mrs. Bradley gave him a shilling, which he put into the top of his sock, and went back to George, who was waiting impassively in the car.

Still in the broad sunlight of the middle day they came through a white-washed village to the sea, and a few miles further on drove past Miss Foxley's home, and then pulled up, to have a look at it without attracting too much attention.

Chapter Six

THE DEAR DEPARTED

> The world's a bubble and the life of man
> Less than a span ;
> In his conception wretched, from the womb,
> So to the tomb ;
> Curst from his cradle, and brought up to years
> With cares and fears.
> Who then to frail mortality shall trust
> But limns on water, or but writes in dust.
>
> BACON.

IT was rather an extraordinary house to have chosen, thought Mrs. Bradley.   Granted that the owner's main object had been to obtain complete privacy, it would have been reasonable enough to choose this white-washed cottage, but from the point of view of one who, presumably, was in hiding from the curiosity of neighbours and possibly that of the police, there was a good deal to be said in favour of a flat in London.   This cottage, remote, situated on the edge of a moor and within sound and sight of the Bristol Channel (an old turnpike house, no doubt), and its solitary tenant, would be bound to arouse local interest. Besides, it was the sort of place at which hikers and cyclists were apt to call, demanding teas, or water with which to make tea. The tenant of it could scarcely be said to have chosen the best kind of cover.

Mrs. Bradley, shaking her head, told George to drive on and find a convenient place to park the car at the side of the road, and she herself went up to the door and knocked.

Too bad, she felt, if Miss Foxley should not be at home. But Miss Foxley was at home, and came to the door. Mrs. Bradley recognized her at once from the photographs in the album which Miss Hodge had shown her.

" Yes ? " said the owner of the cottage.

" Miss Foxley ? " said Mrs. Bradley.

" Yes."

" My name is Bradley. I called to see you about the house which you let to me for some spiritualist . . ."

" I suppose you didn't get any results. Well, I'm afraid I can't help that, you know. Come in," said Miss Foxley. She pushed back a moist-looking strand of iron-grey hair and held the door open wider. Mrs. Bradley, apologising, stepped slightly aside and then did up her shoe-lace before she went in. The cottage consisted, it seemed, of two rooms downstairs and two bedrooms. The front door opened directly into the living-room. " Sit down," added Miss Foxley. She dabbed at her chin with a handkerchief specked with tiny red spots. " Been squeezing them out, and made rather a mess," she said. "Have to excuse me, I'm afraid. Not expecting a visitor this morning."

" Mercolized wax," suggested Mrs. Bradley.

" Tried it. Not much good. Martyr to the things. Complexions are God-given," Miss Foxley responded brusquely. " Now, then, about this haunted house. I can't help it, you know. I don't guarantee anything. The spirits won't come near some people. It's just a matter of luck."

" Ah," said Mrs. Bradley, " but I don't say the spirits didn't come near. All I say is that they were the wrong kind of spirits. Not what I expected, and, really, rather alarming."

" Say on," said Miss Foxley. " Are you new to the game ? "

"I have never taken much interest in spiritualism," said Mrs. Bradley, deliberately giving the science its old-fashioned name, "but somebody discovered, quite by accident, that people of my colouring almost always have mediumistic powers."

"And you have?"

"Well . . ." said Mrs. Bradley deprecatingly.

"You mean you have. Well, go on. What did you see? The headless coachman the villagers talk about?"

"No. I saw two little boys."

"Materialisation of the *poltergeist*, I should say. I think all *poltergeist* phenomena must be produced by entities with the mentality of little boys."

"And then I saw a woman," Mrs. Bradley continued. "Do you believe in ghosts?" she suddenly demanded.

"No," replied Miss Foxley, "not in the way you mean. Go on about this woman. My sister, I suppose?"

"She didn't say who she was. She merely said, 'Tell Bella I'll be there.' She repeated this three times, and then we broke up the sitting."

"Well, I don't see how you can tell Bella anything," said Miss Foxley in a practical tone. "Bella—if it means my sister Bella—has been dead for years. Still, I don't discredit what you say. The house belonged to Bella once, you know. I inherited it, along with the rest of her stuff." She paused, and then said briskly, "And now, what the hell are you getting at?"

"I want to know whether you will sell me that house," said Mrs. Bradley.

"Oh?—I see." For some reason she seemed taken aback by this simple statement, and repeated it aloud. "You want to know whether I'll sell you that house."

Mrs. Bradley waited. Miss Foxley, slatternly in a blouse which refused to remain tidy at the waist, and a skirt which revealed that one of her stockings was laddered, brooded, her black brows drawn together, her large and very well-kept hands irritably pushing back her hank of greasy hair. Suddenly her brow cleared.

"How much are you offering?" she demanded.

"I hadn't thought of a price."

"You can have it for—— Look here, why don't you rent

it ? Then you could give it up when you were tired of experimenting with it."

" So I could," said Mrs. Bradley. " But I don't want to experiment with it. I want to pull it down."

" Pull it down ? "

" Yes. I think it is a dangerous house. It is too much like Borley Rectory."

" Never heard of the place. Oh, yes, I have, too. Isn't that the place Cousin Tom used to blether about ? "

" There's a book on it," said Mrs. Bradley vaguely. " I believe your sister had read it."

" Poor old Bella ! What a rotten life, and what a rotten end ! I was fond of her, in a way, you know. Surprised at the *felo de se* and all that."

" Ah, yes. You identified the body, I believe."

" Sure I identified the body. Nobody else to do it."

" Did you have to go all the way from here ? "

" No. On the spot."

" Staying with her ? "

" Staying with her ? Living with her. She'd got the creeps, and asked me to come for good. Good thing for me I'd got a fool-proof alibi, or I might have found myself in the jug, you know. Looks bad to inherit a couple of thousand through the sudden death of a sister. Don't you think so ? "

Mrs. Bradley demurred politely, but Miss Foxley was not to be put off.

" I'll say it does," she continued, with truculent emphasis. " Anyway, the vicar swore to me, so that was all right. At a Mothers' Meeting I was, addressing them on Manners and Morals, or some such tripe. Poor old Bella ! She was a deep one, she was. I'd never have put it past her to have choked Aunt Flora for the money. She swore she didn't, but . . . I wouldn't have a bet on it with the Recording Angel."

" Then what about Cousin Tom ? " asked Mrs. Bradley.

" Tom ? Oh, Tom was a goop," replied Miss Foxley roundly. " And as for that . . . but there ! I never knew her, except by hearsay from Bella."

' Never knew whom ? " asked Mrs. Bradley.

" That redundant little wife of his—Muriel."

"Oh, I see. But the inquest went off satisfactorily, didn't it?"

"Did it? Would you say that? After all, they nabbed old Bella for slugging him, didn't they? Not that I think *she* did that. Aunt Flora, yes. Cousin Tom, no. No point in it, for one thing. I reckon Muriel did it."

"I meant the inquest on your sister."

"Oh, that? Yes, that went off all right. There was plenty of motive for suicide knocking about. Only wanted putting together and re-shuffling. Anonymous letters, general feeling of depression, dark hints to one or two of the villagers she might not live long, the disclosure that she had stood her trial for murder and had expressed remorse (that was my contribution, made privately). Didn't want the reporters nosing around, so that bit never came out at the inquest. Unnecessary, really."

"Were the anonymous letters genuine, do you think?" Mrs. Bradley enquired.

"Well, she certainly got 'em. I saw one or two. Pretty stinking. Oh, well!—Oh, and going back to the ghosts, didn't you get any wall-writing?"

"Oh, I had overlooked that. Yes," replied Mrs. Bradley. "The word *Beads*, or something similar. I wasn't interested. It's so easy to get into a house and scribble on the walls. I had it cleaned off."

"I thought you psychists sealed the place up when you were in it? Haven't I read that somewhere? How did anyone come to get in?"

"We did seal up the obvious means of ingress," said Mrs. Bradley carelessly.

"Well, either you slipped up somewhere, or the writing was genuine," said Miss Foxley. "Well, see here. I'll let you know about the house. I'll have to write to my lawyer. Can't keep you any longer now. Got to go out and pull some vegetables and stuff for my dinner. Living the simple life here."

She showed Mrs. Bradley to the door in an uncompromising manner, nodded with grim amiability at parting, and even came on to the road to see her go. A few minutes later, still at her front door, she watched with narrowed eyes as the car drove eastwards.

"Did you get the snapshot, George?" asked Mrs. Bradley.

"Two beauties, madam, I hope. I caught her fairly each time, one full-face and one profile."

"Excellent," replied Mrs. Bradley. "And now, George, we return to the village of Pond, Hampshire, where poor Miss Foxley was drowned."

In order to reach the south shore of the Bristol Channel by the end of the morning, Mrs. Bradley had left Wandles at dawn and was now extremely hungry. She directed George to drive into Taunton for lunch, and as she very much doubted whether there would be an inn at Pond, she decided to spend the night in Bournemouth.

George enjoyed driving, and, having his private reasons for wishing to spend as many hours in Bournemouth as possible, got his employer to her favourite hotel by six, put up the car, washed himself, and went to a restaurant and thence to the entertainment at the Little Theatre.

Mrs. Bradley, who would have preferred to have come more slowly from Taunton through Ilminster, Chard, Crewkerne and Dorchester, ate an excellent dinner at a table which had been found for her by the head waiter, an acquaintance of many years' standing, and after dinner strolled along the front before she went up to her room.

George had instructions to bring the car round at half-past nine next morning, but, to his delight, the order was countermanded by half past-eight, and he received instructions to spend the day exactly as he pleased, as his employer proposed to go to Christchurch to visit the Priory, and would take the bus.

George hired a bathing suit and a towel, and went for a swim. Then he called in at a pleasant bar for a drink. After that he sat in a deck chair on the front. He wore the grey flannel suit he always carried as one of the ' spares ' in the car, put on his scarlet beret (a regrettable form of headgear of which, in justice to him, it must be recorded that he wore it only at the seaside and out of sight of Mrs. Bradley), and smoked cigarettes. At half-past twelve he went to a restaurant for lunch, and by two was on the front again, this time to play on the putting course and subsequently to walk on the pier. He had another swim before tea, and listened to the band in the evening.

Mrs. Bradley took the bus along the Boscombe Road as far as Southbourne. From there she walked over Hengistbury Head, was ferried across to Mudeford with a boat-load of other people, caught another bus into Christchurch, visited the Priory, inspected an antique dealer's stock, bought a large knife which she would not permit the dealer to wrap up, and caused a certain amount of sensation by lunching with the weapon beside her plate.

After lunch she went a pleasant little trip to Mudeford and back by river launch down to the mouth of the Stour, had shrimps and watercress for tea, and returned by bus to Bournemouth at half-past six. She dined at a quarter to eight, but did not go out again, for while she was still at dinner, having just eaten her fish, a message arrived from George.

" She is here, madam, but does not know we are," George had written. Mrs. Bradley cackled. She had said nothing to him of the reason for her change of plan when she had counter-manded the order for the car. She wrote on the bottom of his piece of paper, underneath his message :

" Drive the car after dark into Poole, and see that you get a lock-up garage. We shall be staying in Bournemouth another two or three days."

She herself remained in the hotel that evening and all the next day. She had no fear that Miss Foxley would recognize George. She herself was the danger. George in his uniform and leggings was like any other stocky, superhuman chauffeur. In his flannel suit and little red beret, which, unbeknown to its owner, she had seen on his head several times, he was, in her view, like nothing on on earth. But then, red was not her favourite colour, particularly that shade of it referred to by Mr. Wooster as a fairly brightish scarlet. George, in his tomato-like crown, might, and did, attract a certain amount of notice, but he was not in the least likely to be connected in the mind of anyone who had only set eyes on him for a brief space of time, and at a distance, and at the wheel of a car, with Mrs. Bradley's sedate and respectable servant.

They had left Miss Foxley at her toll-house on Tuesday morning. On Friday morning George produced for Mrs. Bradley's inspection the developed and printed snapshots.

" Excellent, George," said Mrs. Bradley. " Get some

enlargements postcard size, and then I think the hunt will be up."

" It will be all up, madam," replied George, " if she gets on our track before we've got all our proofs."

" The photographs should set the ball rolling, anyhow," said Mrs. Bradley. " I wonder whether she will have the hardihood to go to Pond to look for us."

" I shouldn't be surprised, madam, if she'd been. She hired a car yesterday and was driven in the right direction."

" Pity you couldn't have followed her," his employer suggested. George looked wounded.

" I've done better, madam, I fancy. I'm in touch with the bloke—chap—garage-proprietor who drove her. What's more, he did all the asking, I shouldn't wonder. I'll get on to him this afternoon, if he hasn't got a job on, and find out where they went and what they did. If he *has* got a job on, it will have to be this evening."

" Excellent," said Mrs. Bradley. Miss Foxley, it transpired, had gone to Pond. She had affected to take some interest in the ruins of Beaulieu Abbey, then they had come back across Beaulieu Heath to Brockenhurst, and so, by way of secondary roads, to Pond. There the driver had been asked to enquire whether a car answering to the description of Mrs. Bradley's— " pretty fair description, too, madam, according to what this chap said, but she hadn't been able to spot our number-plates " —had been seen in the neighbourhood. The occupants also had been described. " The car was referred to as ' chauffeur-driven,' madam," said George, " but she must have described *you* very carefully, very carefully indeed."

Mrs. Bradley cackled, but did not ask for a repetition of the description. She fancied that it might embarrass George to give it. She merely said :

" Strange that so observant a lady did not learn our number-plates by heart, George, was it not ? "

George would not permit himself to wink at his employer, but his left eyelid trembled slightly.

" Perhaps not so very strange, madam," he replied.

" I see," said Mrs. Bradley. " Who sups with the devil must have a long spoon."

George assented, but did not know, either then or afterwards, whether his employer referred to himself, herself, or the painstaking and suspicious Miss Foxley, or whether the proverb was intended as a compliment or a reproach.

On the Saturday morning George was absent. At one o'clock, however, Mrs. Bradley was called away from the table to take a telephone call.

" I am in Minehead, madam, having come here by motor-cycle," said George. " The lady returned home by hired car, leaving at eight-thirty this morning, and the hired car is returning to Bournemouth now. There is no possible train back to you until after four o'clock this afternoon, so if you thought of visiting Pond without fear of disturbance . . ."

" Thank you very much, George. I will go at once," said Mrs. Bradley. Go she did, leaving her lunch unfinished, to the great grief of the head-waiter, who had personally supervised her choice. She took a taxi into Poole, retrieved the car—George having given up to her the key of the garage and the ignition key on the previous night—and drove to Pond by way of Christchurch and Milton, the most direct route she could find.

She arrived in the village before two, and drove straight to the church. She did not know how much time she had at her disposal, but the grave she sought was in a far corner of the churchyard, and she found it easily. Miss Foxley had done her sister proud, Mrs. Bradley considered. A headstone of Purbeck marble inscribed with large clear lettering indicated that Bella Foxley, aged forty-five years, was at rest, and added a pious expectation that she was also at peace.

" Curious," said Mrs. Bradley aloud. If the diary were correct, Bella Foxley at the time of her death must have been at least forty-eight, and her sister Tessa somewhat older. She shook her head in admonitory fashion at the tombstone, and walked along a gravel path to a small wicket gate which led to the vicarage.

There was tennis going on on the vicarage lawn. In fact, it seemed that some kind of fête or a garden party was in progress. The vicar, a handsome, florid man, with curly hair going grey, a round, cheerful face and a grey alpaca jacket with grey flannel trousers, was among what appeared to be the female nobility and gentry of the place, handing cups of coffee. The remains of a cold collation set out on trestle tables in the shade, and now being taken away and generally cleared up by what Mrs. Bradley correctly assumed to be the vicar's wife, daughters and maidservants, explained the presence of the coffee, and just as Mrs. Bradley left the path to make her way across the lawn a small band of musicians carrying those instruments usually associated with the classical kinds of jazz, made its appearance at the front gate which led from the road.

"Heavens!" thought Mrs. Bradley. "Just my luck to arrive in the middle of a jamboree."

By this time, needless to say, she had been seen. There was proceeding a swift conference between the vicar and his wife. The latter then advanced, as it were, to the fray.

"Were you looking for anybody?" she asked.

"Well, I particularly wanted to speak to the vicar, but I am afraid I've come at an inconvenient time," said Mrs. Bradley, making polite motions of backing out again.

"Oh, well, if it is *very* important . . ." said the vicar's wife, adding gently, "I don't think we know you, do we?"

"Lor' lumme, mother. *I* do!" exclaimed a young man who had come leaping across a couple of flower beds. "It's Carey Lestrange's Aunt Adela, or I'm a Hottentot."

He seized Mrs. Bradley's yellow claw and pump-handled it ecstatically. Mrs. Bradley, who had met a good many of her favourite nephew's friends, very easily placed this one.

"You must be Ronald," she said. The young man enthusiastically agreed that this was so, and informed his mother that he and Aunt Adela had knocked 'em cold on Boatrace Night by performing, with a crowd of assorted Londoners, the community dance known as the Lambeth Walk, this up the Haymarket at a quarter to twelve or thereabouts.

"And but that she can run like a deer, and has admission to the brightest little speak-easy I ever expect to attend," concluded the young man, this time on a rare, lyrical note, "we should have been up before the beaks in the morning as sure as eggs. Old Squiffy was, and received a fortnight without the option for taking a policeman's boots off."

Mrs. Bradley, aware that this panegyric was not having, from

her point of view, too gracious an effect on Ronald's mother, was
relieved to see that the vicar was approaching. Ronald, catch-
ing her eye, hastily informed his mother that he had been talking
rot, as usual, presented Mrs. Bradley formally, and, when his
father had been introduced, observed that he would leave them
together, as he was required to make up a four at tennis.

" A very charming, high-spirited boy," said Mrs. Bradley in
obituary tones. " My nephew Carey, whom he mentioned,
is very fond of him."

" Carey ? Then you must be—— Good heavens, Milli-
cent ! " said the vicar, " this is Mrs. Bradley. You know, I've
often talked about her. Don't you remember that Carey was
telling us about some of her cases when he was here ? Do come
along and have some coffee, Mrs. Bradley. Have you had
lunch ? "

Mrs. Bradley said that she had.

" That's fine," said the Vicar, absent-mindedly. He walked
beside her to the deck-chairs. " Don't tell me we have a
murderer in Pond," he added, pleased at his own joke.

" Possibly," Mrs. Bradley replied.

" Ah, poor Bella Foxley, you mean ? I'm afraid we can
hardly say so, though, can we ? She was acquitted, you know.
Poor soul ! Poor soul ! Such a wretched end, and hounded
to it, one might almost say."

" Oh, no, one might not," replied Mrs. Bradley firmly.
" That's why I'm here. I need not trouble you very much," she
added, " but I want to know, first, who this is."

She took out one of George's snapshots of Miss Foxley. The
vicar examined it carefully, almost as though he were handling
Exhibit A at a trial for murder ; as, indeed, thought Mrs.
Bradley, he probably was.

" This, to the best of my knowledge, recollection, and belief,"
he said, " is Miss Tessa Foxley."

" Ah ! " said Mrs. Bradley. " Do you mind writing that
opinion on the back of the snapshot and signing your name ? "

" Not at all," replied the vicar. " My pen . . ." Mrs.
Bradley produced her own, and watched, with a grimness
strange to see upon her dread yet, on the whole, good-humoured
countenance, whilst he wrote, neatly, and, to her great comfort

and admiration, quite legibly, the name *Tessa Foxley*, and signed his own name underneath.

" I should, perhaps, add the date ? " he suggested.

" An excellent idea," said Mrs. Bradley cordially. She had been going to suggest this herself. The vicar added the date, and handed the snapshot back.

" Now," said Mrs. Bradley, " I wonder whether you would be kind enough to describe Miss *Bella* Foxley ? "

" The only thing that I remember is that she had fair hair and rather a nice complexion," said the vicar. " I should not have noticed the complexion, but for the fact that it was so different from that of her sister. One could not help remarking the difference, for one scarcely ever saw one without the other. They were very lonely, poor souls. Both had had their troubles, I understand. To tell the truth, I sometimes thought Miss Bella's troubles had unhinged her."

" When did Miss Tessa Foxley come here to join her sister ?" Mrs. Bradley enquired.

" Oh, she didn't," the vicar answered. " The house was taken by Miss *Tessa*, who thereupon sent an invitation to Miss *Bella* to come and join *her*. She told me all about her sister's dreadful ordeal, said what a mercy it was no newspaper photographs were taken, and begged that we would never mention it to her sister, as it had left her very nervous and depressed. She even asked us not to disclose either of their Christian names. As a matter of fact, it was not until Miss Bella's dreadful end that anybody in the village except myself and my dear wife knew who they were, I believe."

" They kept their surname, I suppose ? They did not go under a false name to the tradespeople, for instance ? "

" No. And when they were together they called one another Flossie and Dossie—childhood appellations, I imagine."

" Did they seem to hit it off ? No quarrels, for instance ? "

" No, I am sure there were no quarrels."

" Did you ever have speech with Miss Bella when Miss Tessa wasn't there ? "

" Never. But I several times spoke to Miss Tessa by herself. She told me how extremely good her sister had been to her. It seems that a wealthy aunt left all her money to Miss Bella, and that she shared everything with Miss Tessa. Then, of course, upon Miss Bella's death, it all came to Miss Tessa, and she moved away. She moved very soon after the funeral. She said she would have wished to stay on in the village, and mentioned our kindness—although I'm afraid I cannot claim that we ever did very much except to keep their little secrets—the trial, you know, and the Christian names, and so forth—and, of course, my dear wife and I used to visit them occasionally, but really a good deal of the kindness was on the other side. We never asked for a subscription in vain, for instance, at that house, and Miss Tessa was an excellent stand-by if we wanted a talk in the village hall or at a Mothers' Meeting. She was also a most excellent cook. Poor Miss Bella couldn't cook at all."

" Really ? " said Mrs. Bradley. " Wasn't Miss Tessa at a Mothers' Meeting when her sister . . . ? "

" Very distressing," said the vicar. " Very distressing indeed. I know that she blamed herself very much. Had she been with her sister, she said, it would never have happened. The meeting was at a quarter-past two, you see, and she came back here to tea. She was here when the news was brought to her. Terribly distressing."

" Have you the same doctor now ? " asked Mrs. Bradley ; and when the vicar replied that they had, and that his name was Sandys, she told him that he had been more than helpful. " All the same, I'm not at all sure you haven't laid yourself open to a charge of having been accessory before the fact," she added.

" Before the fact ? " said the vicar, puzzled.

" Of murder," said Mrs. Bradley. She cackled to see the expression upon his round and amiable face, accepted an invitation to return and take tea at the vicarage, and went off to find the doctor's house. Characteristically, she had not asked where it was, and, characteristically, she found it within five minutes.

" You seem to have been enjoying yourself, mother," said Ferdinand, somewhat austerely. " What the devil have you been up to ? "

" Looking at *Item* one pond, *Item* one cottage, *Item* one toll house, *Item* one murderess, mark of interrogation, as our friend Stainless Stephen would say. Not to speak of interviewing a clam of a doctor, an expansive and genial vicar, and the murderess, question-mark, aforesaid," replied his mother, looking very pleased with herself. Ferdinand, who had been looming over her, sat down on the arm of a chair.

" Not there, dear child. You're too heavy for my furniture," suggested his mother. Ferdinand removed his thirteen stone to the seat of the chair without comment and looked across at her. His expression had altered considerably.

" Are you pulling my leg, Mother ? "

" No, child. I've found Bella Foxley."

" Then who was it committed suicide ? "

" Well, not Bella."

" The sister . . . ? "

" Murdered, possibly. If so, she was held head-downward in the rain-water butt outside the woodshed of their cottage in the village of Pond, transported to the pond at Pond, left there to be found by any who would, and the rest abandoned to Fate and the crass stupidity of a coroner who wouldn't believe that what the village idiot said was evidence."

" What did the village idiot say ? "

" He said that it was the rain-water washed her cheeks so white."

" I seem to have heard that before."

" Yes, I have transposed his rude rustic remark into the key of the poetic."

" You couldn't take that statement as evidence, coming from such a source."

" You could investigate it, though," said Mrs. Bradley. " Instead of that, the boy was told not to waste the time of the court."

" When is all this supposed to have happened ? "

" Well, the doctor put the time of death at between noon and three o'clock. She wasn't found until almost dusk. It was winter, too, which gives the idiot boy's evidence all the more importance. Whenever you would choose to wash yourself in the rain-water butt, you would hardly do so in November, I imagine. Bella must have drowned Tessa, gone straight to the Mothers' Meeting, and then had tea at the vicarage."

" But why should she kill her sister ? "

"That remains to be seen.   Why should she kill Cousin Tom ? We know why she may have killed the old aunt."

"You'll never prove a word of it, Mother."

"Probably not," said Mrs. Bradley, in such tones of self-satisfaction that her son lifted his black brows and grinned.

"Something up your sleeve," he announced.

Mrs. Bradley by this time had the enlargements of the snapshots.

"Ask your friend Pratt to dinner," she observed.   "You see this woman ? "

"Who is she ? "

"That," said Mrs. Bradley, "is for Mr. Pratt to say."

Mr. Pratt, confronted with both snapshot and enlargement, did not hesitate.

"If it was ten years younger—well, say, five . . ."

"Say six, and you'll be about right," interposed Mrs. Bradley. Pratt looked at her out of heavily lidded eyes.

"I should say it was Bella Foxley," he concluded.   Mrs. Bradley produced the snapshot which the vicar had signed and dated.

"And this ? " she said, presenting it so that the ex-journalist saw the photograph.

"The same, isn't it ?   Looks like the same snap to me."

"It is," said Mrs. Bradley.   "And the man who developed the negative can swear to the date.   That is arranged.   Now read what is here."   She turned the snapshot over.

"But the fellow can't be right, unless the two of them were identical twins," said Mr. Pratt.

"They were not in the least alike," said Mrs. Bradley gently, "and neither were they twins."

She then explained the circumstances under which the photographs had been taken, and then produced George's profile view of Miss Foxley.

"Oh, well, that one I'd swear to.   It's the view I mostly saw of her in court," declared Mr. Pratt.

"You've got something there, Mother," said Ferdinand.

"Of course she has," said Caroline, now Mrs. Bradley's firm adherent.   A diversion was caused at this point by Derek, who appeared to say good night, this little formality being observed

on all family and what may be referred to as " semi-guest "
occasions.

" My mascot," said Mrs. Bradley, presenting him, to his great
delight, with ten shillings. " This is the person who found the
diary and put us all on the track, Mr. Pratt."

" Oh, Gran ! " said Derek, wriggling in a pleased manner.
His face became even more radiant. " What's more, I got the
prize. Did you know ? " he said.

There was another source of confirmatory evidence of identity
in Eliza Hodge, Mrs. Bradley reflected. Then, the real work
would begin.

On the Thursday following her departure from Bournemouth
and Pond for Wandles Parva she received a letter, signed Tessa
Foxley, refusing her offer for the house. She could not bear,
Miss Foxley said, the thought of having so interesting a place
pulled down. She agreed that it might be dangerous, but added
that ' the psychic people would know what to do about that.'

There was nothing for it but to find her another purchaser,
thought Mrs. Bradley. Nothing could be done in that house
unless she had complete possession of it. She wrote back, undertaking not to pull down the house, but demanding permission to
have it exorcised if it became her property. She added, and
underlined the words, that she did not see that there could be
any objection to that."

Miss Foxley wrote back, refusing to sell. The interesting
thing was that neither of her letters bore the very slightest
resemblance, either in style or handwriting, to the diary.

" Very pretty," said Mrs. Bradley, and sought another interview with Eliza Hodge. The good old woman was pleased to
see her.

" I wondered what you were at, madam, spending your
money renting my house like this, and never coming back to
live in it," she said.

" I've had a good deal of business to attend to," Mrs. Bradley
replied, " and doubt very much whether I shall be able to settle
down here for any length of time, after all. Did any of the boys
turn up ? "

" Ah, they did, with one of the masters, a very pleasant young fellow. Got them well in hand, too. I told him they could have the run of the garden, if they liked, but he only has 'em gather the flowers and the raspberries like under his eye. Tried their hand at jam-making, I declare, they did, with me to tell 'em what to do. Made a fair hand at it, too, and pleased as Punch with it, time they got it into pots. Laugh! I thought I should have died, to see boys so solemn-like over picking the fruit and then picking it over, and stirring the pans and all that. Oh, dear! It lasted me for days!"

"I suppose it reminded you of the days when Miss Foxley was housekeeper at the Institution," said Mrs. Bradley.

"No, it didn't, as a matter of fact, madam. And, of course, they did wring the neck of one of Mr. Smart's fowls and had a picnic with it over on the common. Still, they paid up, because the master stopped it out of their pocket-money he said you said they was to have, and Smart charged ten shillings although that old hen she certainly wasn't worth a penny more than three and sixpence. The boys told Smart so, too, when they went to pay him, but he only winked at the master and said honesty was the best policy, and they could have bought the chicken for three and six if they'd a-wanted, but being they thought fit to steal it, why then, they must pay for their fun. There was some talk of them waylaying him and setting on him, I believe, but he goes about now with a dog-whip, and I don't think even the boldest fancies the look of him much. 'Young 'ounds,' he says, looking 'em in the eye the first time he met 'em, 'has to be learned their manners.' I think he's got the measure of them, madam, but I don't think he ought to have took all of ten shillings for the fowl."

Mrs. Bradley listened to this artless tale with deep attention, and then resumed her own theme along the lines laid down by Miss Hodge.

"In Miss Bella's time I doubt whether they would have had a chance to help with the cooking," she observed. "After all, you are a good enough cook, I suppose, to be able to give the right sort of help to amateurs, but a poor cook like Miss Bella . . ."

"Miss Bella? She could cook something lovely, madam!"

"I thought that was Miss Tessa," said Mrs. Bradley.

"Oh, no, madam. Miss Bella had got all her diplomas and certificates. There wasn't anything she couldn't cook. Miss

Tessa stopped short at toffee, and, it might be, boiling a potato, although even then you might get either potato soup or potato marbles, just according to how they happened to turn out. You'd have *thought* she was the cook, she was that nice, fair, clear colouring and complexion, but Miss Bella, for all her spotty face, was the one. She used to say she'd have got on better in service as a private cook than at anything, only it seemed a waste of her other education."

" But, surely," said Mrs. Bradley, " the vicar in the village where she was living after her trial couldn't have been mistaken ? This is the one he declared was the cook, and this he also declared was Miss Tessa."

She produced the snapshot and also the enlargement of it. Eliza Hodge wiped her fingers upon her apron and took the photographs. Then she turned them over, but Mrs. Bradley had not given her the one which carried the vicar's signature.

" He must have got it quite wrong, madam," she said. " This is Miss Bella to the life, except she looks that much older. Did she age all that much at the trial, madam ? "

" No, not at the trial," said Mrs. Bradley. " Would you be prepared to declare on oath that that is a photograph of Miss Bella ? "

" On oath, madam ? In court, do you mean ? I should think we've had enough of courts, what with two of those dreadful inquests, and then Miss Bella's trial."

" Well, I mean, are you *perfectly certain* it is a photograph of Miss Bella ? Are you so certain that you could not be persuaded otherwise, even by someone really very clever at persuading people ? A lawyer, let us say."

" Why, of course I am," said the old servant stoutly.

" And no one could get you to declare that it was Miss Tessa ? "

" It's nothing in the world like Miss Tessa. Have you forgot them photos in the album up at the house ? "

" No. That's why I thought the vicar must be mistaken," said Mrs. Bradley. " Did Miss Bella and Miss Tessa have nicknames for one another, do you know ? "

" Not that I know of. Short names, Bell and Tess, when they were younger, before Miss Tessa fell out with the mistress, like, and cut herself out of the money."

" They didn't call one another Flossie and Dossie ? "

" Good gracious, no, madam ! Sounds more like a couple of barmaids, or something not even respectable ! "

Mrs. Bradley agreed, and, to her horror, dreamed about rain-water butts.

Chapter Seven

THE HAUNTED HOUSE

" Now the wasted brands do glow,
  Whilst the screech-owl, screeching loud,
  Puts the wretch that lies in woe
  In remembrance of a shroud.
  Now it is the time of night
  That the graves all gaping wide,
  Every one lets forth his sprite,
  In the church-way paths to glide. . . ."

SHAKESPEARE.

THREE days later Mrs. Bradley, to her surprise, received a letter from Miss Foxley advising her that she might rent the house for a week, if she so desired, but not for longer as ' it kept other visitors away.'

Mrs. Bradley wrote off a brief acceptance, and as the amount of the rent was mentioned she enclosed it, received a formal receipt by return of post, telephoned a number of interested people including her son Ferdinand and Mr. Pratt, and took up her week's tenancy of the haunted house on the following Saturday afternoon.

Altogether she had ten people in the house, but three of them were not at first seen except by Mrs. Bradley herself and by one another.

The other seven consisted of Ferdinand and Caroline, a Roman Catholic priest named Conlan, the Warden of the Institution, Mr. Pratt, a fellow-journalist named Carris (a man particularly interested in *poltergeist* phenomena) and Mrs. Bradley. The unknown three were two boys from the Institution who had come to the haunted house direct from Mrs. Bradley's own care, for they had just concluded their week's summer holiday at the house rented from Eliza Hodge, and the young instructor who had come down in charge of the party. These three were already at the haunted house when the party arrived, and had ' gone to ground ' as Mrs. Bradley expressed it with some accuracy. Father Conlan did not put in an appearance until the Monday morning, and he left on the Tuesday evening with Ferdinand and Caroline. The journalists left on the Thursday morning. On the Thursday evening the two boys and their instructor returned to Miss Hodge's house, and by the Friday morning no one was left except Mrs. Bradley herself, but she had in her possession ten interesting documents, duly signed and dated which she was able, later on, to hand over to the police. Ferdinand and Mr. Pratt returned to the haunted house, in mystified response to Mrs. Bradley's further invitation, on the Friday afternoon.

The first séance was held on the Monday evening, and before the guests settled down in the library, which opened on the left of the hall as one entered the house, Mrs. Bradley earnestly requested them to make a thorough exploration to convince themselves that no unauthorised person and no ' trick ' apparatus was to be found.

The guests, who had assembled much in the spirit of children attending a party, gleefully explored the whole house and then, except for the tiny pantry window, which they forgot, secured with adhesive tape all the entrances. Then they assembled with their hostess in the library and it was suggested by Caroline that they might have the windows open. A vote was taken upon this proposal and it was agreed to in view of the fact that seven people in the fair-sized but not particularly large room would soon produce a stuffy atmosphere, and that they were all witnesses of one another's actions.

The séance was almost ludicrously successful. Scarcely had the circle settled down—in the most informal manner, incidentally, grouped as the sitters pleased about the room, everyone talking, reading, smoking or, in the case of Mr. Pratt's friend Mr. Carris, playing Patience—when everyone was electrified by the sudden ringing of bells.

Mrs. Bradley had had the bell wires repaired, and every

separate member of the party had either tested the bells or watched and listened whilst other people tested them.

The reaction, after the first shock, was disciplined and intelligent. Those who had agreed to do so—Ferdinand, Mrs. Bradley, Mr. Carris, and Father Conlan—went out of the room and made a concerted tour of the house. They went first to the servants' quarters, where the indicator was still vibrating. Each investigator had been provided with a small notebook in which he or she was to record the phenomena, if any, and his or her own reactions to them.

A written entry was duly made by everyone, and by the side of it everyone unhesitatingly wrote *Faked*. Two of the company, Caroline and the priest, also wrote, " But I don't see how," and " Inexplicable, however," respectively. Ferdinand added to his verdict the rider : " I would have said *Genuine* if all the bells had been rung, but the *poltergeist* seems to have avoided coming too near to where we were, in case we heard him moving about. The bells in the hall and in the room where we had been sitting and in the bedroom over this séance room did not ring."

The party returned to the room, and nothing more happened for about an hour. Then came a crash, followed by smaller tumbling noises, and the party, all this time, running out into the hall, beheld parts of a bedstead, three chairs, a candlestick and five metal trays lying on the floor at the foot of the staircase.

The company, not as well-controlled this time, went bounding upstairs. Nothing could be seen, heard, or in any way discovered, although every bedroom and every attic was searched. Two earnest seekers after truth even discovered the attic cupboard which had the airholes, but, so far as they could tell, it was empty and, as Caroline expressed it, innocent.

Opinions in the various notebooks varied on the subject of this second phenomenon. The majority wrote to the effect that they supposed the furniture had been thrown downstairs by human and not by super-human agency, but two of these confessed that they could not see how it had been done. Ferdinand wrote that he thought he had the glimmering of an idea of the method, and Mr. Pratt wrote : " I think I know where they hid, but I cannot see why we did not get them on the back stairs."

The priest wrote : " This is trickery, but it is cleverly done and I cannot determine the method. There must be a cellar."

Caroline and Mr. Carris wrote that, failing any feasible explanation, they considered the phenomenon genuine, and Caroline added with her usual naïveté : " I don't think I should like to sleep here alone."

None of the party slept there except the young instructor and his charges, but where they slept remained as secret as did the fact of their existence. The rest of the party spent the night at the inn, in accordance with a previous arrangement, although Mr. Carris demurred.

All day Tuesday the phenomena continued at irregular intervals, and in the evening, when it was dusk, and Ferdinand, Caroline, and Father Conlan were about to take their departure, Mrs. Bradley summoned everyone else to the dining-room and requested them to accompany the three to the gate.

" I will wave to you all from the window of the spare bedroom, the one from which Cousin Tom is supposed to have fallen," she said. Ferdinand, suspecting that some more trickery was toward, glanced at her and raised his eyebrows.

" It's all right," said his mother. " *I* shall not fall out of the window."

When the party was out on the gravel drive they turned to look up at the first floor. There was Mrs. Bradley waving from one of the windows, and behind her could be seen distinctly the outline of a shadowy man.

The priest began to run back, but Ferdinand caught his arm and reassured him. When the other three returned to the house, Mrs. Bradley was in the hall to meet them.

The two journalists made for the stairs, but, carefully though they searched, there was no one to be found in the house except the people for whom they could account.

" Illusion ? " asked Mr. Pratt.

" Oh, no, there was someone with me," said Mrs. Bradley. " What's more, he and his confederates are still in the house."

At these words the journalists, assisted by the Warden, who had been an interested but uncommunicative observer of the phenomena so far witnessed in the house, made a still more thorough search. The journalists came to the conclusion, after some trouble and a considerable expenditure of electricity, that the ventilated cupboard at the top of the attic stairs had nothing to conceal, and the Warden found that there was a communicating door between the chief bedroom and the room adjoining. Mrs. Bradley sat downstairs in the dining-room placidly knitting a shapeless length of mauve wool, adding (apparently as the fancy took her, for she seemed to be following no particular pattern) touches of grey and shrimp-pink, and blandly received reports as they came in. Occasionally she went to the window and stared out. There was never anything to be seen except the weedy drive and the gloomy trees. It was a disconcerting house, in more senses than one.

The searchers did not give up until a quarter to ten, when they, with their hostess, went along to the village for their nightcaps and to their beds. Next day they resumed their labours, and Mrs. Bradley thought at one point that the mystery was about to be solved by Mr. Carris, who stood for nearly a quarter of an hour in the grass-grown courtyard, inspecting it from every angle and sometimes gazing down into the well. Although he had thus the first clue in his hands, he did not follow it up, but merely remarked that wells should be covered in, and that this one, so near the scullery door, was particularly dangerous.

Mr. Pratt found the second clue, but, lacking the first, made nothing of his discovery. He merely remarked to Mrs. Bradley that it seemed as though the foundations of the house might be older than its superstructure, an intelligent conclusion with which she gravely agreed. Not to be outdone by his companions, yet equally unable to apply his information, since neither of the others had thought it worth while to follow up their own discoveries, the Warden observed that it was odd to find no door at the top and bottom of the servants' staircase in a house of that period, especially as close inspection of the walls convinced him that such doors had originally been in position. He supposed they had been taken away for convenience by later owners, but he thought this made the house draughty.

During that afternoon, when the three, tired out by their exertions and slightly bored by the apparent fruitlessness of them, had given up exploring the house, the phenomena began again. Besides the usual destructiveness and noise, the watchers were greatly interested to discover some fresh markings on the walls. Some of these were mere random strokes and loops, but the word ' blimey ' and two unprintable epithets were also among the exhibits.

The three men owned that they were puzzled by this new manifestation, but the Warden remarked that it seemed ' quite like home ' to find that kind of thing scribbled on walls. At this artless remark Mrs. Bradley grimaced, but she did not reply to it, nor indicate to the guests in any way that, among them, they now had the key to all the manifestations in their hands.

When night approached, all three (having sounded one another on the subject) asked permission to remain in the house for the night. She consented, and, having anticipated such a request, produced food and drink from the larder.

After supper it was agreed that Mrs. Bradley and Mr. Carris, who had not been known to one another before the visit, should keep the watch from midnight until half-past two, and the others, who were also strangers to one another, should take over at the end of the first watch and remain on guard until five. Collusion between the watchers would thus be extremely unlikely. Incidentally (as she learned later), Mr. Carris was told to keep as strict an eye upon Mrs. Bradley and her doings as on the ghosts and their performances.

The couples had drawn for watches, and it was agreed that no one should hunt alone. Mrs. Bradley and Carris, having drawn the first watch, saw the others go up to ' bed '—in this case into the bedroom in which Mrs. Bradley had been attended, as all could witness, by the shadowy presence—and then settled down, at Carris' request, in the dining-room. At the end of ten minutes, however, he further suggested that they should not restrict themselves to one guardroom, but should move from room to room about the house, both upstairs and down, at varying intervals, keeping together, but otherwise policing the place as carefully as they could. Mrs. Bradley grinned, and agreed. But, often though they changed their headquarters, the ' ghosts ' were nippier still. Whenever they had left the dining-room or drawing-room unattended, and were upstairs, they would find, upon their return, that one or more objects in that room had been displaced during their absence. If they merely moved from one of these rooms to the other, however, Carris noted that nothing in the empty room was touched. It was clear that the whole thing was trickery and depended largely upon timing. Once or twice Carris felt, he afterwards observed, as though he were on the track, for doors slammed ahead of him, and, in following up the sounds, he thought he could hear light scurrying footsteps. They always remained ahead of him, however, except on one occasion, when he was passing along the kitchen passage, on his way back from the scullery to make sure that the door to the courtyard was still sealed. It *was* still sealed, yet he heard footsteps behind him as he began to walk back towards the hall.

Mrs. Bradley contented herself with remaining close beside or just behind him. Several times he leapt round on her, but there was never anything in her bearing or actions which gave indication that she was a prime mover, or even an assistant, in the trickery which his intelligence told him was being practised, and on the occasion just referred to he turned and darted back, forgot two steps which led down into the kitchen, took a toss, heard a slight laugh, but found no one.

Whilst he and Mrs. Bradley were in the spare room a frog jumped with the most startling suddenness out of one of the corners, and sat there, with pulsating throat and steady little eyes, regarding them with what appeared to be sedate amusement.

" One ought to be able to relate that frog to the well, I suppose," said Carris. " It *did* have steps, so I suppose the frog could get up to the courtyard . . . but how upstairs to this room . . . unless someone brought him ? "

The other two watchers had a quiet time until just before five. But at ten minutes to the hour, when their spell of duty was supposed to end, they were aroused from their sleepy boredom by a succession of loud knocks on the wall. They were in the drawing-room, which was the most comfortably furnished of the downstair rooms, and as soon as they heard the knocking they rushed out into the hall. As nothing was to be seen, they examined the seals of the front door, found that they were still intact, and made for the back of the house.

But for their compact, Pratt said afterwards, he himself would have made for the landing above, but as the Warden ran down the hall towards the passage leading to the kitchen and the scullery, he himself was bound to follow. They went as far as the scullery door, proved that it, too, was still sealed, and, coming back slowly, examining the passage walls and the dining-room as they came, discovered more scribbles.

Sucked-in was scrawled in one place, and *Silly bastards* in another. They went up by the front stairs and down by the back stairs, opening every door they came to and waking Carris, who was lying on the spare-room bed. Mrs. Bradley, in an armchair, was already awake, but her wrist was secured to his by a length of string, to ensure that neither moved about the house without the knowledge of the other.

The string was then detached, and the four went down to breakfast. Experiences were compared, and after breakfast two pillows fell downstairs into the hall. No more phenomena occurred before the departure of the journalists. They went reluctantly, and declared that, with another night on the premises, they could have solved the mystery.

Mrs. Bradley picked up the pillows and replaced them on the spare-room bed, then, watched by the Warden, she erased the new scribblings on the walls, only to find that two more had been done on the wall of the bathroom passage.

" I know that writing," said the Warden, suddenly. Mrs. Bradley chuckled as she erased it.

" I've no doubt of it, Warden," she said, " but you had better forget all that. Tell me, have you enjoyed your experiences ? "

The Warden confessed that he had.

" And what do you really think of the phenomena ? " Mrs. Bradley continued.

" Very interesting and stimulating," said the Warden. " And now—*where are my boys* ? "

" Returned to the fold this morning. They left the house immediately they had done this last bit of writing," Mrs. Bradley replied. " I chose Price and Watermallow for this job, and I think you must agree that they have been most intelligent."

" I hardly know whether the Board . . ." began the Warden.

" Did you know the two boys called Piggy and Alec, who disappeared from the Institution just before Miss Foxley inherited her aunt's money?" Mrs. Bradley enquired, coming adroitly between the Warden and his conscience.

"No. I heard all about it, of course. In fact, if you remember, that was why I was so grateful when you captured those other little scoundrels for us. Perhaps, if they had had your help over the two who got clean away . . ."

Mrs. Bradley shook her head, and assisted the Warden to come to the conclusion that he also ought to be going.

They had lunch together at the inn, and she saw him off. Then she returned to the haunted house. The time was a quarter to three, and the high, untidy grass and overgrown shrubs of the garden, a broken wicket gate on to a paddock and a neglected summer-house on a weedy gravel path gave, at that still, close time of the day, an odd and ghostly effect which the first view of the gabled house did nothing to alter or dispel.

She walked up to the front door and opened it with the key which the caretaker had provided. Sunshine danced in motes of dust in the hall. The staircase, uncarpeted—for Miss Foxley had left the house only partly furnished—turned on itself at the end of the first eight stairs with an air of reserve and chilly watchfulness. Beyond it the dim kitchen passage led direct to the realm of ghosts, and one of these ghosts—so it seemed at Mrs. Bradley's first half-glance within—was already in occupation of the premises.

Mrs. Bradley was quick and lithe as a woman one-third of her age. She flung herself flat, and the bottle flew over her prone body and crashed against the wall of the staircase. She rose and sped forward to grapple with the *poltergeist*. The voice of Miss Foxley, from the point of vantage of cover behind the dresser, called out deprecatingly :

"Oh, Lord ! I thought you were one of the ghosts ! "

"I had the same impression about you," replied Mrs. Bradley, dusting her skirt with her left hand, and keeping her right in the pocket of her skirt.

"You—you needn't shoot," said Miss Foxley, emerging. "I assure you I'm *not* a ghost."

"So I perceive," said Mrs. Bradley, keeping her right hand where it was. "You came to see how we were getting on, I presume ? Well, I'm afraid you've missed all the fun. We did have a little, although not as much as one had hoped."

" I'm glad you don't feel you've wasted your money," said Miss Foxley, nervously. " So often people complain. After all, I can't *make* things happen, can I ? "

As Mrs. Bradley had her doubts about this, she did not reply. She merely asked whether Miss Foxley proposed to stay long in the village.

" Oh, I'm not staying at all," Miss Foxley hastily answered. " I'm due to return on the four-thirty train."

" I'll walk as far as the station with you, shall I ? " said Mrs. Bradley. Miss Foxley demurred, Mrs. Bradley insisted. Miss Foxley caught the train with ten minutes to spare, and, to Mrs. Bradley's great satisfaction, completely obscured her features with a thick veil, and the lines of her figure with a long, loose mackintosh cape, before they set out from the house.

" I am just sufficiently like poor old Bella to look at, that I don't feel I want to give people a shock," she remarked, apparently feeling that an explanation was called for, although Mrs. Bradley had asked for none.

" Very proper," said Mrs. Bradley. As soon as the train pulled out of the station she telephoned for the police, and then returned to the house. This time there was nobody in occupation. She passed from room to room, and then went to the courtyard. There she removed the wooden cover of the well and peered into the depths.

There were footholds in the brickwork, as had already been noted by one of her amateur searchers after truth. She glanced round—at the scullery door, which opened almost on to the well ; at the kitchen window, which overlooked it ; at the pantry window, which, with all their zeal, the seekers had not troubled to seal nor she to point out to them.

" Selah," said Mrs. Bradley, removing all traces of the *poltergeists'* ingress and egress by this means. She returned to the well and soliloquised it :

" In five minutes we were at the well, and for some little time we sat on the edge of the well-head to make sure that no one was stirring or spying on us . . . and so we began to descend cautiously, feeling every step before we set foot on it, and scanning the walls in search of any marked stone . . ."*

Mrs. Bradley began to climb carefully into the well.

The police were as painstaking as usual. Led by Mrs. Bradley, who availed herself of her position as temporary tenant of the house to act as guide and showman, they also climbed warily into the well, felt their way along a narrow tunnel which opened out of its side about a dozen feet above the water-line, and, after groping forward a couple of yards, emerged, as she had already done, into the cellars of the house.

The cellars were ancient, and were interesting, not only from the point of view of their age. Frogs hopped on the floors, for dampness was everywhere, chiefly because of the proximity of the well. The chief interest, however, lay not in the frogs but in the great thick groins of stone upon which the roof of the cellars was supported.

" Good heavens ! " said the inspector, straightening himself as he came out of the passage exit. " Looks like something built to hold up a bridge."

" It was built to hold up the floor, including the stone pillars of a Norman church," said Mrs. Bradley, resting one of her thin yellow hands affectionately on the stonework. " This is a Norman crypt, and, I should say, one of the most interesting in England."

" No wonder there's been funny goings-on," said the sergeant, who was inclined to be superstitious and was marked for promotion because of it, his superiors being under the impression that it betokened imagination, about which they had been hearing in staff talks.

Mrs. Bradley nodded, and suggested to them that in order to obtain the results she thought probable, they would need to dig. As they had brought nothing down with them—indeed, they could not have transported spades down the well—the inspector looked at her as respectfully as circumstances, and the crude illumination of his countenance by the beams of electric torches,

---

* " The Treasure of Abbot Thomas." From *Ghost Stories of an Antiquary*. By M. R. James.

would permit, but did not reply. Mrs. Bradley did not relieve his mind by picking up a very beautiful frog, caressing it gently with her forefinger, and cackling loudly, and with a horrid echo from the vault.

" This way," she said. The overhead arches of the vaulting descended to earth in the form of thick, heavy, crudely-carved, round-capitalled pillars. Mrs. Bradley suddenly disappeared behind one of these, and the inspector, thinking to follow, discovered that she was gone. Unpardonably, since the place must at one time have been consecrated, he swore nervously, and turned round to speak to the sergeant.

" Disappearing trick," he said, introducing a regrettable adjective.

" Snatched away . . . and no wonder, with a physog like that," said the sergeant. Suddenly Mrs. Bradley's voice spoke right in his ear.

" Tell the inspector to mind the step," she said. The flight of stone steps was immediately visible to the sergeant. He blushed—fortunately in the darkness—and followed the inspector up to a little square trap-door.

" So if the one entrance or exit was not feasible or available, the other was," Mrs. Bradley explained, as the three of them emerged at the foot of the servants' staircase. " This passage, you see, is to the kitchen and scullery, and from the scullery the door opens almost on to the top of the well. The well is a good deal later in date than the crypt, of course, and may have existed independently of it for a hundred years or so. I know very little about such things, but I should put the date of the crypt as not much later than 1090. The well may have been sunk in the fifteenth century, and the passage connecting the two I should be inclined to associate with Tudor times, although I have nothing much to go on apart from the type of brickwork. I should think the connection was made to give protection to a Catholic priest. The Jesuits, I believe, were active towards the close of the sixteenth century.

" Anyhow, that's how the *poltergeist* worked. He could always be somewhere else—the essence of a good game of hide and seek. Let us return to the cellars. I have more to show you."

It was, the sergeant declared afterwards, as good as a film.

They returned to the cellar by the way that they had used to ascend to the kitchen passage. A short length of linoleum had been removed to give free access to the trap-door.

" Accounts for the cold that people have noticed, I daresay," the inspector remarked, peering into the aperture which the open trap-door disclosed.

" And yet how necessary an adjunct to the presence of the supernatural," said Mrs. Bradley.* " There is a way into this passage from the back stairs," she added. " You will have noticed that the back stairs have no doors."

The inspector could not see that this had anything to do with it, and said so, but received no answer except an accidental dig in the back from the sergeant who, at Mrs. Bradley's request, had provided himself with one of the crowbars which the police had brought with them in their car.

Upon reaching the cellar (or crypt, as Mrs. Bradley preferred to call it), they examined the floor with great care, but for some time could find no indication of anything out of the ordinary except a slight depression near the well-side entrance, which was to the west. The wall on this side was extremely damp, and the sergeant twice stepped into a pool of water before it occurred to him or to the inspector to enquire why there was water on the floor in this spot.

" Must be a depression, and fills from the well," he said. He climbed up the well again as the nearest way back to the house, and procured a birch broom which he brought back by way of the inside staircase. When he had swept away the water the cause of the sinking still was not apparent, but by testing the bricks with the crowbar he discovered that they were loose and could be prised up. Whilst they were being moved, however, a rush of water filled up each hole as it was made.

" Put 'em back," said the inspector, helping in this part of the work. " I'd say you've given us enough to go on, ma'am," he added, when the three of them were in the house once more,

---

* " Such cold air currents, or psychic winds, have been experienced, we should add, with many mediums. . . .
. . . the chill feeling upon wrists and forehead which is a recognized sign that contact has been made and that the mysteries have begun."—Sacheverell Sitwell.—"*Poltergeists*."

"and I'm inclined to pass on the information so that we can get our hooks on the lady before she makes a getaway. You say she was here this afternoon, so she can't have hopped it very far. Once we've got her, we can examine that cellar more carefully, and if we don't find what we expect to find, well, we shall still have enough to go on for a bit. She'll have to explain the sister's suicide, if nothing else, and why she's been passing herself off as her. You've no doubt about getting her identified, I suppose ? "

" No doubt at all," replied Mrs. Bradley.

As they re-entered the kitchen the sound of footsteps was heard outside, and the caretaker came in by way of the scullery door.

" Ah, so you be still here, mam ? " he said. He looked at the two policemen. Mrs. Bradley took out one of the snapshots.

" Is this your employer ? " she asked.

" Never set eyes on her," replied the old man, " as I telled 'ee before. This . . . ? " His face changed. " Why, this be the lady as was tried for the murder of the gentleman what fell out the window."

" Are you sure ? " enquired the inspector. " No photographs were taken at the trial," he added, turning to Mrs. Bradley.

" Ah. But her was living here in the village when the poor fellow fell," said the caretaker.

Mrs. Bradley put the snapshot away and then glanced at her watch.

" I'm staying the night here," she said. " Are you expecting visitors to-morrow afternoon ? "

" Ah. A lady and gentleman named Lee-Strange wants to look over the house," replied the caretaker, " so you're bound to clear out before then ; Miss Foxley's orders."

" I shall be out by twelve noon," said Mrs. Bradley. The old man pattered away, and the inspector wished her good-bye.

" You know," said Mrs. Bradley, detaining him out of earshot of the sergeant, " I think you ought to finish that business in the cellar, or you may be too late to find what we think may be there."

The inspector looked sharply at her.

" It wouldn't do not to find them if they're there, ma'am," he agreed.

"Leave the sergeant to keep an eye on me, so that you're sure there will be no monkey-business," Mrs. Bradley tactfully observed, "and get back as soon as you can with something to mop up that water and a few more men to dig."

The inspector was back in less than an hour. Meanwhile, Mrs. Bradley and the sergeant had tea just outside the summer-house and discussed old-fashioned flowers, women's fashions (of which the sergeant proved to have far-reaching and extraordinary knowledge), and the breeding of pedigree Airedales.

The inspector brought back with him a posse of six men, about a hundredweight of sacking, two more crowbars, a waterproof sheet, some spades, rubber gloves, a coil of rope, three dark lanterns, and a doctor.

He left two men on guard over Mrs. Bradley, who sat with her escorts in the drawing-room, and regaled them with stories of *poltergeist* activity both real and faked, asked the doctor to remain in the kitchen (upon whose table he proposed to lay the results of his researches in the cellar), and took the rest of his party and their accoutrements with him into the crypt.

They emerged an hour and a quarter later. The inspector himself summoned Mrs. Bradley. He had a triumphant and congratulatory expression, but swallowed from time to time, as though it would have done him good to be sick.

"We've found 'em all right, ma'am," he said. "As you're a doctor, and put us on the track, as you might say, perhaps you'd like to be with Dr. Ellis, who is going to give them the once-over, what there is of 'em. Seems to be two boys, according to him, though I couldn't stick it long enough, myself, to be sure of anything. Buried before death, he reckons."

The gruesome and pitiful task concluded, Mrs. Bradley again found the inspector at her elbow. Half apologetically he laid his hand upon her arm.

"And, although there's, maybe, another explanation, ma'am," he said, "it is my duty to warn you that anything you say will be taken down, and may be used in evidence."

Chapter Eight

THE WIDOW'S MITE

Ah ! when will this long weary day have end,
And lend me leave to come unto my love ?
How slowly do the hours their numbers spend ;
How slowly does sad Time his feathers move !
SPENSER.

MURIEL was hysterical in her denials. She knew nothing about *poltergeist* phenomena, she said, and nothing about the well in the courtyard. Her husband had earned an honest living, she declared ; it was not his fault, poor man, that he had been duped and victimised by that wicked Cousin Bella.

Oh, yes, the photograph was a very clear one. She would have said it was Bella anywhere. No, she could think of no reason why Bella should pass herself as Tessa, unless it was because she had had such a bad scare over the trial for Tom's murder that she thought she ought to take advantage.

Take advantage of what, the police enquired. Why, of the fact of the death ; the suicide, Muriel vaguely explained. They pressed the point, and this frightened her, as Mrs. Bradley could have told them it was bound to do. Muriel crawled back into her shell, and the utmost they could then achieve was an alarmed squeaking from her that she did not know a thing more, not a thing.

" The most valuable witness simply thrown away, Mother," said Ferdinand, after Mrs. Bradley's release and the inspector's apologies. " Couldn't *you* do something with the woman ? They'll never prove their case without her. She must know all about it, really. She simply wants handling, and the witness-box won't be the best place to do it. She's full of venom against Bella Foxley, and these flat-footed idiots have gone and stamped it all out of her. She's out to save her own skin now ; nothing more."

" I know," replied Mrs. Bradley.

" After all," pursued Ferdinand, " they can't continue to hold

Bella merely for impersonating her sister. They will have to prove she killed her, and that won't be any easy matter. The evidence at the inquest on Tessa Foxley was pretty straight-forward. Not a doubt in anyone's mind but that it was acci-dental death, except for that idiot boy, and no one is going to take any notice of him after all this time, even supposing he remembers a thing about it, which he probably doesn't. And it's tricky work, anyway, having the woman up for murder again. There's certain to be a bat-eyed, pudden-brained sec-tion of the community who'll paint the newspapers red swearing poor Bella is being victimised. You see if there isn't. The police want a cast-iron case, and they haven't any such thing, unless and until Mrs. Turney comes across with what she knows."

"The trouble is," said Mrs. Bradley mildly, "that the police have succeeded in convincing Muriel that once she owns up to having known about the cellar she might as well adjust the hangman's noose about her own neck. It is most unfortunate, but there it is."

"Well, something will have to be done," her son observed. His mother grimaced, but promised nothing. She, like Sherlock Holmes, had her methods, but they required, she felt, careful application.

She left Muriel alone for a fortnight, and concentrated all her energies upon finding out all she could about the history of the haunted house. The prosecution would have to establish that Bella could have known of the cellar. The tale of the hauntings, and the chronology of the buildings, she found in the County History. She perused the account twice, and then copied it out.

There were legends and ill-authenticated stories of the coach, a headless driver, a headless Cavalier, a hanging figure supposed to date from the time of the French Revolution, and, in short, all the usual nonsense. Of true *poltergeist* phenomena there was no mention in the County History nor in any other printed account of the house. That, however, scarcely mattered. Such phenomena rarely persisted long.*

---

* The longest recorded case of *poltergeist* activity seems to have lasted about twelve years. This was at Willington Mill, Northumberland. One of the shortest was the famous haunting of the family of Wesley, which lasted for two months.

The history of the house itself as a building next engaged her attention. The County History informed her that it had originally been built on the site of a former monastery, which had been suppressed by Henry the Eighth and reconstituted under Mary. The original dwelling-house had been built in 1541, after nearly all the monastic buildings had been destroyed, but upon the accession of Mary Tudor, the monks were brought back, the Abbey Church was returned to the community instead of being used as a Parish Church, and part of the ' new ' house was used by the Abbot as his lodging.

In the next reign, however, the monks were again dispossessed. The house was enlarged by the addition of another wing, and the Church was neglected. The cloister garth became a bowling green, and it was said that the earliest hauntings of the house derived from this period in its history.

During the eighteenth century the house was purchased by members of the Hell-Fire Club, and the hauntings became more serious. One of the members, whilst engaged in his childish anti-godliness, was killed, and, later, the house was burnt down and the last ruins of the church destroyed.

In 1851 the present house had been erected on the site of the ruined building, except for the north rooms which helped to enclose the courtyard. These had been added about thirty years later. The names of previous tenants, with the varying degrees of ill-luck which had attended them, members of their families or any of their servants or friends resident in the house, were appended to the rest of the historical account, sometimes with considerable detail of the hauntings, sometimes baldly.

Of the well in the courtyard there was specific mention, and it was clear that Bella Foxley—or Cousin Tom, for that matter— could have deduced the opening of the passage from the well into the crypt.

" It is supposed," one writer had alleged, " that there must at one time have been a priest's hole in the house. This would have been constructed during the short and unlucky tenancy of the Catholic family of Merrill. . . . There is a strong hint in one of the family papers that access to the priest's hole could be gained by means of the ancient well in the courtyard. This, however, only seems to lead to a cellar under the house. . . ."

That was all that Mrs. Bradley could glean of the history of the house. The tales of the hauntings were ill-authenticated, but at least there was no mention of anything which suggested the activities of a *poltergeist*. Not that this negative information was of much value, she reflected again, since *poltergeist* phenomena, besides being usually of fairly short duration, are apt to be episodic, spasmodic, and to attend upon the presence of certain living persons* rather than upon historic wrongs and infamies past and gone.

Mrs. Bradley gave up the records, and returned to Cousin Muriel, again without result. Cousin Muriel, in fact, expressed the opinion that she would go off her head if people did not stop worrying her about those poor little boys. As Mrs. Bradley, looking at her frightened eyes and a twitching muscle just above her mouth, considered this more than likely, she forbore to press her, remarked that it was a pity that there was no one to exact vengeance for the murdered children, and, leaving this grim phrase to do what work it would to Cousin Muriel's conscience and such superstitious fears as she knew her to possess, went off to the Institution to find out what help the Warden could give in tracing the boys to Bella Foxley's company.

There was one hope in her mind, and one only, so far as this was concerned. The diary had named a certain Larry, and from the entry in which his name appeared, Mrs. Bradley had deduced that this Larry, if he could be found, might prove to have some knowledge of the means of escape used by Piggy and Alec, and some knowledge of where they had proposed to go. The difficulty, as she saw it, would be to get in touch with Larry. He might prove to have cut his connection with the Institution so completely, once he had left it, that it would be impossible to track him down. He might be dead, in prison, in another continent—anywhere. He might be out of touch with English newspapers, so that an advertisement would never reach him. He might be unable to read, or, even more likely (and she knew

* " Its powers, then, seem to be fixed or loaded in the person of someone in the house, preferably a child in the most impressionable months of its life."— Sacheverell Sitwell.—*"Poltergeists."*

On the other hand, this is not invariably true. Cf. the phenomena at Borley Rectory, during the investigations carried out there by Mr. Harry Price and his observers from 1929 to 1939.—G.M.

how completely illiterate some members of the criminal classes could be), he might be unwilling to come forward and expose himself voluntarily to police questioning.

The sooner all this was put to the proof, the better. She telephoned the Warden as soon as she arrived in the town nearest to the Institution, which was situated about two miles away on the slope of a treeless hill, and received an invitation to come immediately to see him.

He looked less like a frog, and a good deal more animated, than usual. He seemed, in fact, pleased to see her.

" Larry ? Larry who ? " he enquired, when Mrs. Bradley had stated the object of her visit.

" I don't know. He was here six years ago, with Piggy and Alec."

" That's another thing," said the Warden. " Who were Piggy and Alec ? "

" Alec we should be able to trace, I think, from your records. It sounds to me like a reasonable, if shortened, form of Alexander or even Alexis."

" And it may not be short for anything. He may have been christened Alec," argued the Warden. " And Larry might be traceable. Yes, indeed he might."

The records were conveniently to hand. An exploration of a stock-room, a mounting of library steps, and the records were identified and produced for inspection and research.

" Larry ; Larry," said the Warden, tracing Christian names with a patient and experienced forefinger. " Harry ? "

" Laurence ? Lawrence ? " suggested Mrs. Bradley.

" Got it in one, if that's it," replied the Warden. " And if it *is* it, you're in luck. Only one boy named Lawrence for the whole of that year, either Christian or surname. Here we are. Henry Nelson Lawrence. Now, I can give you the next stage in his career from this."

He opened another register. Mrs. Bradley leaned over, and followed the zealous forefinger as it passed swiftly down the page.

" Ah ! We *are* in luck ! Here it is, look," said the Warden. " Lad went into the Navy. Now, granted that he continued to be respectable, you'll have little difficulty in following him up, I imagine."

It was not quite as easy as the Warden had indicated, but,

fortunately for Mrs. Bradley's plans, Henry Nelson Lawrence, A.B., proved to be one of the Institution's successes. Furthermore, he happened, by great good luck, to be on leave at Plymouth. He proved to be a large, docile young man, whose embarrassment at being brought up against the past was almost equalled by his desire to assist in tracking down the murderer of Piggy and Alec.

" Who *were* Piggy and Alec ? " Mrs. Bradley enquired. " Can you remember their names ? "

" Pegwell and Kettleborough," the young seaman promptly responded.

" Thank you very much. And now, Mr. Lawrence, I wonder whether you have any idea of the means by which they escaped from the Institution ? I ought to warn you that you may have to make this statement in court."

" In court ? " He looked doubtful, but only for a moment. "They was good little chaps," he remarked. " I liked 'em. The cook-housekeeper—I forget her name—she got 'em the files, and she hid 'em in the kitchen while they was being looked for. But that's all l know, lady. I never cottoned on where they went, or aught else about it."

It was good enough, if not too good, thought Mrs. Bradley. She tested the statement carefully and with *finesse*. There seemed no doubt that Larry fully believed that Bella Foxley had assisted the escape and had hidden the fugitives until the first hue and cry had died down.

It was not easy to decide, after that, to what extent Larry ought to be taken into her confidence. She thought she would risk it. After all, Bella Foxley was under arrest. She was not in a position to attack the witnesses.

" I ought to tell you, Mr. Lawrence," she said, " that we suspect Miss Foxley of having used the two boys for her own ends, and that, when they were of no further use to her, she murdered them by shutting them up in a cellar and starving them to death."

The simple face of the young man hardened.

" I wouldn't put it past her, mam," he said.

" And you would be willing to give evidence ? " Mrs. Bradley enquired.

"Yes, I reckon so. I've gone straight since I joined the
Navy. I've got my record. There's nothing again' it. I don't
see why I shouldn't speak up, and tell what I know. 'Twasn't
nothing to do with me they made their getaway."

"All right," said Mrs. Bradley. "Tell me all you know."

"Well, I know she got 'em the files and I know she done some
of the filing through the window bars, because Piggy told me.
He said she could get in the dormitories without being questioned,
being, like, the housekeeper, and able to go where she wanted."

"Why did they think she was willing to help them?"

"She never said. Only spilt 'em some dope about she knew
they'd go straight if they got the chance, and she was going to
see they got it."

"Where were they to go when they had escaped?"

"I dunno."

"Had they any money?"

"No, I don't reckon they had, but we didn't let on to one
another about that. Next thing you knowed, somebody had
swiped it off of you, and you couldn't complain because we
wasn't supposed to have no dough. Them that had it swiped it
off of the instructors."

"How long before they went did Piggy tell you they were
going?"

"About a week, I reckon."

"Do you think they had any plans?"

"No, barring getting some work. The cook-lady, she put 'em
on to that, because Piggy said so."

"He didn't say what sort of work?"

"I don't reckon he knowed. All he said was she was going
to hide 'em up till the police 'ad done lookin' for 'em, and then
she was going to find 'em some work. Then, when they got jobs,
see, they was going to look out for something to suit 'em better."

"And get them into trouble with the police?"

"I don't know. I couldn't say what ideas they got. Racing
stables, more like, from what they said. I reckon they was the
kind to go straight all right, give 'em a chance, so long as it
wasn't too dull."

"Were they obedient boys?"

"Never got into much trouble that I remember. The beaks

was a bit surprised they lit out. Didn't think they was the sort, the Warden said."

" He questioned you at the time, I believe, Mr. Lawrence ? "

" Oh, he dickered me a bit, but I never let nothing come out. If ever you get in a jam, lady, stick to Don't Know. I've never found nothing to touch it."

" Thank you," said Mrs. Bradley gravely. She had had exasperating evidence from Muriel Turney of the impenetrability of this simplest of defences.

The interview with Larry, however, although very unsatisfactory from the point of view of actual information, had outlined clearly the path she had to follow. Whatever her fears and objections, however tiresomely obstinate she had made up her weak little mind to be, Cousin Tom's relict would have to be browbeaten into acknowledging that she had known of the boys' presence in the haunted house.

Before she could return to Muriel's lodgings, however, a message from Ferdinand informed her that he had precise information from the police that Muriel had ' skipped.' As it was in their own interests to find her in order to produce her as one of the chief witnesses at the trial, they were ' on her track, baying like hounds,' Ferdinand's letter continued.

Mrs. Bradley did not believe that Muriel, whatever her state of mind, would acknowledge complicity in Bella Foxley's crimes by running away, so she sought her straightway in the most likely place—the house which Aunt Flora had left to Eliza Hodge. From there she telephoned to Ferdinand.

" She's in that state," said Miss Hodge, " poor thing, that I don't know what to do, and that's a fact. She says she'll go out of her mind, and, upon my word, madam, I almost believe she will, she's that worried and upset with it all. And no wonder, either, if the half of what she's been telling me is true."

" Look here," said Mrs. Bradley. " I've got to see her. I haven't come to frighten her, but I've got to know what she knows about those boys."

Muriel, however, had locked the bedroom door and was at the window, threatening, in high, hysterical tones, to throw herself out if Mrs. Bradley did not go away at once and stop worrying her.

Mrs. Bradley, standing on the lawn, said clearly :

" Now don't be silly, Mrs. Turney. Come down at once, and tell me what you know. I have just telephoned the police that you are here. Your best chance is to tell me the truth before they arrive. Come, now. Don't waste time."

Whether this appeal or Muriel's own common-sense won the day Mrs. Bradley never knew, but scarcely had she entered the house when Muriel came down the stairs and motioned her to the drawing-room. There, on heavy chairs and surrounded by Aunt Flora's *bric-à-brac*, the two conversed, and gradually Muriel disclosed to Mrs. Bradley the story of the *poltergeist* phenomena, the part played by Piggy and Alec, Bella Foxley's contributions to the hauntings and her share of the proceeds, together with other strange and diverse matters.

Most unfortunately, although Muriel was prepared to admit that she had known that the boys had originated the *poltergeist* tricks, she insisted that she had not known of the terrible death which they had suffered. From this assertion she could not be moved, and Mrs. Bradley had to accept it, although she could not believe that it was the truth.

" You see, as I told you, poor Tom got his living with the séances and all that," Muriel said, " and Bella often put us on to the houses. Of course, we had the usual troubles. The Society for Psychical Research used to try to check up on Tom, but he wasn't having any, and he said he didn't mind if they called him a fraud, even in print, because the people who were any good to him were not the kind to read the Journal of the Society.

" Well, about a month before Aunt Flora died, Bella wrote to us, and said she was fed up with the Institution and if she didn't get away from it for a bit she'd die. She said she had had all the sick leave she was entitled to, so either she'd have to go sick without pay, or else she'd have to resign, but she couldn't stand the life any longer.

" Well, she said she'd find us another haunted house, and a good one, if we would agree to take it on and have her live there with us for a bit until she found something she liked better.

" It sounded queer, coming from her, and I asked Tom what he thought she'd got up her sleeve. He said he didn't know, but that it was her own business and that he didn't mind if she came, so long as she didn't stay too long. He said he had done all he could with Hazy, because you had to have more helpers to get the results any better, and, besides, we had been there so long that the landlord wanted to put up the rent, and Tom said it wasn't worth that, because the house was a bit too much off the beaten track to keep on attracting people when they could go to séances in London. And the flat, of course, had entirely petered out.

" So I wrote off to Bella and told her she could do as she liked, and she wrote back and said she had found just the house and knew just the way to work it for us.

" Now she'd never suggested helping us in that way before, and Tom didn't know what to make of it, quite, and neither did I. Tom said that what he could make would keep two of us, but certainly not three, especially as Bella's helpers would expect to be paid. He wrote off and said that he didn't want extra help, and that amateurs would only mess things up. Bella wrote back and said that the helpers she meant wouldn't mess things up, and wouldn't want anything except their food and somewhere to sleep. She didn't say who she meant, but Tom soon guessed she meant two of those dreadful boys.

" Well, he was dead against it, right from the first. He said he wouldn't be able to depend upon boys like that, and he said that, anyway, as soon as they got fed up they'd sling their hook— that was his expression—and then he would be left with a lot of disappointed clients who were not getting their money's worth.

" Well, Bella didn't argue. She just turned up with the boys. That was late in January——"

" Yes. That was on January 24th," thought Mrs. Bradley, "if the dates in the diary are to be trusted." She did not speak, however, and Muriel, after frowningly trying to recollect the date for herself, announced that she thought it was somewhere round the twentieth, and continued :

" She came along with them about supper-time, and locked them up in one of the bedrooms, and said she must get back quickly to the Institution in case she was missed. I ought to say that we were in the haunted house by this time. Tom had rented it for a month ' to test its possibilities,' he told Bella."

"So you were in the haunted house before the twenty-fourth or twenty-fifth of January," thought Mrs. Bradley ; but, afraid of startling this shy song-bird into silence again, she made no remark.

"I didn't like it," Muriel resumed. "I knew what dreadful boys they had at the Institution, and I didn't know what they might get up to, away from all the discipline and that. Tom didn't seem to mind. He took them up some supper, and locked the door again, and I must say they behaved quite quiet and orderly, I was quite surprised and pleased ; not that I ever got fond of them, mind you, and right to the end I was afraid of what they might do if they took it into their heads.

"Well, then came the news about Aunt Flora. That must have been the next day, I rather fancy. Anyway, Bella sent us the telegram, saying she'd already been sent for by old Eliza Hodge, as the doctor didn't think poor old Aunt was likely to last.

"Tom didn't see any point in going at first. He said we'd never had much to do with Aunt, and that she'd only think we'd gone there to see what we could get. Anyway, I persuaded him—poor Tom !—and then, of course, Aunt began to get better, and then Bella killed her."

"Bella or your husband or you," thought Mrs. Bradley. Aloud she said, "And what were the boys doing while all of you were staying at Aunt Flora's house ? "

"I don't know, I'm sure."

"Oh, yes, you do, Mrs. Turney. They were in the cellar, weren't they ? "

"I don't know where they were," repeated Muriel. "I didn't know anything about the cellar then. I asked Tom what had happened to them, and he said not to worry ; they were quite all right where they were, and had plenty to eat."

"And had plenty to eat," thought Mrs. Bradley, nodding soberly. "And Aunt Flora had had too much to eat, and was dead." Again she said none of this aloud.

"Bella went back to the Institution for a day or two, but not for long. Then she joined us at the haunted house, and Tom began his séances," Muriel continued. "Well, of course, they were ever so successful, as you know. The boys were really wonderful, I will say that for them. They cottoned on ever so quickly to what was wanted, and thought up all sorts of extra things for themselves. Quite got the spirit of it, Tom said, and he and Bella were getting on like a house on fire, which usually they didn't really do, Bella being sharp and impatient in her manner on account of her work, and being a spinster, I always thought, but never said so, of course, being the last to want to make trouble.

" Well, the cellar was Bella's idea. It seemed she had read up about it before we took on the house, and before even we got there she had had the wooden cover off the well. Of course, she didn't usually put it back, because of the boys getting up and down that way to be able to do their stuff when the spiritualists came, and get away again safely without being seen.

" Well, the next part is all, like, about my fancies, and you needn't believe it unless you like, but, after a bit, the house got on my nerves. Of course, you can say it was really the boys I was scared of, and, in a way, I think it was. You see, when Tom kept saying to Bella at the first that this game was all very well, but where were we going to be when the boys got fed up and left us, she turned round on him one day and said the boys would leave when *she* was ready, and not a minute before. She said she'd got the tabs on them all right, because if they didn't do what she said she'd only got to give them up to the police and they'd be taken back to the Institution straight away, and well they knew it.

" Well, things went on all right for quite a bit after that, and then I began to get those fancies."

" What fancies ? " asked Mrs. Bradley gently, to end a lengthy pause.

" Well, you'll no doubt think me very silly, just like Tom and Bella did," confessed Muriel, " but, the fact is, I began to feel that there was something *really* funny about the house ; not just the boys and their tricks. You see, up to then, I'd always believed that Tom was an honest investigator—lucky, but honest—and that my help wasn't to help him go in for tricking people, but to help with genuine what-do-you-call-it——"

" Phenomena ? "

" Manifestations ; that was Tom's word for them. But this *poltergeist* business with the boys was different. It was just simply hoodwinking the people, and I'd always felt the spirits were kind of sacred, and that I'd been kind of initiated into the great mystery of it all when I married Tom and my right hand went luminous, and I was in a trance and told people things, and all that. And it sort of came to me that if we weren't careful, playing about with all this *poltergeist* stuff, we might offend *something queer*, and be very sorry for it. It seemed to me I heard whispers and footsteps nothing to do with the boys, and once I thought I heard a kind of a horrible laugh just at my elbow when I knew the boys were up in the attic cupboard being told by Bella and Tom what the next stunt was to be.

" Well, I got thoroughly nervy and run-down, and in the end I said I should leave the house ; I couldn't stand it. Rather to my surprise, Bella and Tom made no objection, except Bella said that it was a bit of a nuisance, because she'd have to come, too. She said it wouldn't look right for her to stay alone with Tom, even though they were cousins. I begged Tom to send away the boys, but he said he couldn't do that, and he wouldn't join us at the inn because he said we couldn't leave the boys alone in the house because they might escape. When he did come to see us, he locked them up in the attic cupboard, where he didn't think they could come to any harm. He didn't think they could get out of it, either, but, of course, they did. . . ."

She paused and shivered.

" Of course they did. And they thrust your husband out of the bedroom window when he returned from a visit to the inn," said Mrs. Bradley.

" How did you know that ? I've never told anybody that ! "

" It was fairly obvious. Bella, of course, knowing the boys so much better than your husband did, was afraid that something of the sort would happen. She went along to see whether Mr. Turney was all right. It was when she discovered that he was going to use the incident to lay a charge against her of attempting to murder him because he had evidence against her for the murder of Aunt Flora that she realized it would be safer for her if he were out of the way. It would be easy enough, she thought, to accuse the boys of the murder. What I can't understand, and what I should like you to explain, if you can, are these points :—"

Muriel shied like a startled horse at the sight of Mrs. Bradley's little notebook.

"I don't suppose I can tell you anything at all," she said wildly. "And I don't know at all why she wanted to kill poor Tom and those poor boys. All I know is . . ."

"Now, listen, Mrs. Turney," said Mrs. Bradley. "First, I can't understand why, with the death certificate duly signed by the doctor, she was afraid of anything which your husband might have to say about the cause of Aunt Flora's death. After all, even an exhumation of the body couldn't have proved the doctor wrong. It was Bella Foxley's word against that of your husband."

"Ah, but there was the motive, wasn't there? All Aunt's money, except for the little bit left to Eliza Hodge."

"Ah, yes, the money. But, don't you see, Mrs. Turney, that, even granted a motive, there would be little to gain by accusing Bella of a murder which could not possibly be proved? If your husband had gone to the police with his story he would have been thought a malicious man who was jealous because the woman he was accusing had inherited a fortune to which he may have thought he had some claim. If he had been able to produce other witnesses, or some sort of circumstantial evidence . . . but even you yourself could not have supported his statement, could you?"

"Don't you believe, then, that Bella *did* murder Aunt Flora?" Muriel demanded, without attempting to answer the last question.

"That is not the point. At the moment I am pointing out that belief isn't proof, and that the unsupported testimony of one man could not be accepted in a court of law. Now, come along, Mrs. Turney! Why *did* Bella Foxley murder your husband?"

"I don't know anything more than I've told you already," said Muriel tearfully. "I don't see why you won't have it. I don't suppose Bella knew any more about the law than I do. I still think she believed Tom would give her away."

"And I still believe that that is nonsense," said Mrs. Bradley crisply. "Oh, well, if you won't tell me, I must seek other means of finding out."

"I'm sure I wish you success," said Muriel, perking up a little.

" As long as she's punished for it, I don't mind what means you take."

" It is the death of the boys I am investigating," Mrs. Bradley reminded her. " Bella Foxley has already been acquitted of murdering your husband."

" Well, the boys were killed because they knew she was going to kill Tom," said Muriel. Mrs. Bradley looked at her for a little time in silence. This apparently caused her some alarm and discomfort, for she added, dropping her eyes, " Oh, no, it couldn't be that ! How silly of me to say that ! Unless, of course . . ."

" Unless what ? "

" Unless, as you thought at first, I believe, it was Bella who pushed Tom out of the window the first time, and not the boys at all."

" It was not Bella," Mrs. Bradley responded. "If it had been, Tom—your husband—would not have exposed himself a second time to be attacked."

Chapter Nine

COUNSEL'S OPINION

> Love forbid that through dissembling I should thrive,
> Or in praising you myself of truth deprive !
> Let not your high thoughts debase
> A simple truth in me :
> Great is Beauty's grace,
> Truth is yet as fair as she.
>
> CAMPION.

THE trial of Bella Foxley for the murders of Frederick Pegwell and Richard Kettleborough began on Tuesday, November 5th, and was concluded on Friday, November 8th. It was not a sensational trial, as trials go ; it had none of the historic horror of the trial of Burke and Hare for the murder of the Widow Dogherty ; it did not enhance the reputation of the Counsel for the Defence as did the trial of Mrs. Maybrick for the murder of

James Maybrick, her husband; neither did it achieve that almost sublime position in the annals of the Sunday press which was granted to the trial of Hawley Harvey Crippen for the murder of his wife, Belle Elmore, Cora Turner or Cunigunde Mackamotzi; to the trial of Ronald True for the murder of Gertrude Yates, alias Olive Young; and to the trial of Patrick Mahon for the murder of Emily Kaye in the bungalow on the Crumbles at Eastbourne. Nevertheless, it had its own interest, and received, as Mrs. Bradley admitted to Mr. Pratt later, a very good press.

The trial opened on a fine but chilly morning, with Bella Foxley pleading ' Not Guilty ' to the charges brought against her. Muriel and the young seaman, Larry Lawrence, should have been the most damning witnesses for the prosecution, but Muriel made a bad impression, was confused, hesitating, contradictory and nervous, and the defence scored several points in the cross-questioning. Larry, however, was unshakable. He was slow-minded, sure of his facts, unimpressed by his surroundings and obviously certain of Bella Foxley's guilt. Unfortunately, however, his early lapses, for which he had been sent to the Institution, told against him, although they were not referred to in so many words. It was enough that he had been an inmate.

Gradually the story of the crimes emerged, but the most interesting part of the trial from the point of view of the spectators was when Bella Foxley herself went into the witness box to give her own version of the occurrences.

She had heard of the haunted house through an agency, she averred, which sent her advertisements from time to time of such houses. Knowing (she did not give Cousin Tom's name at this point, and was not asked for it in case it should prejudice the jury if they remembered that she had been tried for his murder) that some relatives on her mother's side were interested in psychical research, she had informed them that this particular house was in the market and that she had already visited it and had been greatly impressed by some unaccountable happenings which she had witnessed.

Later (she did not refer to Aunt Flora's death) she went to visit them after they had taken a lease of the house, and they agreed with her that the house was under supernatural influences. She visited them on three or four occasions. The longest single visit that she made lasted from a Friday evening until the following Sunday afternoon. On other occasions, two or three in number, she could not remember exactly how many, she had stayed a single night.

It was represented to her by the prosecution that she had once spent more than a week in the house. She denied this, and then, looking very uncomfortable for the first time since the proceedings had begun, she admitted that she had stayed for several days in a hotel not far from where the house was situated. As this week covered and included the time of Cousin Tom's death, she was not asked to enlarge in any way upon her answer, and it was doubtful, Mrs. Bradley thought, whether the prosecution had scored a point or not, since the jury were not to be encouraged to realize that they were trying a woman who already had been acquitted on one murder charge and was fortunate to have escaped a previous one.

Bella then denied completely that she had had any part in the escape of the two boys from the Institution, that she had connived at it, or that she had the slightest idea of what had happened to them after they had got away.

The defence of stout denial is always a good one, Mrs. Bradley reflected, particularly if the accused does not commit the error of embroidering the denial by producing facts in support of it. Bella Foxley produced none. In effect, she challenged the prosecution to prove that the bodies which had been found in the crypt were those of the two boys who had escaped from the Institution, and she challenged them to show that she had had any knowledge of the whereabouts of the boys after they had escaped.

" All over bar the shouting," wrote Mr. Pratt to Mrs. Bradley in the court. She grimaced at him in reply. It was Larry against Bella, she knew, for Muriel could not have done more to prejudice the case in favour of the prisoner if she had been on the opposite side ; and Larry, poor fellow, still had his boyhood to live down. Bella herself appeared to have no doubt of the result. She remained calm, almost phlegmatic, self-assured and clear-headed.

A scale model of the haunted house had been prepared, and from it Mrs. Bradley had made clear her discovery of the passage connecting the well with the crypt and of her further discovery of how simple a matter it was, with the aid of two boys, to re-produce psychical phenomena of *poltergeist* character. This, she inferred, had been Bella's motive in assisting the two boys to make their escape from the Institution.

The old caretaker had referred to screams, shouts and moans which had come up ' through the floor ' of the house, but his evidence did not stand the test of cross-examination by the defence, for he was confused as to dates, and ended by agreeing (although he did not, to the end, realize this !) that he had imagined the whole thing. Miss Biddle's charwoman fared no better at the hands of Counsel for the Defence.

" You'll never get her, Mother," said Ferdinand, gloomily. " She's as guilty as hell, but old Crodders has got you on toast. You see, you yourself can't speak to anything except the finding of the bodies, and although Muriel ought to have been able to slam the nail on the head that they were the bodies of those particular wretched kids, she didn't do it. Scared of finding her own neck in the noose ; that's the trouble with her."

" Oh, I knew she'd make a thoroughly bad witness," said Mrs. Bradley comfortably. Her son gaped at her, but she did not enlarge upon her answer.

The cross-questioning of Bella Foxley nevertheless remained the high spot, as Caroline called it, of the proceedings. There was a ' sensation in court,' for instance, when in reply to questions the prisoner at last admitted that she *had* known of the presence of two boys in the haunted house, and agreed that the *phenomena* were fraudulent. She persisted in maintaining, however, that she had had nothing whatever to do with introducing the boys into the house, and declared that they were there at the invitation of those relatives of her own in whose name the house had been rented.

" You helped these boys to escape ? " the enquirer persisted.

" No."

" Do you deny that you helped them to file through the window bars of their sleeping quarters ? "

" I deny it absolutely."

" Do you deny that you supplied them with the files ? "

" Yes, I deny that, too."

" How do you think the boys got in touch with your relatives ? "

" I mentioned that two boys had escaped from the Institution and were at large."

" I suggest that your relatives knew from you how to get hold of these boys."

" No, not from me."

" From whom, then ? "

" I don't know."

" I suggest that you know perfectly well."

" I'm sure I don't. It seems to have been coincidence."

The judge intervened at this point to remind the prisoner that she was on oath, ' like any other witness.'

" When you knew that the boys were in the house, did you take any steps to inform the police that you knew where they could be found ? " the prosecuting counsel continued.

" No."

" Why not ? "

" I believe in the idea of ' live and let live.' "

" But you knew why these boys had been sent to the Institution ? "

" Well, yes, more or less."

" What do you mean by that ? "

" I mean I knew they were supposed to have done something wrong."

" Something so wrong that one of them, at least, was a potential danger to the community."

" I didn't know that. We were never told the reason—not any particular reason, I mean—why any boy was at the Institution."

" Even so, did you not believe it to be your duty, as a citizen, to inform the police as to the whereabouts of the boys ? "

" No."

" Would you call yourself an anti-social person ? "

" No. I'm unsociable, but I liked the boys."

" When you had made up your mind not to hand the boys over to the police, did you set about organizing their activities so as to benefit yourself and your relations ? "

" No."

" You didn't help to exploit these boys for gain ? "

" Certainly not. As I explained before (this had been during her statement to her counsel) I had no reason to want to make money, either with or without the help of the boys. I had plenty of money. The boys were amused at playing the *poltergeist* tricks, and it was such a change to see them laughing and happy."

"But when their laughter and happiness grew too dangerous, you battened them down in that cellar with frogs, newts and all kinds of slimy and disgusting creatures, and left them there in the dark and the wet to starve."

"I never did that! I swear it! This is all a mistake. I am not the person who ought to be accused."

"When did the boys become a nuisance?"

"Never. I did not find them a nuisance. I had very little to do with them. I was at the Institution most of the time they were at the house."

Counsel had led up to this point very well, Mrs. Bradley thought. The next part of the argument did not take her by surprise, but it seemed to flummox the prisoner. Pointing at her (one of the few histrionic or dramatic gestures he made during the trial) Counsel for the Prosecution said clearly:

"You were not at the house during most of the time that the boys were there?"

"No."

"You were still at the Institution?"

"Yes, certainly."

"Will you tell the court the amount of your salary at the Institution?"

"I —let me see—I think I was getting about a hundred and sixty."

"And your board and lodging, of course?"

"Yes, except during holiday periods."

"Quite so. When did you begin to receive your legacy?"

"About—on—let me think. It would have been—I think I had the first payment towards the end of February."

"Towards the end of the February?"

"Yes, I believe that's right."

"And the boys escaped from the Institution on January twenty-third, according to the records kept by the Warden."

"Yes, I suppose that would be right."

"It *is* right. We can call witnesses to prove it, if necessary.

Now, tell me : did you know, when those boys escaped—that is to say, on January twenty-third—that your aunt was going to die and leave you all this money ? "

" No ! No, of course I didn't ! "

So she did not, even now, perceive the trap, thought Mrs. Bradley.

" Well, then, I suggest that perhaps your financial position, at the time that these boys escaped and found their way to this house which your relatives had rented, was *not* quite as assured and as satisfactory as you would have the court to believe ? "

" Yes, but—No, I know it wasn't, but, don't you see——"

" I am afraid we do see," responded the learned gentleman, with a satisfied smile. " We see that your protestations that you did not need to exploit the mischief-making powers of the boys for your own gain are not, in the light of your own evidence, either acceptable or true, and I forbear to enlarge upon the point, which is, I am convinced, perfectly comprehended by the jury, but it was a very odd coincidence indeed that these boys, with no help from you, should have managed to find their way, not only to your relatives, but into a house where their services could be utilized in such a gainful way to their employers."

" I know all that. I agree," said Bella Foxley desperately, " but I didn't kill the boys ! I didn't shut them up ! There are those who know far more about that than I do ! ' "

Counsel for the Defence cited the ' long arm of coincidence ' in his closing speech. He insisted that coincidence was an every-day happening. He begged the jury to remember strange co-incidences in their own lives and to attempt to explain them away in the light of ordinary reason. His client did not deny, he said, the presence of the boys at the house ; she did not deny the purpose for which their services had been used. But the faking of spiritualist miracles was not murder, nor was it in any sense akin to murder, and it was for murder that his client was being tried, the murder of these boys she had befriended.

She had a long and honourable record in the Institution of which they had heard so much. She had a reputation, even, for kindness. One of the witnesses for the prosecution had been, himself, a boy at the Institution, and, in spite of the fact that his evidence had been given against the prisoner, he had had to agree that she had been a kind woman, bringing into the lives of these poor boys—victims of our social system rather than sinners in their own right !—something of a mother's care and love.

Was it likely, was it probable, in fact, was it possible at all, that such a woman could have done the deed attributed to her by the prosecution ?

"Not a bad effort," said Ferdinand. "Really not bad at all. I'm prepared to lay you a monkey to sixpence that that jury will let her off. The missing link is vital. You can't put the job on to Bella without something better than that wretched hysteria-patient of yours, and that's that. After all, Crodders ain't so far wrong about coincidences, and the jury, curse them for super-stitious fatheads, know it."

Mrs. Bradley agreed.

"We have to allow for the fact that there are three women on the jury, though," she added, "and we have yet to hear the summing-up."

"Yes. Shouldn't think Nolly would be particularly prejudiced in her favour," Ferdinand agreed, more cheerfully. "After all, he must remember her former trial, even if the jury don't, but he can't manufacture evidence, much as he might like to. He can only throw his weight about, and he's always scrupulously fair. No, I take it that the priceless Bella will drive off amid cheers come this time to-morrow. Cousin Muriel has dished us. She had the whole thing in her hands, and she chucked it clean away. She and the Naval rating, between 'em, ought to have cooked Bella's goose, but it's all over now, I fancy, bar the enthusiasm of an exhilarated populace."

Chapter Ten

REACTIONS OF AN ELDERLY PSYCHOLOGIST

> Strength stoops unto the grave,
> Worms feed on Hector brave :
> Swords may not fight with fate :
> Earth still holds ope her gate.
> Come, come, the bells do cry :
> I am sick, I must die.
>
> .   .   .   .   .
>
> Wit with his wantonness
> Tasteth death's bitterness ;
> Hell's executioner
> Hath no ears for to hear
> What vain art can reply ;
> I am sick, I must die.
>
> .   .   .   .   .
>
> NASHE.

MR. JUSTICE KNOWLES commenced his summing-up by emphasizing to the jury the point at issue in the trial. The question for them to settle was whether or not the prisoner had, by her wilful act, murdered, by starving them to death, two boys named respectively Frederick Pegwell and Richard Keitleborough.

That two boys had died of starvation (an even more sinister report by the medical witnesses was not referred to) and had been buried beneath the floor in the cellar or crypt of a house known as Nunsuch in the village of Tonning, there could be no doubt. The facts and cause of the deaths were not disputed by the defence, and the medical witnesses who had appeared for the defence, as well as those who had appeared for the prosecution, were agreed upon the approximate date of the deaths.

It was not disputed, either, that the accused had visited, and even lived in, the house. As to her assertion that she and her relatives believed the house to be haunted, the jury must make up their own minds to what extent the accused really believed this. The question here was not whether the house really was or was not haunted, but whether the prisoner believed that it was, for this might have some bearing upon their verdict.

The question, then, resolved itself into this : Did the accused murder Frederick Pegwell and Richard Kettleborough ?

The prosecution had produced a witness to show that the prisoner had connived at, and even assisted in, the escape of these two boys from what was a remand home for young criminals. The jury might ask themselves whether this young man, who had also been for some years an inmate of this home, was a reliable witness. . . .

Here Mr. Pratt looked at Mrs. Bradley and held his thumbs down.

. . . or whether it could be expected that he should remember clearly all the details of his life there. On the other hand, the jury must remember that this witness, like all the other witnesses, was on oath, and that he had given his evidence straightforwardly and undoubtedly had so far improved his way of life that he was to-day in an honourable calling, the most honourable, perhaps, in the world, that of an Able Seaman in the Royal Navy.

The jury had also heard another witness declare that the two boys Pegwell and Kettleborough had been employed by the accused to counterfeit psychic phenomena in order that the reputation of the haunted house might be exploited for gain.

On the other hand, the jury would remember that this witness had contradicted herself on several important counts during the hearing of her evidence. First she had said that she tried to dissuade her husband from employing the boys, and then that she had agreed to it. She had also stated that the accused had received a share of the profits, and then she had denied that this was so. Furthermore, she had stated expressly that she had left the haunted house because she did not like what was going on there; she believed, she said, that the house was verily and indeed the haunt of supernatural beings, yet she had also made the statement that she knew that all the extraordinary occurrences which were experienced there were the work of these two boys, and she insisted that they were acting under instructions from the prisoner.

It surely would not be contended, as learned counsel had pointed out (observed his Lordship), that all these statements could be true.

" Why not ? " wrote Mr. Pratt, passing the note to Mrs. Bradley. She glanced at it and grinned, pursing her lips almost immediately afterwards into a little beak, and looking again at the judge.

There were tales of screams, shouts and moans, Mr. Justice Knowles continued, but if it were so, why had nothing been said or done about them at the time ? Why were they dragged into the light of day for the first time more than six years afterwards ?

On the other hand, there was the actual evidence of the bodies. Two bodies had been found under the house in circumstances which indicated foul play. If the bodies had been left unburied it might be argued that a horrible accident or even criminal negligence had taken place. But the fact that the bodies of two starved children had actually been buried, and buried in secret, and in a place where it was most unlikely that they would ever be found, indicated—in fact, insisted—that there had been foul play.

There was also the evidence of the ex-Warden of the Institution. The jury would remember that this witness had stated that no trace of the missing boys had ever come to light. The jury would also remember that this witness had stated, further (and in this part of his evidence he was supported by the testimony of the present Warden), that for the police to fail to track down two such boys, of whom a full description could be circulated and who would be most unlikely to have money with them to assist them to get away from the environs of the Institution, was most unusual.

His Lordship elaborated this part of his theme, and concluded with an exhortation to the jury to remember to give the prisoner the benefit of any reasonable doubt. Then he invited them to retire and consider their verdict.

In the interval which followed this retirement, Mr. Pratt again scribbled a note to Mrs. Bradley.

" What a pity we couldn't produce the *motive* for the murder of the boys ! "

Mrs. Bradley wrote in reply on the bottom of the same sheet of paper :

" What *was* the motive for the murder of the boys ? If you could tell me that I should be delighted."

Pratt wrote on the other side of the paper (thus offending,

Mrs. Bradley pointed out later, against all the canons of journalism and other authorship),

" Why, what about the murder of Cousin Tom ? What a blight on us that it has to be hush-hush, isn't it ? "

To this Mrs. Bradley wrote in reply :

" Cousin Tom was not murdered until *after* the boys were imprisoned in the cellar. You've got the wrong notion. I had, too, at first, and it led to Bella's arrest. Tom may not have been a party to the killing of the boys, therefore he may have been a nuisance ; he may have known facts about the death of Aunt Flora, therefore he may have been a menace ; but the death of the boys must have had some connection with another matter, I think, and certainly with another person."

" The thing is," said Ferdinand to his mother that evening, when, the jury having failed to agree, the trial was postponed until the next sessions—a matter of a few weeks—" you will have to go further into the alleged suicide of the sister. There's still some sort of mystery about that. Nobody is going to get me to believe that anyone as completely hard-boiled as Bella Foxley wanted to fake a suicide because people were sending her anonymous letters. Besides, the villagers didn't know who she was, did they ?—Although, of course, you can never be sure about a thing like that. Because the shepherd doesn't know there's a wolf in the fold, it doesn't stand to reason the sheep don't."

" They would be likely to betray the fact to the shepherd, though, don't you think ? " observed Mrs. Bradley. " But I think, all the same, dear child, it is your metaphor and not your reasoning which is at fault."

" Pratt showed me your note about the motive for the murder of the boys," continued Ferdinand. " I thought you had made up your mind that they were killed because they knew she had murdered Cousin Tom, until you suddenly presented me with that contrary opinion of yours the other week, about Muriel."

" I did think so at first, but the evidence of the caretaker and his daughter, plus the evidence of Miss Biddle, caused me to change my mind, and the medical evidence confirmed everything. You see, Bella Foxley was arrested so soon after the death of, and the inquest on, Cousin Tom that she would have had no chance of returning to the house to bury the bodies of the two

boys until they would have reached an advanced state of de-
composition. Now the bodies, as I saw them when they were first
disinterred by the police, did not bear out this theory. The boys
had been buried, I should have said, *before they were quite dead*,
and the medical evidence at the trial bore out this suggestion
of mine. Q.E.D."

" It is indeed," agreed Ferdinand. " Well, it will be a very
serious thing if you *don't* get her at the next attempt. What are
you going to do ? "

" I am going to rent a cottage in the village where Tessa
Foxley was drowned," Mrs. Bradley replied. " There may be,
as you suggest, a more powerful motive for that impersonation
than the desire to put an end to anonymous letters, and there
may be a motive for the murder of the boys which has no
connection whatsoever with the death of Cousin Tom or else a
different connection from any which we visualized at first.
I had better interview the prisoner, I think, before I go to Pond.
Can you arrange that for me ? "

" I don't know that she'll agree to have you visit her," replied
Ferdinand.

" I know what you mean," said Mrs. Bradley, with her harsh
cackle. " I did my best to get her hanged, you think. Well, let
me know as soon as I can get permission to visit her."

She had few questions to ask Bella Foxley when they met.
The prisoner was as uncommunicative as when they had
conversed at her toll-house in Devon, so perhaps it was well that
Mrs. Bradley was prepared to be brief.

" Don't worry. They'll probably get me next time," Bella
announced, as soon as she was seated opposite the visitor.
" What do you want ? "

" Answers to a question or so," Mrs. Bradley replied, " and
I will guarantee not to use what you tell me in a manner detri-
mental to your interests."

" Perhaps you think the gallows might serve my interests
best ? " said Bella with an ugly look and an even uglier laugh.
Mrs. Bradley shrugged, and then, fixing her bright black eyes
on the prisoner, looked at her expectantly.

" For my own satisfaction, if for no other reason, I should like
to establish the truth," she said. " Now, Miss Foxley : suppose,

instead of being charged with the murder of those two boys, you were charged with the murder of your sister, Miss Tessa Foxley?"

Bella half-smiled. Mrs. Bradley waited. Her clients knew that expression of patient benevolence. It seemed to have hypnotic powers. She exercised them now upon Bella, and, to her relief, although not altogether to her surprise, the prisoner spoke almost good-humouredly.

"Poor Tessa! Of course, as you've guessed, she was mental. That's why she was taken advantage of. That's one of the reasons why I hate men. I had her to live with me after the other trial because I had nobody else, and I thought I ought to keep an eye on her as I was letting her have half the money, and—I suppose I might as well confess it and get it off my conscience—I was hoping something would happen, and it did. She was the suicide kind, I suppose. My aim was to assume her identity if anything happened to her. I suggested to her we should call each other by nicknames, and I always told people—not that we got to know many; I saw to that all right—that she was Bella and I was Tessa Foxley.

"People didn't seem to suspect anything; I suppose they thought she was what people were like when they'd been acquitted of murder.

"Anyway, one afternoon I got to her in time to pull her head out of the rainwater butt. Silly of me, because it would have done the trick all right, but, somehow, you can't watch people die. Anyway, next time she did it in the village pond, and it was all up with her by the time she was discovered."

"And you had an alibi, I believe, for the time of her death?" said Mrs. Bradley in very friendly tones.

"Yes. Good enough for the coroner. I thought I told you. I had been let in for giving a talk to the Mothers' Meeting. Nice fellow, the vicar. Very good to both of us. Glad to oblige him."

"What made you so anxious to assume your sister's identity?" asked Mrs. Bradley. Bella gave her a curious look, and then replied off-handedly:

"Oh, I don't know, you know. I suppose I wanted a chance to forget all about the trial and all the unpleasantness. Still, I don't seem to have got far with it, do I?"

"It couldn't do any harm to tell me the truth, you know."

Mrs. Bradley suggested. " If you wanted to begin life afresh, as they say, after the trial, why couldn't you have adopted an entirely new name ? After all, the names Tessa Foxley and Bella Foxley are not so extremely unlike that you would have been able to hide yourself much behind your sister's name—except to people who knew you ! Come, Miss Foxley, be reasonable."

But Bella shook her head, and her heavy face set obstinately.

" It's neither here nor there," she answered. " I reckon I've had this coming to me all my life. I haven't had a happy life, you know."

" But I suggest to you that you had a better reason than the one you've given me for assuming your sister's name," Mrs. Bradley persisted. " You knew those boys were dead."

" Forget it," said Bella tersely ; and as Mrs. Bradley had no more questions to put she took her leave.

" Come again," said the prisoner in tones more genuine and less sardonic than Mrs. Bradley had expected. " It's something to talk to somebody a bit intelligent."

" Thank you," said Mrs. Bradley. " I have two or three more questions I want to put to you, and I shall be glad of an opportunity."

" Pleasure ! " responded the prisoner, but more in good-humour than contempt.

Mrs. Bradley returned to the Stone House at Wandles Parva full of cheerfulness, and remained there for five days. At the end of that time she had given up the idea of her proposed stay in the village where Tessa Foxley had been drowned, but had paid three visits there. There was no doubt, it seemed, that Bella Foxley's alibi for the time of the murder was, although slightly shaky theoretically, almost fool-proof from a practical stand-point. The tremendous risks attendant upon transporting her sister's dead body in daylight from the rain-water butt outside the back door of the cottage to the village pond were a deterrent to any but a maniac, Mrs. Bradley decided.

Bella Foxley, whatever her peculiarities, was no lunatic, and Mrs. Bradley abandoned, without regret, the theory that the idiot boy had been a witness of the murder of Tessa Foxley. The more likely explanation, it seemed, was that he had been a witness that Bella had indeed saved her sister from a suicidal drowning.

The next task, that of tracing the man who had bigamously married Tessa, proved less difficult and complicated than she had feared. The man, who had served a prison sentence, was working in a Salvation Army shelter. He responded readily to Mrs. Bradley's advertisement, established his identity by appeal to the Court missionary and admitted that Tessa had been ' kind of weak in the head.' He also stated that it was not for her ' or the likes of her ' he had ' done his stretch,' that he believed she had had money, but that this proved ' the biggest washout of the lot,' and that he was ' going straight ' and didn't ' need to be afraid of no-one.'

Painstakingly, Mrs. Bradley sifted fact from opinion, and opinion from lies, and convinced herself that she was left, at the end, with a residue of truth which, if not particularly valuable in itself, had its point as contributory evidence. Tessa had been weak. vacillating and of suicidal tendencies.

" In fact, I wouldn't help to hang Bella Foxley or anybody else. . . ."

" Even the rice-pudding Muriel . . ." interpolated Ferdinand, with a grin . . .

" . . . upon such evidence as we have in connection with Tessa Foxley's death," said Mrs. Bradley.

" So what ? " her son not unnaturally enquired.

" So—another interview with the prisoner so that I can explore fresh avenues," said Mrs. Bradley, with a cackle of pure pleasure.

" ' So we sought and we found, and we bayed on his track,' " quoted Ferdinand unkindly. But his mother's only response was another cackle.

" Something up her sleeve," thought Ferdinand uneasily. " Now where have we all slipped up ? "

This second interview was not, in some ways, either more or less satisfactory than the first one had been. The prisoner, puffy under the eyes and with skin as unsavoury as ever, raised sardonic eyebrows and greeted Mrs. Bradley ironically.

" What, you again ? " she said. Mrs. Bradley agreed, cheerfully, that it was.

" And when do we go through the performance again ? " enquired Bella Foxley.

" I don't know exactly. But, tell me, Miss Foxley—that

diary of yours. Your own unaided work—as they say in competitions for children—or not ? "

" Diary ? Oh, diary. I suppose Eliza Hodge handed it over ? "

" Well, yes and no. A small boy, my grandson, discovered it in your aunt's house. Eliza lets the house during the summer months, as I daresay you know."

" Very nice, too. Yes, I believe I did keep a diary. Why ? I haven't kept one for—since—Oh, well, you probably know the date of it."

But she looked hopefully at Mrs. Bradley as she said this, as though anticipating that Mrs. Bradley might not know.

" Well, the date of the year was on it—printed on it—and although that, in itself, is not, perhaps, proof positive that the items were written in that same year, the chain of events with which the diary seems to be concerned dates it without doubt. Tell me, Miss Foxley—for I gather you do not propose to answer my former question . . ."

" Which one ? "

" Whether the diary was your own unaided work."

" Oh, lord ! Of course it was ! What a silly question ! "

" You will take back that unkind remark later on, I think."

" Maybe. And—maybe ! Well, go on."

" By all means. Time is short, of course."

" You're dern tooting it's short," Bella agreed. " They'll get me next time, I reckon. Well, I should worry ! I've not had so much luck in my life that I expect to get away with this. Shoot ! "

" These Americanisms—the cinema ? " Mrs. Bradley enquired.

" Oh, possibly. I used to live there, nearly, in the evenings. Only thing to do, and the best way, anyhow, to get away from the atmosphere of that poisonous Institution for a bit."

" Ah, yes. You weren't happy there."

" When I say I'd sooner be here," said Bella vigorously, " I'm not saying one-half. Does that convince you ? "

" I don't need convincing. The diary would have convinced me."

" The diary ? But I didn't put anything in the diary about the Institution, did I ? I used to be pretty careful about that."

" Really ? You surprise me," said Mrs. Bradley, grinning like a fiend.

"I don't remember any of it," said the prisoner, scowling in the effort of recollection. "But I do want to ask *you* something. Exactly what is your object in pushing in here? You were against me at the trial, you and that precious Muriel, and that oaf Lawrence. What's the big idea of turning prisoner's friend all of a sudden?"

"Not prisoner's friend; seeker after truth," Mrs. Bradley corrected her. "And, of course, you are at liberty to refuse to answer my questions. You are at liberty to tell me not to come again."

"Oh, it makes for a good laugh once in a while," said Bella, "and, as you say, I needn't answer; and, not being quite so gone on the truth as you are, I can always tell a lie."

"So you can," replied Mrs. Bradley, unperturbed. "I think I know most of the truth, mind you," she continued. "Enough of it, anyway, to be able to pick out your lies. Did you tell the truth in court, by the way, about the boys?"

"Not exactly, but near enough to make no difference to the jury."

"You mean that you did send them to Mr. Turney?"

"No, I didn't *send* 'em, but when he offered to *have* them I let them go."

"Do you ever wish you hadn't?"

"No, I don't."

"It was a terrible death," said Mrs. Bradley, her eyes leaving those of the prisoner and wandering vaguely towards the door.

"It's over now," said Bella, "and they're better out of the world, two kids like that. What chance did they ever stand? Who'd give them a chance? Poor little wretches! Thieves and murderers before they'd hardly begun their lives at all."

"I saw in the diary that you held strong views on the subject," said Mrs. Bradley.

"You saw—Don't be daft! I never put any of my real opinions in that diary, that I'm positive I didn't!"

"Well, at any rate, it seems to have got round that you held strong views of that kind."

"Oh, maybe. I generally used to say what I thought, to one person and another."

"Especially to one person," said Mrs. Bradley, with peculiar emphasis. To her great interest, an ugly, purplish flush spread over Bella Foxley's face and down her thick neck.

" You're wrong ! " she said, huskily. " I never told Tom all that much."

" No, I'm not wrong," replied Mrs. Bradley. " Now, this question of mine which seems so long in coming. Do you happen to know—I ask it in the most disinterested and scientific sense—but *do* you happen to know how your Cousin Tom met his death ? "

" Considering I was tried for murdering him," said Bella, in strangled tones, " I suppose I ought to know ! "

" Ah, but you were acquitted. Tell me what you really think." Bella looked at her suspiciously.

" What *is* all this ? " she said.   Mrs. Bradley nodded mysteriously.

" We are coming to something, I do believe," she said. " Come along, Miss Foxley. Do your best. It won't seem as strange to me as it might to some people."

" I don't see it would sound strange, exactly, to anyone," said Bella, recovering herself a little. " After all, one of the little devils had committed murder already . . ."

" Ah," said Mrs. Bradley. " So you think the boys killed Cousin Tom ? "

" Well, I suppose it was a fact that they'd already pushed him out of the window once."

" That would account for his having made no particular complaint, I suppose," said Mrs. Bradley, as though she agreed with the supposition.

" Well, he couldn't very well inform against them, considering how he'd been hiding them from the police and using them, could he, poor fellow ? "

" I suppose not," said Mrs. Bradley ; but she seemed to have lost interest in the subject. " You do realise, though, don't you, that the boys were already in the cellar when your Cousin Tom fell out the second time ? "

She looked expectantly at Bella. The prisoner's face was livid.

" I heard that in court, but it didn't—it wasn't true. I happen to know that for a fact, if it's facts you're after," she said. Her sombre eyes smouldered. She did not speak again for a minute or two. The heavy, rather turgid mentality behind that ugly forehead and those angry, defeated eyes was accustoming itself to a new and terrible conviction, Mrs. Bradley surmised. She rose.

" Think it over," she said, almost kindly. " And when you go next into the witness box, I think I should tell the truth, the whole truth and nothing but the truth, if I were you. Even if it does no good, you'll feel the better for it. And, you know, Miss Foxley, if I were you—and I mean this in the most . . ."

" Disinterested way," said Bella, with a return to her former irony.

" If you like. Anyway, I should make up my mind to tell the court exactly what you were doing and where you were when the boys . . . need I say the rest ? . . . when the boys were dying."

" And now," said Mrs. Bradley brightly, " for another go at our patient Griselda."

" That fatheaded widow, I suppose you mean ? " said Mr. Pratt, who was again a weekend visitor at the Stone House. " That woman ought to be stood on hot bricks or something, to wake her up and bring her to, I should say. She simply threw away the case for the prosecution—simply threw it away."

" *Mea culpa*," said Mrs. Bradley inexcusably. Pratt, lighting a pipe, looked at her steadfastly.

" You're up to something," he said. " Don't tell me we've got to whitewash the unspeakable Bella ? "

Mrs. Bradley grinned and asked him whether, in such case, she could count upon his assistance.

" Count on me in any way you like," responded Mr. Pratt gallantly. " But tell me all first. I am all ears and curiosity."

" Well, come with me to interview Muriel Turney, then," said Mrs. Bradley. " We can do it to-morrow. It isn't so far from here. I don't need to notify her that we are coming. She is pretty sure to be at home. And this evening, between now and the time you go to sleep, I wish you'd re-read Bella Foxley's diary. I am going to confront her with it when I visit her next time. I think I may get some interesting reactions."

" You know, you're a public menace," said Mr. Pratt.

" I am wondering," said Mrs. Bradley, " whether—but let me begin at the beginning."

Muriel looked at her in perplexity. Her weak face was pale, and she had given a cry of surprise and, it seemed, of relief, when she had opened the door to find Mrs. Bradley waiting on the step.

" Yes, certainly," she said vaguely. " Sit down, won't you ? "

Mrs. Bradley sat down.

" To begin at the beginning, then," she said——" or, rather, at the end, if you do not object to a paradox—what are you going to do if, after all, Bella Foxley is acquitted ? It is a fact we have to face, you know, that she may be. What further steps are you prepared to take ? "

" Why—why, I don't know, I'm sure. Do you mean you think she *will* be acquitted ? "

" I was surprised that they did not acquit her this time."

" Yes, I suppose—that is, it would have been dreadful, wouldn't it ? Do you really think she'll get off ? "

" We must be prepared for it," repeated Mrs. Bradley. " Now, then, what do you say ? "

" Why, nothing. Poor Bella ! I suppose she's been punished already. Perhaps it would be for the best."

" Did your husband possess a sense of humour ? " asked Mrs. Bradley. Muriel, not unnaturally, looked completely bewildered by this question, which appeared to have no bearing whatsoever upon what had already been said. She begged Mrs. Bradley's pardon nervously.

" That's all right," said Mrs. Bradley benignly, waving a yellow claw. " Don't mention it."

" I—I don't think I heard what you said."

" Oh, yes, I expect you did. What did you think I said ? "

" Had—had Tom a sense of humour ? "

" That's it. Well, had he ? In his writings, more particularly."

" Well, he—sometimes he would be a bit what he used to call jocular—about the spirits, you know, and what they said."

" He used to be a bit jocular," said Mrs. Bradley solemnly. Then she shuddered—or so it seemed to the unhappy Muriel.

" Of course, a lot of his writing had to be very serious. It was kind of technical," Muriel added. " The Society of Psychical Research . . ."

" You don't tell me that he wrote for their journal ? "

" I—Oh, well, perhaps he didn't, then. I really don't know what he wrote for. He never bothered me with it. He always said I needn't trouble my head."

" And—was all the love-making on one side ? "

" I . . ."

" Don't beg my pardon," said Mrs. Bradley gently. " Yes, that was what I said."

" But—I mean—isn't it rather—married people don't talk about such things."

" Why not ? "

" Well . . ."

" I thought most of the divorce cases were because of it."

" Because of . . . ? " Muriel's colour heightened. She half rose from her chair. " I don't think I understand what you're talking about."

" Well, this : the boys were starved to death—or nearly to death, we'll say. The bodies—alive or dead—that didn't seem to matter very much to a cruel and wicked woman—were buried. Well, it struck me afterwards—after the trial, I mean—that there was a discrepancy somewhere. Do you see what I mean ? "

" No. No, I don't."

" Curious."

" I don't know what you're getting at," said Muriel wildly and shrilly. " But if you say any more about those wretched boys I shall scream."

" Are we alone in the house ? "

" I don't know."

" And yet you came to the door. Do you answer the door all the time ? "

" Yes. It is an arrangement with my landlady. She answers all the knocks some days, and I answer them the other days. It's just an arrangement."

" Very sensible indeed. What were we saying ? "

" I don't remember."

" I do. I mentioned a discrepancy. I wondered whether you would help me to understand. Possibly it is perfectly plain and straightforward, but I can't quite follow it. You remember the first time your husband fell out of the bedroom window ? "

" Yes, of course I do, but I thought we said . . ."

" Well, on that occasion, your husband was in the house with the boys, and you and Bella were at the inn. Is that correct ? "

" Of course it is. You know it is."

" Very well. Now, your husband was hurt by the fall, I presume. Did you nurse him ? "

" No. He wouldn't have us put about. He made light of the fall."

" I see. I obtained so little information about this part of the story from Bella's diary that I thought perhaps you might be able to enlarge on it for me."

" But this won't help to get the wicked woman hanged ! "

" I'm afraid not, no. You see, the diary mentions the fall, and then Bella announces that she went to the house to see whether she could discover any explanation of it, but, most tantalisingly, she leaves out any account of this visit and merely reports, the next day, that your husband had decided to give up the house as too dangerous. He wasn't in the house when he made that decision, was he ? "

" I can't remember whether he was or not."

" I deduced he could not have been, because she goes on, after a mention of other matters, to state that three gentlemen and two ladies interested in psychical research came to the house and asked to be shown over it. She then states that, as she felt sure your husband ' would have wished it '—indicating that he was not able to be consulted on the matter—she herself showed them over the house. You, I suppose, Mrs. Turney, would have been with your husband at the inn ? "

" I suppose so. Yes, of course. But I feel so dim and hazy. You see, poor Tom being killed so soon after . . ."

" Quite so. Yes, I see. So Bella had the house to herself except for those strangers ? "

" Well, yes, she would have had, except for the boys, wouldn't she ? "

" Well that's the point. Were the boys there then ? "

" Well, unless she'd murdered them by that time."

" But she hadn't. You see, if, as we think, the boys pushed Mr. Turney out of the window—as we have agreed they must have done, haven't we ? . . ."

"Yes, I suppose we have, but . . ."

"And if, when these ladies and gentlemen came to see the haunted house, they had no manifestations of any kind . . ."

"Didn't they?"

"Apparently they did not. Well, what does that tell us about the boys?"

"But . . ."

"I know. They couldn't have starved to death in two days. In fact, they were alive when Bella was arrested."

"I don't know what you're trying to get me to say," said Muriel. "I can't explain it, if that's what you mean. Either these people didn't come, or else Bella was lying. I don't see why we should have to believe what she put down in that diary."

"Curiously enough, neither do I," said Mrs. Bradley. Muriel looked at her. There was fear, unmistakable, on the shallow little face. Mrs. Bradley nodded, slowly and rhythmically, still keeping her eyes fixed on those of her victim. Muriel was like someone in contact with electricity—writhing, yet unable to drag herself away.

"You know what caused the jury to fail to agree?" said Mrs. Bradley at last.

"Oh, I know everybody on our side blamed me," said Muriel, recovering herself a little. "But, after all, I wasn't any worse than that half-baked sailor. How could you expect he would be believed! You must have known that his boyhood would tell against him. Nobody likes evidence from criminals."

"No, I agree about that. I had weighed that up very carefully, I assure you, before I suggested that he should be sought for to give evidence at all at the trial."

"There's one thing I ought to ask you," said Muriel, abandoning the subject of Larry. "Do I have to go into that awful witness box again? Because I don't believe I can do it."

"Needs must, when the devil drives, I should imagine," said Mrs. Bradley, with brisk, assured unkindness. Muriel looked at her, puzzled and slightly annoyed by these extraordinary tactics.

"What did you mean about love being all on one side?" she enquired in a voice of mingled curiosity and alarm.

"Oh, that!" said Mrs. Bradley. "That brings me back to my discrepancy, I believe. It's like trying to find a mistake in a column of figures. Ten to one you add it up again incorrectly, making the same mistake as you had made before. Have you ever done that ? "

" Yes," said Muriel, looking pallid. " But what's this all got to do with me ? "

" What indeed ? " said Mrs. Bradley with an unpleasant leer. " What, indeed ? Well, good-bye, Mrs. Turney. I shall hope to see you again before the new trial."

" But you must tell me . . . You must tell me what to expect," said Muriel wildly.

" Blessed is he that expecteth nothing," quoted Mrs. Bradley solemnly, " for he shall be gloriously surprised ! And I shall be surprised," she added, as though to herself, " if I do not find the last clue I want in the haunted house."

" You are going there again ? "

" To-night."

" Alone ? "

" Well, I don't suppose there will be any point in taking Bella Foxley's lawyer with me, or the gentleman who led for the prosecution at the trial. Were you, by any chance, offering to come ? "

" Me ? Oh, I couldn't ! As I told you before, my nerves simply wouldn't stand it."

" Yes, you did tell me, and I fully sympathise. You remember by the way, what you said about the *poltergeist ?*"

" What—what do you mean ? "

" Don't you remember telling me that you were always afraid that something inexplicable would happen in that house ? I believe you used the expression 'playing with fire.' Do you believe that something outside human agency can function as a result of human interference with the province of the immaterial ? "

" Something from *beyond the veil*, do you mean ? " asked Muriel, with a shudder.

" I mean . . ."

" Yes, I know what you mean. Well, I must say I'd rather *you* went there now than that *I* did. In fact, I couldn't do it. I really couldn't do it. I should die of fright if I so much as put my foot over the doorstep. After all, you never know what you might be invoking."

" True. Or provoking. That is what I mean. And, of

course, three people were murdered there—one quickly, and two very slowly and horribly, weren't they ? "

Muriel went so white that Mrs. . Bradley thought she was going to faint or be sick. She looked at her fixedly, until the widow showed signs of recovery.

" I expect I shall get to the house by about eleven to-night," she went on. " I suppose the electric switches are still functioning ? Then I shall remain until people turn up to be shown over the house next day. If nobody comes, I shall leave as soon as I have made a thorough exploration of the place."

" Well, I wish you luck," said Muriel tremulously. " Be—be careful, won't you ? "

" Very, very careful," said Mrs. Bradley, with her horrid cackle. " By the way," she added, " I have advised Bella to remind the court where she was, and what she was doing whilst those boys—whom I pledge myself to avenge !—were starving to death in that cellar."

The caretaker had no authority to admit Mrs. Bradley to the house, but made no objection to doing so.

" Come to see how them there old ghosties be getting on, like, I do suppose ! " he said, with jocular intent.

" Exactly so," replied Mrs. Bradley solemnly. " And now, I want you to let me have this key until to-morrow. Will you ? "

He scratched his head.

" I take it to be Miss Foxley, her's still the owner ? " he said cautiously. " Although they do have her still in gaol ? "

" Certainly she is. Who else ? "

" Why, nobody. Think they'm going to hang her ? "

" Who can say ? The gentleman who defended her told me afterwards how well you gave your evidence."

He looked pleased, but observed anxiously :

" Ah, but, you see, I never told all I knowed."

" How was that ? "

" Well, they didn't ask me, see ? And they do take ee up so sharp if so be you answers out of your turn."

" Yes, that is perfectly true. I suppose you could have told them that Mrs. Turney visited the house alone, after the death of her husband and after Miss Foxley was arrested."

The old man gaped at her.

" That do be right, that do," he declared. " But how did ee know ? "

" You told me so yourself."

" Oh, so that's it, is it ? There isn't nothing in it, after all."

" I wouldn't say that. If you look out, a little later on, you may see her visit the house again. Take no notice. She has her key."

" Ah, yes, so she have. Her and Mr. Turney and Miss Foxley, all of 'em had keys. But I should have thought Miss Foxley might have collected of 'em up when she bought the house for herself."

" Well, I don't think she did. So don't worry Mrs. Turney when she comes, if you happen to see her. She has her reasons for visiting the house again, and as they are connected with the murder, I don't suppose she'll want to be disturbed."

" I know how to respect folks' miseries," replied the ancient man. He shuffled back to his cottage, and Mrs. Bradley went to call upon Miss Biddle.

" I've come with an extraordinary request," she said. " I want you to let me remain here, more or less in hiding, until about seven to-night. Will you ? "

" Why, of course," replied her friend. " And I suppose I mustn't ask why, so I shan't put out even the littlest tiny feeler."

" You shall know all before morning, if you wish," said Mrs. Bradley. " Now, where can I hire a slow-witted, heavy, mild, obedient horse ? And I want to borrow an iron well-cover, the heavier the better."

" Well, it had better be Mr. Carter for the horse. I expect he'd let you hire Pharaoh. As for the well-cover, you can have mine, but you'll have to let me help you lift it if you want to take it away. Oh, dear, how you excite my curiosity ! But I ought not to speak of that now ! "

" What kind of man is Mr. Carter ? " asked Mrs. Bradley.

" Well, he's very lame, poor man, since his accident, but if you wanted someone to help you in any way, you couldn't do better than to have young Bob, his eldest son. Look here, let me do the arranging for you. I know the family quite well."

So Mrs. Bradley explained what had to be done, and, as it

was obviously cruel not to take Miss Biddle completely into her confidence, she told her everything.

By five o'clock, the plan had been completed and partly tested. Young Bob proved to be an intelligent, grinning lad, dependable, however, and very much interested in the game that Mrs. Bradley proposed to play.

" Won't be the first time there's been ghost-faking round this house," he observed, when Mrs. Bradley had rehearsed him in his duties.   " But I've never heard tell before of having the bobbies out to arrest a ghost ! "

By seven o'clock Mrs. Bradley was in her chosen position in the attic which commanded the approach to the house from the road.   She had had the forethought to borrow a cushion or two from Miss Biddle's house, and had brought her knitting, so that she could recline in comfort and occupy herself during her vigil. She had no idea how long this would be likely to last.   She had returned from Muriel's lodgings by car, driven very fast by George, who thus obtained one of his rare treats, for Mrs. Bradley's preference was usually for a more leisurely progress.

Muriel would probably come by train, and, at the earliest, could scarcely arrive at the haunted house before eight, for the railway journey was across country, and involved three changes. The connections, too, at the exchange stations were poor. Mrs. Bradley did not expect her to approach the house before dusk, even if she got to the village earlier than that.

It was dark, however, before Muriel came, and Mrs. Bradley had to retire to her vantage point, the attic cupboard in which she believed Cousin Tom used to lock up the boys when they were not wanted in the cellar.

At about half-past ten she heard the slam of the front door.   She had heard no footsteps on the path, and no sound of a latch-key in the door.   She listened intently, but Muriel must have gone straight into one of the downstair rooms, or remained in the hall, for she could not hear her walking about or mounting the stairs.

She had put away her knitting and had taken out of the capacious pocket of her skirt a small harmonica. Quietly she pushed back the door of the attic cupboard, and played a few soft notes.

Like faery music, they seemed to float all over the empty

house. She stopped, and listened again. Nothing was to be heard for a full minute, and then a sound of footsteps below caused her to put the instrument again to her beaky little mouth and play another series of disconnected notes.

This time Muriel's reaction was more definite. She began to run up the stairs, and as she ran she called out :

" Are you there, Mrs. Bradley ?   Are you there ? "

For answer, Mrs. Bradley blew a long discordant confusion of notes from the harmonica, a pre-arranged signal for her friends, the inspector and the sergeant, who had been in hiding in the scullery. Taking their cue, the police officers began to hurl furniture and pots and pans out of the kitchen into the hall.

Muriel ceased to run upstairs. She gave a strange, loud yelp of terror, and then shouted :

" Mrs. Bradley !   Please don't do it !   I'm frightened. And, listen !   I want to speak to you."

Mrs. Bradley waited until the din below had ceased, and then blew on the harmonica again.   The noises broke out worse than before ; upon this, and, under cover of the really appalling sounds, she raced down the back staircase and then slipped out through the scullery as soon as it was safe to negotiate the array of furniture which was now piled up outside the kitchen.

She made her way to the front of the house, walking briskly on the gravel path, and opened the front door of the now almost eerily silent building.   At that, Muriel came flying down the stairs to meet her.

" Oh ! " she cried.   " I'm glad to see you !   Oh, I'm thankful to see you !   This house !   *It's come awake at last !* "

" Whatever do you mean ? " asked Mrs. Bradley.   Muriel did not answer until she had groped for and discovered the main switch.   Then she put on the lights and both of them looked at the wreckage.

" Not the *poltergeist ?* " said Mrs. Bradley incredulously.

" Unless it's someone playing the fool," said Muriel with weak annoyance.

" Bound to be," said Mrs. Bradley reassuringly.   " If we look about we're almost bound to find them, unless they've cleared off by now, which I rather suspect they would do if they've been here on mischief bent."

"But they couldn't have known I was coming. I didn't even tell *you* I was coming. It was just—just a sudden fancy to see the place again. Of course, I'd never have dared to come alone, but as you said you would be here. . . ."

How well she did it, thought Mrs. Bradley, dispassionately interested in such a convincing display of protective colouring ; how extraordinarily well, the nervous, over-strained, weak and clinging little . . . murderess. Her voice hardened.

"Yes, but I'm here with work to do. I don't require, or particularly desire, company."

"Oh, you won't mind me. I shan't interfere," said Muriel. "I expect, as you say, it was someone thinking to scare us. Ah, well, it all seems quiet enough now. But, you know, when I first heard that mouth-organ thing which seemed to come from the top of the house, I really thought for a minute that it was—that it was the fairies, or something."

"Oh, no," said Mrs. Bradley, "you did not. You thought it was those poor . . ." She watched the razor coming slowly round from behind the murderess's back, and suddenly cried, "What's that ? "

She cried it out so loudly that her voice rang through the house. At the same instant a shrill whistle came from the direction of the scullery, and, as Muriel's face grew pale, a sound stranger and more eerie than any that had so far been heard that night seemed to come from the courtyard outside. Part of it was homely enough—the steady clop, clop of a heavy horse, the sound of the hoofs muffled by the courtyard weeds—but, mingled with this was another sound, unusual to most men's ears, but apparently familiar, in some horrid and personal sense, to the wretched, guilty woman who had now dropped the razor on the floor.

"The cover of the well! They're here ! They're here ! They've come to be revenged on me ! Go away ! Go away ! Go away ! Leave me alone, you little fiends ! " she shrieked at the top of her voice.

The sounds ceased. Mrs. Bradley picked up the razor.

"I think you dropped this," she said.

"I ? " faltered Muriel, recoiling. "I don't know what it is ! I never saw it ! Didn't you hear what I heard ? "

" I only heard someone screwing down a coffin lid," said Mrs. Bradley, quietly as before. " Or could it have been the trap-door down to the cellar ? Listen ! Do you hear it too ? "

She half-turned, and at that instant Muriel opened the razor and made a sudden slashing attack. Mrs. Bradley, who had been waiting to do so, side-stepped, and banged her on the elbow with a cosh which she had drawn from the deep pocket of her skirt when she had half-turned away.

" *Listen !*" she said again.

Muriel was moaning with the agony of the blow on the elbow, but her moans of pain changed suddenly to a dreadful cry of terror. From beneath their feet came the sound of someone digging. She was in a state of hysterical panic when the inspector stepped out of the kitchen to make the arrest. She made a full and babbled confession on the way to the station.

Chapter Eleven

THE DIARY

> " Hark, now everything is still,
> The screech-owl and the whistler shrill,
> Call upon our dame aloud,
> And bid her quickly don her shroud ! "
>
> WEBSTER.

" THE thing is," said Ferdinand, " when did you first suspect her, mother ? "

" I don't know," replied Mrs. Bradley.

" Genius," said Caroline, without (her mother-in-law thought) much justification for the compliment.

" I thought you were convinced of Bella's guilt."

" I was."

" Well, then, you must know when your ideas changed."

Mrs. Bradley was silent for a minute or two. One would have said that she was in contemplation of the hedge which divided part of her garden from the paddock. " I don't know," she repeated, "but if I am being asked to hazard an opinion, I would say that I was convinced of Bella's guilt until I went to see her down in Devon."

Ferdinand nodded, as his mother turned her basilisk eyes on him.

"Personally," he said, "I did not think anything could disprove Bella Foxley's guilt. The ancient, wealthy aunt, the blackmailing cousin, the dangerous and criminally minded boys, and the golden opportunity of making herself safe for life by assuming the identity of a murdered sister—the thing seemed self-evident, fool-proof, satisfactory and horrible."

"But it *wasn't* altogether satisfactory," said Mrs. Bradley, " as I realized the moment I began to examine it from Bella Foxley's point of view. If you assume for a moment that Bella was *not* guilty, you get a different impression entirely of the course events may have taken. You get the impression, for instance, that every ill deed we had attributed to Bella could just as well have been performed by Muriel."

"That means, though, that the aunt died accidentally," said Ferdinand. "Bella was the only person to have had a motive there for murder."

"Not necessarily," replied his mother. "Bella certainly had the motive, for she stood to gain by the death, but if she could be blackmailed successfully, Tom and Muriel stood to gain something too. It was a clever plot, but it was apparent, before I suspected Muriel at all, that Tom was somewhere involved. It was evident that Bella had not written that diary."

"The diary ? "

"Yes. You've read it. You know what the mistakes and discrepancies were. Some of the mistakes could, but others could *not*, have been made by a single author, especially if that author were Bella. Collaboration was indicated—an unheard-of thing in a genuine diary."

"I see what you mean. But there was no way of telling which part was Bella's own work, was there ? And, even if there were, the only other part-author of the diary, as you say, could have been Tom. At least, let's put it that the collaborator couldn't have been Muriel."

"There was no need for it to have been Muriel. I spoke just now of a plot. But, to revert to the diary itself, it seemed to me to indicate that the writer had a rather pleasing style, and a definite, although possibly rudimentary, sense of form. Of course, we must admit that Bella may have possessed both these literary qualities, but Tom, as a practising writer (he made some of his income out of articles for journals devoted to psychical research, you will remember), was the more likely author, on the whole, in my opinion. Still, one cannot generalise about such things, for it is a well-known fact that people whose powers of conversation are crude, boorish, unready, or even, for all social purposes, non-existent, can sometimes contrive to express themselves, when in receipt of pen and paper, in unexceptionable prose."

" I don't see, all the same, why you think two people wrote the diary between them," said Caroline.

" I don't know that they did. Bella was an unconscious collaborator. What interested me, and caused me to investigate the matter in the first place, were the ending of the diary, abrupt yet undramatic, and the mistakes in fact which were apparent almost at a glance and which became ludicrously obvious as soon as one began to examine the matter.

" Then came the very odd fact that, although the diary continued long past the time when everyone concerned had left Aunt Flora's house, the diary itself remained there. That seemed very curious."

" Last entries faked ? Written beforehand ?" said Ferdinand.

" It added to my idea that there was a plot. The plot, of course, came into being when Bella helped Pegwell and Kettleborough to escape from the Institution. Well, the arrangement between Bella and Tom was that the boys should remain hidden in the haunted house, where Tom could make good use of them in faking the *poltergeist* phenomena, and where, Bella hoped, they would be safe from the police.

" That, I fancy, was as far as Tom was prepared to go, and, apart from Muriel's confession, I could not prove much of what follows.

" One thing which Tom never allowed for, of course, was the horrid jealousy which his necessary collusion with Bella over the boys evoked in Muriel. This jealousy led Muriel, later on, to kill him and to see that Bella was charged with the murder."

" Didn't Bella know who had killed Tom ? " Caroline enquired.

" She thought it was the boys. She does not seem to have suspected Muriel of that until now."

" Then did Muriel kill the aunt ? "

"It is most likely. But it doesn't matter now, in one sense, whether she did or not. The death of the aunt suggested to Tom this further plot to continue to blackmail Bella—not that he did anything so crude, I imagine, as to extort money by threats, or anything of that kind. Bella loved him, and he found it easy enough to get the money. It was, of course, very much more than those small amounts suggested at the trial. It was, very possibly, the half which was supposed to have gone to Tessa, although Bella did not admit it."

" Well, he wrote the diary, intending to type it out later and threaten Bella with it if ever it became necessary to apply a little pressure. He purposely sent it to the house to Eliza Hodge, being pretty sure that the old servant would take care of it without being unduly curious about it. Then he wrote the anonymous letters and drove Bella almost mad, I should imagine, by the accusations of murder contained in them. Then he fell out of the window that first time, and allowed her to believe that the boys had pushed him out."

" And that gave Muriel the idea of how to kill him without being suspected ? " asked Caroline.

" Yes. She has now confessed it. I had an inkling of what had happened—I think we all had—when we heard about the button which was found in the dead man's hand."

"Well, it was rather silly of Bella to go and visit Tom so late at night," said Caroline. Mrs. Bradley looked benevolently at her daughter-in-law, and agreed.

" There is one thing I don't understand," said Ferdinand. " How did a comparatively frail woman such as Muriel contrive to get the two boys battened down under hatches in that cellar ? I should have thought the lads would have popped up the well whilst she was screwing down the trap-door, or vice-versa."

" Oh, Bella helped her over that."

" So Bella *is* partly guilty ? "

" No, but it flummoxed her at the trial. Tom must have

told her that the boys had pushed him out and were dangerous. She suggested that they should shut the boys up until they had decided what was the best thing to do about them. She knew, of course, that, following the information which she was going to give at the inquest, it was almost certain that Bella would be arrested for murdering Tom. After that, Muriel dared not keep the boys alive in case they could witness against her. The probability was that they had been fast asleep at the time, but her guilty conscience would not allow her to run any risks.

" When Bella had been acquitted of the murder of Tom, she knew, from the way in which Muriel had given her evidence, that she had an implacable enemy, and she knew the reason for it. It was to escape from Muriel's hatred, I think, that she assumed Tessa's identity, although I am certain that she never suspected that Muriel had killed Tom. She did think, though, that Muriel had choked Aunt Flora.

" I myself had some glimmering of the truth, I think, when I realized that there was a curious little entry which seemed to leave a kind of time-gap in the diary. This gap was that the diary failed to explain what on earth made the whole four of them—Bella Foxley, Tom, Muriel and even Eliza—leave the old lady alone in the house on the day that she died. I could not believe that even the most irresponsible and heartless people would have done such a thing, and, when I questioned Eliza, I discovered that, as a matter of fact, they did not. Eliza herself was there, and either Bella or Muriel.

" Now there was, in connection with this entry, too, an interval unaccounted for by the author—whether Bella or Tom—between seven o'clock and that ' little later on in the evening ' during which Aunt Flora died."

" But it doesn't prove anything," protested Caroline.

" It proves that whoever wrote the diary was a liar, and a liar about the most important event mentioned," said Ferdinand. " Mother, presumably, became interested in Bella Foxley before she obtained Eliza's evidence, but the discrepancy between that evidence and the evidence of the diary was proof-presumptive, I should say, of foul play."

"Yes, but Tom *wanted* to indicate foul play," persisted Caroline.

" I know," said her husband soothingly, " but it was that—

and I expect, the other curious mistake about the colour of the old lady's hair—which made mother think that there might be something worth investigating."

" I am glad you mention the hair," said Mrs. Bradley, " for that indicated that whoever wrote the diary could not have gone in to see the old lady. The fine imaginative passage about. the dirt in the parting—you remember?—proved positively that whoever the author was, it could scarcely have been either Bella or Muriel, both of whom, according to old Eliza, spent time in the sick-room, a thing which Tom did not do, being afraid, on the one hand, we are asked to believe, that the old aunt might think he had come for what he could get—a thought repugnant to his nature—and, on the other, that he detested illness—a more likely explanation, I feel."

" And were you positive, before Muriel confessed, that she was the murderer of the two boys? " asked Caroline.

" Yes. I don't want to go into details which you would not care to hear, but it was obvious that the boys' bodies had been buried before they had decomposed. Now they could not have been buried by Tom, for he was dead, and they could not have been buried by Bella, because before they were dead she would have been in prison. That left Muriel, and I have a statement from the old caretaker to show that Muriel visited the haunted house some days after the inquest to do some gardening, he thought."

" Silly mistake to bury them at all," said Ferdinand.

" I can't see how you knew she would confess if you could get her to the haunted house to try to kill you," said Caroline.

" I based the theory upon a discovery I made earlier in the investigation," explained Mrs. Bradley. " I discovered that Muriel was superstitious. She indicated to me once that she didn't really think it was wise to counterfeit psychical phenomena. Therefore, when she came to the haunted house that night to kill me because I had allowed her to know what I had against her, she concluded that the sounds she heard, striking home as they did to a mind over-burdened with guilt, were proof of something that she had half-believed all her life—that there really are such things as ghosts, and that occasionally they take a quite uncomfortable interest in human affairs."

www.vintage-books.co.uk